Steve Sem-Sandberg was born in 1958. He is the award-winning Swedish author of *The Emperor of Lies*, an international bestseller and winner of the August Prize. His most recent novel, *The Chosen Ones*, was awarded the Prix Médicis étranger in 2016. He lives in Stockholm.

Dr Anna Paterson, an ex-neuroscientist, is a writer and award-winning translator from the Germanic languages into English.

Further praise for *The Tempest*:

'His prose seems to break every rule in the creative writing handbook, and yet does so joyfully, recklessly and utterly convincingly ... That such stylistic complexity is rendered in a manner that feels entirely natural is testimony to the great skill of the translator, Anna Paterson ... It's as if the book's most significant borrowing from Shakespeare's play is not the island setting, but rather Prospero's total control of narrative, the omnipotence of the author-magician.' *Spectator*

'The Swedish author Steve Sem-Sandberg's novels worry at Nazi atrocities as at a loose tooth ... His latest, *The Tempest*, tackles Nazi collaboration in Norway – but he approaches his subject circuitously, peeling back layers of secrecy, evasion and guilt . Sem-Sandberg captures the relentless, dark dream-fl prose.

With Kaufmann as a Prospero figure, and his monstrous farm manager Mr Carsten as his Caliban, there are echoes of Shakespeare's play in this *Tempest*. But themes of forgiveness and repentance aren't so obvious here; the lingering shadows of complicity remain dense and murky.' *The Times*

'Through the accumulation of detail, Sem-Sandberg conveys the atmosphere of a corrupt Eden suffused with dread. Planes shriek constantly overhead; the inhabitants' festering hatreds periodically erupt into violence. Yet the island's dreamlike beauty, as much as his childhood memories, still casts a spell on Andreas.' *TLS*

'Thrums with building intensity, the writing deceptive in its simplicity but with a hypnotic rhythm and cadence which echoes the novel's dreamlike exploration of the past, of the shadows which loom.' *Irish Times*

'A small masterpiece.' *Expressen*

'A tale that both shimmers and threatens.' *Svenska Dagbladet*

---

by the same author

THE EMPEROR OF LIES
THE CHOSEN ONES

STEVE SEM-SANDBERG

The Tempest

A STORY

Translated by Anna Paterson

FABER & FABER

First published in 2019
by Faber & Faber Ltd
Bloomsbury House
74–77 Great Russell Street
London WC1B 3DA
First published by Albert Bonniers Förlag, Stockholm, in 2016

This paperback edition first published in 2020

Typeset by Faber & Faber Ltd
Printed in the UK by CPI Group (UK) Ltd, Croydon, CR0 4YY

pp. 74–5 Quotation from travelogue: *Aspects of Nature in Different Lands and Different Climates* (*Ansichten der Natur*) by Alexander von Humboldt, translated into English by Mrs Sabine, Lee & Blanchard, Philadelphia 1850, p. 27.
p. 76 Quotation from *Meditations* by Marcus Aurelius, translated by Gregory Hays, The Modern Library, New York, 2002.
pp. 113–14 and 117 Quotations from Baedeker guides to Germany, translated by Anna Paterson from the Swedish versions of the texts by Barbara Knochenhauer.

A CIP record for this book
is available from the British Library

ISBN 978-0-571-33452-0

MIX
Paper from
responsible sources
FSC
www.fsc.org FSC® C020471

2 4 6 8 10 9 7 5 3 1

I'll show thee the best springs; I'll pluck thee berries . . .

WILLIAM SHAKESPEARE, *The Tempest*, II 2

I should not have gone back to the island but did it all the same.

It is April. It has rained and, as always at this time of the year, strands of mist cling to the ground, enveloping the two sentry boxes at the bridge head and what remains of the iron post for the old barrier across the road. The mist reminds me of the white net curtains that Johannes used to drape over the Morello cherry trees to stop the birds from getting at the fruit; now, behind the filmy haze, the trees are bare of leaves and fruit. The surface of the water reflects only rocks and gnarled branches. Johannes always boasted that he had helped to build the bridge, as a navvy who worked with his bare hands. Before it was built, a cable ferry came and went from a ramp a few hundred metres further along. The ferry could carry vehicles, not that the roads on the island were up to much in those days. When Johannes first came to the island, he brought his motorbike across. Later, he toured the island on the bike and often took Kaufmann along in the sidecar, both wearing goggles and lined, belted leather coats with high fur collars. To cross the strait in the ferry could be hard work. The cables threatened to break in strong winds and two men on land were needed to secure the ferry to the jetty while the ferryman hauled at the cable. Everyone expected that, in the end, Kaufmann would have to agree to build a permanent connection to the mainland, though many were taken by surprise when his decision was actually announced. He and his family had for a long time treated the group of islands as their private fiefdom, to be entered only on Kaufmann's say-so: he tolerated the few other owners of private property, the patients in the Sanatorium on West Island, and the doctors and nurses who worked there. As soon as the bridge was ready, Kaufmann ordered the construction of two bricks-and-mortar sentry boxes on each side of the bridge head on the island and hired the ferry workers as guards. In the beginning, the road barrier was in use but it grew increasingly pointless and, once Kaufmann had begun to sell off more and more land, it was simply kept upright. Roughly six years later, it was removed, leaving only the posts behind. How long ago was that, from now? I can no longer remember. Or, rather: my memory is no longer a useful measure of island time. As I walk the five hundred-odd paces it takes to cross the bridge, I have a curiously familiar sensation of being transported centuries into the past. It is as if, all around me, the landscape is taking on greater depth and breadth and colour, yes, as if even the air is becoming denser. Johannes, with the overdone pedantry of his later years, would explain that the climate is different out here on the islands. It has to do with warm sea currents: you must have noticed how jellyfish flock into the strait? Jellyfish always seek out warmer waters. On dark August nights, he often spread the star maps out on the kitchen floor to instruct me and Minna about the positions of the constellations: Andromeda, Pegasus, Cassiopeia, and, if I could make out the seventh star in the Pleiades cluster, my eyesight was unimpaired and would stay that way. By then, Johannes was already half blind but did not care to admit it and instead led us, torch in hand, out into the garden so that we could see the stars in reality and I remember thinking that if all that crumbled around us, and grew mucky and stained – like Johannes, who drank all day long until he was senseless and fell asleep wrapped in his piss-smelling blankets, or like the overgrown garden, the mouldy, decaying house or the way Minna's raucous teenage voice terrorised the whole neighbourhood – if everything about our messed-up life together could be swapped for one single moment of peace and stillness, then this would be it. A moment when the silent darkness surrounded us and the stars shone impassively. And things would simply continue to be as they were, up there in the warm black sky. Night after night. As comfortingly safe every time, under the same fixed and always recognisable constellations. This was how I thought.

This is how a child thinks.

*

That something is closely remembered does not always mean you recognise the reality of it, and, least of all, the geography. Because I had decided to walk rather than take a taxi, I had to carry a heavy backpack for more than a kilometre. And because I had no idea what shape the Yellow Villa would be

3

in, I had brought enough kit to deal with the worst possible conditions. The rucksack contained a sleeping bag and mat and, in case nothing edible was left in the house, tinned food and even a small gas stove. Still, walking had the advantage that I would be able to observe at close range all those posh newly built villas that Johannes had found so hateful, the kind of house that invariably turned its back to the road because the conservatory and the overwrought bay windows had to face the sea, a layout that once upon a time would have been unthinkable. As Johannes would have said, they are all graves, complete with carports and parabolic aerials, shrines to new money spent without restraint. The road, too, seems to follow a different route, or maybe that is how it looks to me, now that it has been widened and asphalted. It follows the rocky shoreline in long shallow curves, down to the narrowest part of the island, an isthmus like the waist of an hourglass, where the eastern and western coasts almost meet, and then the road begins its rise to the top of the slope and the Kiwi supermarket. Opposite Kiwi stands the old wooden barn of a building which once upon a time housed both Brekke's colonial grocery store and the ironmonger's where Johannes used to buy nails and gas canisters. The building is still there but has been extended and refurbished in what is intended to be fashionable farmhouse style and its windows display an estate agent's glossy ads, though the supermarket chain of course runs the trading side of things. It is Sunday and the parking lot is almost empty apart from scattered shopping trolleys, as if people had shuffled them about at random and then suddenly left. A road

4

called King's Road starts at the supermarket. It got its name from the way it encircles the whole island on that side of the isthmus. What was once a humble path off King's Road leads to the Mains Farm Road and, if you follow the path past the *Private Road* sign, it ends at the Kaufmanns' farm. The family villa, with its tall, pointed and turreted roof and long veranda, still stands on one side of the yard opposite the barns and outbuildings. The old pump house is further away, where the drive merges with the meadows and woods, and to the right are the paddock and the horse exercise arena that Mr Carsten built, regardless of Kaufmann's approval. When I was a child, a white horse used to stand beside the enamelled tub used for his drinking water, in the meadow with closely cropped grass over where the woods proper began. I remember being in bed during the short, light summer nights when I could watch the horse through my bedroom window, fascinated by its ability to stand there, absolutely still, hour after hour. It might have been sleeping while standing up, as animals often do; or perhaps the horse was the only creature awake while everyone else was deep asleep. I see Minna, half-naked, running across the field below the white horse's paddock. Once again, the summer is burning hot and the taste of sun-baked soil is in my mouth just as it is in hers. I share the stinging sensation when ears of the wheat scrape her bare arms and legs. We run, with me a pace behind her as always, or it could be that I am in the attic, watching her through Johannes's binoculars, seeing her run and then fall. A small hollow has formed in the surface of the field but the stalks close in tightly around her body. From

up here, I can still see her: she is lying on her back and looking straight up into the sky, her face twisted into an inaudible
howl, and then I see the old man come from the farm and
walk down the road, dark stains of sweat have formed where
his braces press against his body; or is he actually Mr Carsten?
The whole scene is like a freeze-frame. Minna is on her back
in the field, her body is still, and he is closing in on her, a
dark shadow that hovers at the edge of the image. That is
all. A dream or a memory: I can't tell. Now I have reached
the Yellow Villa. I go to stand at the back door. Beyond the
trees, Johannes's beehives look like square skulls just showing
above the tall grasses and the air carries the sour smell of stale
soil, as it always does here: it smells of things that have been
in the shade for too long. The mist is growing denser again
and, through it, I hear a plane approaching slowly, then see it
passing in and out of capricious clouds while the roar of the
engines turns into a high-pitched wail and ends in an almighty
bang. Then it is over, the blinking wing-tip lights disappear at
Bird Hill, behind Kaufmann's farm. The key jams in the lock.
I put my shoulder to the door until the top panel gives way
with a noise of splintering wood and I tumble into the dust-
laden darkness with its familiar smells of mouldy cellar and
kerosene. I am home.

*

It was Ebba Simonsen who called to let me know that Johannes
had died. She and her husband had been Johannes's neighbours

ever since the pre-war days when Kaufmann, generally speaking, owned the island. The Simonsens were childless at first but then children came along, one after the other, so that I still remember Mrs Simonsen, even from when I was a small child, with her deep dimples and tired eyes, always surrounded by noisy children while she, her blond hair falling around her face in untidy, damp strands, bent over whatever she was busy with, like baking or laundry. Her husband – I simply didn't know his first name and never called him anything except Simonsen – was a radio sound technician and used to be at work all day long. He eventually retired but was no more present in the home than before. Simonsen had joined actively in the fighting against the Germans (once historians began to write about the resistance movement, their books would always include at least one chapter about Simonsen's work on encrypting radio messages and cracking coded transmissions), but even so, there was no enmity between him and Johannes. After the war, when Kaufmann was in prison and his wife Sigrid and their daughter Helga lived on the farm under a kind of semi-official house arrest, there were many who thought and also said aloud that justice should have been done to the old Nazi's former associates as well, and told Johannes so in no uncertain terms, because he had worked for all those years as Kaufmann's chauffeur. A crowd of several hundred outraged men had gathered outside the Yellow Villa to demand precisely this, when Simonsen had stepped forward to warn them not to do anything they would regret later and instead walk home quietly, each to his own, and leave justice to take its course. Ever since, a spare key to the Yellow Villa had a permanent place on a hook next to the fuse-box in the hall outside Simonsen's workshop. When we were children, Minna and I used to love being allowed to visit Simonsen in his cellar studio, where his remarkable store of sounds, thousands of tapes in tin cans, was housed on wide shelves that covered the wall behind his desk. You could listen to the scraping and grinding of glaciers calving, the astonishing snap of a crocodile's jaws closing around its prey or to long tropical rainstorms, so fierce that they seemed not even to make distinct noises but sounded like a loud hum, as when you have stuffed your ears with cotton wool. If Minna and I were bored in the evenings or during weekends, we often went along to plead with Simonsen to play us some of his sounds. The live voices he had managed to capture made the best listening. He used to say that the pheasants' hoarse double call was like a death-cry – there were lots of pheasants on the island, so many you would see them out on evening strolls like gentlefolk (the cocks anyway, the hens were often cowering in the verges) – and that the noise of Brekke's dog barking was as if it were strangling itself as it tugged at its long leash. We could hear Mr Kaufmann coughing and clearing his throat, and listened to Mr Norvig, the school teacher, giving a complicated lecture on how to fold and unfold the national flag, and Mr Carsten boasting about something in his heavily accented almost-Danish. All the time, while the island was paraded, as it were, in front of our ears, the key hung on its hook by the fuse-box. If we were locked out for some reason, perhaps

8

because Johannes had gone off in the car on an unexpected errand, we could always borrow the Simonsens' key, although Minna preferred to try to enter our house through any unlocked window. So much more fun to climb on downpipes and roof edges than getting the key. But the key's existence meant that Ebba could get into the Yellow Villa after Epiphany this year. In the normal order of things, Johannes always dropped in to wish them Merry Christmas but this year he had not called, not even for the New Year, and his letterbox by the gate had been filling up for a long time with uncollected bills and advertising leaflets. He must have been dead for a couple of weeks by the time Ebba found him, and only the chill in the unheated house had prevented the stench of the corpse from being any worse than it was. He had been sitting in the kitchen to 'rest awhile' after the midday meal, as was his habit, squeezed into the *nook*, as he called the narrow space between the larder door and the small drop-leaf table he ate at. His arm was twisted into an unnatural angle against the table top as his head, like the rest of his body, tilted backwards against the wall. It was in the nook where he would sit down to write to me, year after year. His letters were long, as many as ten or fifteen pages, and must have taken many evenings to write. I had received a letter like that last year, as late as the middle of December, and apart from the stomach pains he always complained about – caused, so I believed, by him not eating properly, only bread and tinned food – it had not suggested that there was anything wrong with him. Johannes's letters were unmistakably his, written in small, tightly packed capitals (he wrote everything in capitals) on coarse squared paper pulled from the poor-quality pads that he bought from Brekke and, before that, from Brekke's father. He pulled each page off once he had filled it, until nothing was left except the glued strip that had held them together, and then he burnt the strip in the ashtray before starting on a new pad. (It has stuck in my mind from when I was little, the distinctive smell of the writing-pad strip as it caught fire and the glue began to smoulder: acrid and nasty.) As the years passed, the tone of his letters grew more and more querulous. The older he became, the more convinced he was that others were ganging up against him. And it was always me whom he felt he must provide with all the evidence he had gathered about local conspiracies. Johannes saved the details of everything and everyone he had dealt with over the years: the records were kept in a large, black, bulging ring binder that he called Carthage. Carthage contained private letters, cuttings of 'Letters to the Editor' in the local paper (penned by himself and others), receipts of bank transactions, letters to the tax authority, the heating oil suppliers, the electricity and water boards and to the island community trust; never-ending disputes about things like where site boundaries went, how to pay for snow clearance, how *the volunteering* would be distributed over the year, how to manage the permanent jetty moorings that belonged to Johannes and the others in the group known as *the twenty site owners*. Et cetera, et cetera. The twenty site owners were the original island residents to whom Kaufmann had partitioned off plots of land. They were always at each other's throats, and the moorings in particular caused endless conflict because some owners wanted to free them up while others – van Diesen was one of them – were intent on buying as many as possible so that, come time, the entire jetty could be turned into a private marina. This is something I'll have to write up for Carthage, Johannes used to say when something had happened to upset him, like this latest issue about van Diesen's plans. Or he could say: I think you'll be interested in something I've got in Carthage. He mostly said this on the phone, and I must confess that, more often than not, the prospect of being subjected to hour-long readings from Carthage was why I produced one feeble excuse after another to avoid going to the island. With passing years, Johannes grew more and more absorbed by these local disputes. I would have a vision of him going through drawers and cardboard boxes, taking days to look for a piece of paper that would set him free from whatever it was he wanted to be free of. Actually, it was remarkable that Johannes wrote anything at all. His sight was growing poor, and his reading glasses often went missing and stayed lost for days, even weeks. His back troubled him and his right leg was nearly paralysed after a fall that fractured the femur, which had left him shuffling about on a pair of crutches. Because he couldn't be bothered with washing properly, he gave off a sour odour of stale urine and sweat, tinged with acetic acid. He claimed to be afraid of falling over if he tried to climb into the bathtub on his own. Not that climbing into the tub would have been of any use: the local council had become fed up with the pile of unpaid bills and shut the water off, once and for all. It was just as well that the rainwater butt under the downpipe was almost always full. I used to go outside, scoop up enough to fill several buckets, pour the water into the big pan to heat on the cooker, and leave some warm water to do the dishes, should he, against all expectation, feel the urge to wash up. I would then carry the buckets to the bathroom and help him get into the tub. There's no telling what comes out of the taps, you have no control, he said as I unbuttoned his shirt and pulled off his trousers. Nonsense, I said. Surely it was you who told me of how the folk round here went off their heads at a rumour that *the old hag* had poisoned the water? But that was when we at least had our own water, from here on the island, he replied, not realising that he contradicted himself. I used the phrase 'the old hag' about Mrs Sigrid Kaufmann because that is how she was traditionally referred to on the island. In past years, he would catch my eye as he corrected me: Mrs Kaufmann, if you please. This time, he didn't look me in the eye but I noticed that he was upset. As I helped him into the dirty tub, he was trembling, and then he stood still, squeezing his arms between his knees, scrawny and grey with a swollen belly and greying hair in his armpits. Show respect, he said while I soaped him once, and then again, while he crouched under the water I washed him down with. Kaufmann let no Germans cross the bridge, he said. For as long as there was a war on, you'd see none of those bastards on the island. Just look at the people who live here now and what they are dragging in, riff-raff, all of them, nothing but scum, foreigners who think they're somehow entitled to live here just because they have money! To shave him, I had to take off my own clothes and climb into the bathtub: two naked bodies, both past their best, facing each other in the frozen light. Don't let your hand shake, he said. You're the one who's shaking, I told him. It must have been the last time I saw him alive. I grew concerned in the New Year, when he had not replied to my letters and Christmas greeting, so, when Ebba phoned me, I had just started to prepare for a trip to the island, packing food and water and a small coal-fired room heater I had picked up. Apart from the usual line about there being something wrong with his heart, no cause of death was recorded, though I am inclined to think that his proud victory over the authorities had also entailed his defeat. He simply froze to death. I did not have to travel to the island for the funeral, which took place a few weeks later, because he had seen to it, long ago, that his grave would be in the same cemetery as the Kaufmann family grave, at Vidarudden on the mainland. The Simonsens came but not many others: Jonas Brekke, the grocer's son, and Peder Kolding, a Dane who lived up on the ridge above the Simonsens' land, with his wife and one of their sons (the eldest), and Sigurd Hansen, who had taken over as chairman of the island community trust when van Diesen stood down. Hansen presumably attended in his official capacity, as it were, because he and Johannes never got on. Most of the letters in Carthage were actually addressed to Hansen. Many of the islanders, who insisted for years that Johannes was an old Quisling, had died before him and those who had not yet passed on shunned him out of long habit. And, of course, no one from the Mains Farm turned up. Who would have gone? Sigrid Kaufmann had died many years earlier. The Kaufmanns' daughter was thought to be alive but it was uncertain, too, since no one had clapped eyes on her. And what of the manager at the Mains Farm, Mr Carsten? He still lived up there with his dog and his horses but, even if he had cared to come to the funeral, no one would have wanted his presence there. Ebba Simonsen often caught sight of him driving down the road with a trailer in tow. As for me, I would have preferred the funeral to have brought the entire sad business to a close, but the house and its contents had to be dealt with. Sure enough: only a couple of months later, I had another phone call from the island. This time, it was Simonsen himself. People come knocking on our door to ask about your house, he said. What sort of people? I said. What sort do you think? Well-heeled ones, obviously. Folk with money. They haven't a hope, I said. That's what I keep telling them, Simonsen replied, and continued: but if that's how you see it, you had better come and make it clear because if people think there might be an opening, they'll just get keener. The house is a ruin, I said. Always has been. That wasn't exactly what I meant, Simonsen said. The silence between us might have been on one of Simonsen's recordings. Just think it over. What would Johannes have wanted? Simonsen said in the end. And think of your sister. It was his mentioning my sister that finally made me overcome the distaste I felt. Or, rather, the certainty that if I only gave myself long enough in the house, Minna, too, would have to come back. In some shape or form, anyway. To help me rescue what little there was worth keeping, and then to get rid of the rest.

*

The island: it seemed as if it had always existed, full of wailing, enigmatic life forms, long before anyone set foot on it. The earliest arrivals must have crossed the strait either in boats or in sledges during the rare winters when the fjord was ice-bound. They went to the lake in the middle of the island, where they cut the ice into large, rectangular blocks and packed them in sawdust for transfer to one of the shipping ports on the mainland. Some time after the ice traders had stopped coming to the island, a few enterprising farmers managed to cross the strait. They tried to farm it but gave up soon enough and returned to the mainland: transportation of goods to and from the island was still far too expensive to make large-scale agriculture profitable. Kaufmann's father, a minister in one of the pre-war Conservative governments, had bought a site on the Main Island's rocky western side where he built himself a summer villa (it is still there) and, while he was at it, had taken the opportunity to purchase all the available land and hire tenants to look after it. Apart from buying up most of the Main Island he also owned land on the nearby West Island and Net Rock. His most important purchase was the Mains Farm, with the fields and large forests around it, which included a lake, or tarn, as the locals called it. Jan-Heinz Kaufmann senior was not particularly interested in farming but acquired land because he reckoned that if he did not, sooner or later another buyer would come along. In practice, the management of the tenancies fell to Kaufmann's only son. The few resident families must have found Jan-Heinz Kaufmann junior an odd sight: a pale and shy youth but also a bafflingly arrogant copy of his father. He was tall and gangly, with a long, thin face, high forehead, pointed chin and small eyes, alert and curious behind his steel-rimmed glasses. Young as he was, he never stepped outside the house without his hat and walking stick, but he hardly ever put on an overcoat or jacket, and usually wore a rough linen shirt, wide and collarless, with his braces, later to be one of his trademarks, slipping off his sloping shoulders. Even though the two Kaufmanns looked so alike, mentally the son was his father's opposite in almost every way. The older man was a conservative pragmatist who understood how money worked, while the younger one was a free-thinking idealist, impressed by foreign utopians and social thinkers such as Charles Fourier and the transcendentalist George Ripley, who founded Brook Farm. Kaufmann would, come time, set up his own alternative community on the Inner Islands, an unstructured association of reform-minded idealists, normally referred to simply as the colony. With his father's tacit approval, Kaufmann started to experiment with new approaches to agriculture such as dynamic crop rotation and new or newly rediscovered types of grain, including emmer wheat, which turned out to give excellent harvests on the drier, relatively more exposed fields on the Inner Islands. To extend the harvest season on Main Island, he tried a late sowing with rapeseed once the autumn wheat had been brought in. On the islands, experimental seed types and oil-rich crops were unheard-of innovations and people laughed at him to begin with but Kaufmann obviously had good contacts and went on to sign a contract with a Lübeck company that produced cheap rapeseed cooking oil; it didn't take long before the entire harvest was exported by ship and rail to Germany. Just a few years later, Kaufmann started to recruit a new workforce. Each one of the new employees was given an illustrated twenty-four-page leaflet entitled *On the Nutritional Requirements of Nature and of Mankind* written by Kaufmann himself. He left no detail unexplained, from the special growing conditions on the islands to the proper formation of a person's character, and in order to make sure that people took his ideas on board, he ran regular house catechisms. The colony grew, not least because he was a decent employer: new workers were offered family quarters as long as at least two members of the household joined one of the colony enterprises. In the early 1920s, he followed Fourier's recommendations and set up a phalanstery building on West Island, which housed up to twenty-five working families. A teacher came across from the mainland every morning to instruct the children. Kaufmann had wanted to found his own local school to make sure that the teaching would be in his spirit, as it were. The plans were quite advanced but the school never materialised or, more precisely, he never received permission to build. At this stage, the authorities had grown suspicious of his utopian ideas. The satirically inclined caricatured him as a wild and woolly eccentric, the very essence of an old-style feudal laird who promised everyone honest work but actually kept his workers in bondage. Still, it was neither police pressure nor bureaucratic obstacles that caused the final dismantling of the colony but mundane financial reality. In the wake of the depression, Kaufmann began to put pieces of land up for sale in order to raise the necessary capital to continue with agriculture in any form on the Inner Islands. By then, he no longer took any personal part in farming and instead spent his time in politics, having changed his party affiliation from the old Farmers' Party to the newly launched National Front. From 1933 onwards, the people on the islands knew him above all as a passionate botanist. The wetlands and the noble deciduous, abundant woodlands around the lake on the eastern side of the Main Island were natural growing grounds for a great variety of plants that were not found elsewhere at our latitude. Kaufmann mapped the species and described the places where they grew in a book that is regarded as unique to this day, especially because of the beautiful illustrations, hand-coloured by Kaufmann himself. His passion for ordering, categorising, surveying and fencing off took many other forms. A small pumping station built by the lake sent the dark forest water to the new homes on the island. Everything that grew fascinated him, as did the potential for growing things to be improved or transformed into something else. As Johannes used to say, Kaufmann was something of a magician. Not that *he* ever changed. He was all of a piece, a committed idealist, if rather lacking get up and go; instead, he grew more introverted, capricious and despotic. And then the war broke out; before long, the Nazis occupied Norway, the Quisling government was set up and Kaufmann was appointed junior minister in the Department of Trade. To his enemies, and there were plenty of them by then, joining the new government was just the predictable next step after the elitist ideas that led him to found the colony. Others assumed that he acted on an opportunist impulse, probably also responding to pressure from Kaufmann senior, who was still alive (he lasted until 1942) and insistent that the land and buildings should not slip out of the family's grip. As for Johannes, he always said that it was nothing but malicious gossip to call Kaufmann a Nazi. The colony, at least in its early version, was imbued with ideas of good will and mutual trust, the opposite of suspicion and hatred. And that much should be obvious to each and every one who looks up even a single page in *On the Nutritional Requirements of Nature and of Mankind*. Johannes argued that Kaufmann collaborated with the Germans only because he had no other choice and, besides, everyone should examine his or her own conscience before trying to decide if Kaufmann had made a virtue of necessity or acted to save his own skin. Then again, when he was convicted after the war, he bore the punishment as if it were a price he had to pay. Did any of the people who called him a traitor ever ask what he had done for his country? Johannes demanded. It was something out of the ordinary for Johannes to be upset, but this time he really was. He had removed his glasses and had been rubbing his forehead red and shiny with his fingertips. Once the crisis years began, he said, when our ports were under blockade and only ships in convoys could cross the Atlantic, Kaufmann had led a small delegation to Berlin on behalf of the government, and managed against the odds to persuade Germany to increase the export quotas for agricultural seed. It was in the autumn of 1942. The German army was victorious on all the fronts and the topic of the day was how to feed the growing population of the Third Reich by exploiting the enormous, newly vanquished territories in Belarus, Ukraine and further eastwards. Hitler was taking a personal interest in the subject, and Kaufmann, who had even been granted an audience with the Führer, used it to elaborate on the methodological hows and whys of improving different cereal seeds and increasing farm productivity. I remember Johannes's faraway smile when he spoke of Kaufmann's German visit. Or perhaps he smiled just because he recalled how proud the old boy had been over his unexpected diplomatic victory. It was part of the story that Johannes had driven Kaufmann from the Mains Farm to the mainland airport, where the rest of the delegation was already waiting, and that he, Johannes, had stayed around for long enough to see the DC-3's sluggish, croaking take-off into the fog. It was a late, damp evening in November, when all of Europe was sodden. Despite Kaufmann's time being swallowed up by his work for the War and Food Supplies Ministry (this was its actual name), during the early war years he would often be seen out on solitary walks along the paths near the lake. Fifteen years earlier, his wife Sigrid had given birth to a daughter, Helga, who at the age of two had been diagnosed with the 'type three' form of spinal muscular atrophy, a slowly progressive condition that with time would confine her to a wheelchair. If you ask me, Johannes said, this was a terrible blow to Kaufmann, as it would be to anyone of his mental outlook and character. Did you ever meet her? I asked. Helga? Johannes replied. Oh yes, many times. Father and daughter were very close, he would have done absolutely anything to make her well and did all he could. He failed simply because nothing worked. After all, it is an inherited condition. He had the trait himself. Now it comes back to me: a swarm of Johannes's bees had escaped from the hive and built a nest for themselves under the roof ridge, so Johannes had propped the ladder against the wall to get close enough to smoke the bees out. It was summer again and the dust-laden air hanging over the Mains Farm Road trembled in the heat, making the farm building at the top of the slope look vaguely blurred in the warm haze. I asked: Then what happened? And he said: What, with Helga? Or Kaufmann? And I: With everything? And Johannes: Well, you know, it was peace-time then, the Germans were gone and NATO had come to take over, here as everywhere else, the airport was in their hands and civilian air traffic was expanding, so the old flight paths were redrawn and came to cross the island. Sigrid Kaufmann protested against the aircraft noise, the level was unhealthy, she claimed. But no one bothered about what she said, she had sided with the enemy, of course, he said as he reached the last few rungs of the ladder, with the bee smoker in one hand and the mask covering his face. The insects were swarming around him and around the opened windows. In the summer, the bees often took off from his rather neglected hives, swarmed and then settled on branches in the trees or under the roof tiles. Next, Johannes removed the waxy comb and held it with his gloved hand. The bees were crawling along his arm and I remember how unbelievably alien his net-covered face looked as I stood at the foot of the ladder, looking up at him: a mask of restlessly crawling insects.

*

I am not sure what I expected, but most things in the Yellow Villa stand exactly where I remembered: Johannes's room was the one he had claimed while Minna was living at home and, in later years, he slept there except when he withdrew to the attic to get pissed. His narrow iron bedstead is still in the far corner by the door where the bedside lamp is, and next to it, the three-legged stool where he would keep a pile of books and assorted medicines. My room and the room that was Minna's are both untouched, except for a lot of stuff that would normally have ended up in the garage: large, brown cardboard boxes full of discarded clothes, a folding ladder smeared with white paint, pots of paint and bottles of turps and paint thinner. Into the room that became mine once Minna moved out, Johannes had dragged the TV set from where it used to stand in the Small Room, as we called it, a cubbyhole between the sitting room and the hall, and the set is still there, plugged into a socket even though the electricity supply was disconnected ages ago, and looking absurdly coquettish thanks to its top being covered by a small lacy runner, presumably crocheted long ago by one of the housekeepers, and quite out of keeping with all the heavy objects piled up around the room; mostly outdoor furniture, loungers and other stuff that someone (surely not Johannes?) must have hauled in. Everything that used to be outside in the yard before, and in the garden and the garage, seems to have been slowly and steadily transferred into the actual house. The rugs are in the same place as always in the hall and the sitting room, as if to give the place at least an aura of respectability, and in the front room, lit by bleak daylight filtering in through the flimsy curtains, the old pieces of furniture stand in pools of shadow. There is the large armchair covered in studded, oxblood-coloured leather that Johannes was so proud of but had never been seen sitting in. Scattered everywhere, in every single room, there are garishly coloured plastic buckets. They smell as if they once contained rubbish or leftover scrubbing water. From the toilet and bathroom next to Johannes's former room comes a thick stench of mouldy wood, bad drains and dried urine that makes my stomach churn. I do not dare to enter the kitchen but have a quick look to make sure the old drop-leaf table is in its usual place in the nook by the larder and Johannes's well-thumbed black address book with telephone numbers is still on the table, next to the wall. His stack of neatly folded newspaper pages, grown enormous over many decades, is also in the kitchen. He kept items like the reportage of the inauguration ceremony for the bridge across the strait, in 1923 or 1924 or whenever it was: an event recorded for posterity in a photograph of the team of construction workers against the backdrop of the bridge, where, among the men, a very much younger version of Johannes can be spotted furthest to the right in the front row, his arms crossed and a sweater carelessly knotted around his shoulders. Then there is the story written fifteen years after the inauguration, on the occasion when a sergeant in the Norwegian air force flew his biplane fighter, a Gloster Gladiator, under the span of the bridge without having told anyone except a photographer on the local paper, who watched the derring-do from a strategically located sea-side rock, took photographs and wrote it up. The published picture shows the plane flying so low over the strait that the two wheels in front almost touch the surface of the water, its twin wings elegantly angled to make sure of passing cleanly under the bridge. A thin layer of snow covers the ground and the bridge is abandoned apart from an anxious-looking guard leaning over the railing to watch from near the shelter. As it happens, the very same flight sergeant, flying the same plane, was shot down over the Oslo Fjord on the morning of 9 April 1940, after having been ordered out on a reconnaissance flight when it had become clear that the German invasion forces were taking the fjord route. Johannes had of course not saved any cuttings about that. I notice how easily I find my way around the Yellow Villa, as if I were still a child. As soon as possible, I go to the room that became mine once Minna suddenly left us, after the long night she had spent up the hill in the Mains

24

Farm. The room is next to Johannes's and the window looks out on the broad field that slopes up towards the farm, where the lamp on the stable wall usually burns all through the night, in summer as well as winter. I remember being frightened by the light and also by the large damp stain on the ceiling that I thought at first was a monster, then some kind of god and later realised was a horrible animal, breathing as it was moving across the ceiling in the dark. I imagined how the animal woke every time the light moved as it fell on the curtains. When it rained and the wind blew and the light swung and rocked in time with the swaying motions of the trees, I dreamt that its black, shadowy body mounted Kaufmann's white horse and rode away. One night, the dream was so vivid that I climbed out of bed, or perhaps it was a sleepwalking version of me who got up and ran outside to walk through the rain along the forbidden road all the way to the horse paddock, where the large enamelled bathtub seemed to shine as white as the stable lamp in the darkness, and opened the gate to let the horse out. Or was that really what happened? Am I mixing my memory of the dream with the time the procession circled the island and Minna suddenly came running down from the Mains Farm with one of Mr Carsten's hunters at her heels? Minna always inflamed me and made me do the wildest things: like that time she forced a group of us to take all our clothes off in the Simonsens' playhouse, or several years later, when she told me to lie in wait in the forest for Kaufmann coming along on one of his botanical and entomological rambles. The idea was to make him stumble on the partly overgrown path by the lake, and then hit him with a stone until I killed him, an act I very nearly managed to complete. Later, shortly after Kaufmann's death from other causes, a doorbell rang – at *the front door*, for a change – and Mr Carsten stood in the doorway, his bulk and height almost filling it, talking to Johannes in the manner of the master addressing a farmhand or, rather, deputy master and stand-by farmhand, since Mr Carsten by then had taken over the running of the Mains Farm in every practical sense. Now, Johannes, Mr Carsten said, this devilry must cease, somehow you'll have to get rid of that girl, and Johannes said nothing or, if he did, it was in such a low voice I couldn't hear it, or else I didn't want to hear because however badly Minna behaved towards me, to live in the house without her was unimaginable and that night, the stain above my bed had grown to twice the size and covered almost half the ceiling. When Johannes came in, he smiled in that absent-minded way of his and told me that the stain was not a monster, and not a god, and, if it was special at all, it must be an axolotl. An axolotl is a Mexican salamander that is awake at night. It can walk and swim equally well, breathing with proper lungs when on land but with gills in the water. It lives practically forever if you give it the right things to eat and isn't one gender or another but has many different shapes, which it can change any number of times. Then he went on to speak about the great German explorer Alexander von Humboldt, who returned home from his travels in South America with one specimen of these strange creatures of the dark. Or probably two specimens, Johannes said, the shadow on the ceiling in my room being cast by one of them.

Johannes had a strange way of smiling. Everyone who knew him will say so. When he removed his small, round, steel-rimmed glasses and smiled, his face looked almost childishly innocent and unguarded. But his eyes would evade yours, as if the smile was no more than a mask to cover his face so that no one should know what he *really* thought. It made some people uneasy; they felt it was false and a sign that he was not to be trusted. Others thought it was just additional proof that he was in a constant state of confusion caused by his incessant *imbibing*, a word that people used in those days. They said that he had started to drink immediately after signing off from his last ship or else that he hit the bottle well after the end of the war, around the time he was sacked from his job at the Mains Farm. That was when the islanders went for him in earnest, threw stones at the walls and windows of his house, over-turned his beehives on the hillock and broke into the garage to slash the tyres of his lovingly cared-for Renault Dauphine. To us children, his boozing was in the nature of things, like his mood swings and censorious hatred of everything and every-one. We had become used to the stale smell of alcohol, both bitter and intensely sweet, oozing from his pores when we tried to shake him awake in the mornings, clinging to his clothes and suffusing the air in the house. When he drank, he usually grew more uncommunicative and distant, and retreated to the attic, where he could stay holed up for days before his con-science forced him to come down and try to find us something to eat. At other times, drinking could make him sentimental and chatty, and then he might tell us about growing up in Blylaget village on Nesodden, and about relatives who had gone to sea, as he had done, even though he would have preferred to study geography or maybe *the natural sciences*, like Nansen or Amundsen. Johannes had crossed the North Atlantic and the Pacific Ocean, and knew his way around the harbours in the Strait of Malacca and French Indochina. He had stories to tell about practically everywhere he had been and would show us the places on maps and postcards. One of his recurring stories came from a tour with a ship carrying propane and butane gas from the Black Sea port of Constanta to Liverpool in England. The ship had just passed through the Bosporus when the seaman on guard duty discovered that one of the gas containers in the hold had started to leak. The captain ordered the crew to go below immediately, locate the faulty container and pump the gas out. The crew refused, to a man. The captain's next move was to promise the sum of £50 from his personal cash allocation to the first man who volunteered. This was quite a fortune at the time and a man whom everyone called Cheery Harry stepped forward. Harry got his nickname, Johannes explained, because he was the sort of chap who never missed a chance to tell a joke or a tall story or attract attention in some other way. There are people like that, Johannes said, they are somehow *raging* inside, have to be in on everything straight away and can't let a challenge pass them by. At this point in the narrative, Johannes would stop for a moment, take his glasses off and rub his face before continuing. There was no diving suit on board but they tied an oxygen canister on to Cheery Harry's back, stuck a rubber tube on its nozzle and told Harry to keep the other end of the tube in his mouth and breathe through it. Then they wrapped his face in several layers of damp linen cloths, put goggles on him and a helmet on his head, and lowered him into the hold by a rope round his waist. Johannes said that Harry had been moving around down there at first: we watched the flickering beam of his torch but then the light disappeared and the rope went slack. When we hauled him up on deck, the helmet and the mouthpiece had come off and the linen cloths were covered in vomit. Some of his mates cut his shirt open and tried to give him artificial respiration, but it didn't help. The poisonous gas was *inside him*. I remember seeing bubbles of gas the size of oranges slip along his spine and his eyes protruded, like fish eyes. As soon as the ship's doctor had confirmed that he was dead, the crew demanded that the ship should go to the nearest port, but the captain refused and said he didn't dare to, not with a gas leak on board. We sailed on with the hatches open round the clock and a total ban on fires and open flames. For several weeks, we lived inside a stinking cloud of gas and kept throwing up, until we were so drained and exhausted we could hardly stay upright. They say that one finds true freedom at sea. Once there, you know soon enough who's in charge: you're owned by the ship's officers and the shipping firm, take my word for it, Johannes said. I never felt as free as the day I signed off. Still, if it were true that the man with gas bubbles in his body had sacrificed his life in vain because he belonged to *a different kind*, as you said, why keep coming back to that hot, sun-pierced morning in the Sea of Marmara when you all stood lined up on deck and the captain held out his fist with fifty quid in it, on offer to the first man to step forward? Could it be because, deep inside, you had a sneaky feeling that it was *you*, Johannes, who were of a different kind? Because you would not see that, to get somewhere in life, you can't keep moving anxiously sideways, like a crab, whenever a demand is made of you. But you smiled, Johannes, nothing more: your usual accommodating smile. Of course, as you would stubbornly remind us, it's a fact that you survived and Cheery Harry did not. And who could deny that?

*

After signing off, Johannes drove a beer delivery lorry for a brewery in the city. It was his first job on land and he always said his good looks got it for him. And that, for the same reason, he had also been given the use of a motorbike: a robust Harley-Davidson with a Steib sidecar. The sidecar had been rebuilt to hold a gigantic beer barrel with the brewery's name and logo painted on its side and, below this, the words EXPRESS DELIVERY in large capitals, as if to suggest that in the event that a licensed venue should suddenly find itself short of beer, a young biker with a fine head of hair would instantly come to the rescue. Obviously just a publicity stunt. When Johannes was not posing for photographs, like some mobile advertising pillar, he drove around in a perfectly ordinary lorry, loading or unloading crates of full or empty bottles in dark, smelly dock-side bays. But he really was good-looking. His thick, straight hair, which would grow thin and lanky with age, was slicked neatly back over his head from just above the fold of skin made by the sweatband of the brewery driver's peaked cap, and his prominent nose, which later made him look crafty and sly, gave strength and character to the young man's face. One of his first deliveries was to the Inner Islands, probably in 1919 or 1920, when Kaufmann had recently installed himself in the Mains Farm and was about to set up the first colony. The bridge to the mainland was not yet built. Because the brewery lorry was too wide to be taken across on the ferry, the crates of beer had to be loaded separately. At the ramp on the island side, a farm cart stood ready to pick them up. Kaufmann himself was waiting in the yard as the cargo of beer bottles came clattering up the Mains Farm Road, and he still stood there, his thumbs hooked under his braces, when Johannes jumped down from the cart and started to unload the rattling crates. No one knows what went through young Kaufmann's head just then, but Johannes was definitely wearing his grey service coat, taken in at the waist and with wide lapels, and of course the cap, complete with sweatband, peak and lacquer emblem, and then Kaufmann asked, having found out the brewery man's name: tell me, Johannes, are you a family man? And as soon as Johannes shook his head emphatically, the decision was already made in principle. Kaufmann often gave an impression of being *distrait*, even confused, but he always knew what he wanted and, once he had made up his mind, arguing was out of the question. Now, can Johannes see the house down there? Kaufmann had said, pointing at a shack on the other side of the road, on the site where later the Yellow Villa was to be built. The place was just a wreck at the time, a man called Brandt lived there and used the outbuildings to breed animals like mink and foxes for their fur. But no more of all that from now on, Kaufmann said, rocking on his heels. Come time, he might well try his hand at animal breeding, he said, but under more rigorous and sanitary conditions. The tannery and those tin-roofed box things meant to be breeding sheds stink to high heaven and must be demolished! Instead, two garages would be built on the site, Kaufmann explained, one to house the new Ford car he had just ordered (though, for practical reasons, it had not yet reached the island) and the other for a diesel-engine Daimler van that he had purchased with the intention of starting up a local omnibus service. Johannes would be responsible for the driving as and when required and, otherwise, for the maintenance of the two vehicles. To that end, he would move into the Brandt house, the Yellow Villa to be, and the land that went with it. He could dispose of it all as he saw fit, but Kaufmann offered to help with supplying wood and other building materials if Johannes wanted to refurbish or even rebuild. Besides, there were quite a few skilled tradesmen on the farm who could lend him a hand when needed. Tell me, in that situation, what was I to do? Johannes asked us. I couldn't say thanks-but-no-thanks just because of the man's political opinions, even if I had known about them at the time. And then Johannes would show us the photos from the year it took to rebuild the Yellow Villa; actually, it was more like a year and a half because the work had to be put on hold during the winter, which was a hard one. There was a picture of the tannery site; in it, Johannes stands in a ploughed field. He and his helpers had been dynamiting and it took weeks to get the blocks of stone out of the way. They are standing side by side, arms around each other's shoulders, possibly at dusk, or else the light might come from the front, it is impossible to say because it is a black-and-white photograph and slightly overexposed. Their string vests are bright white against their tanned bodies, which look so dark they almost merge with the newly tilled soil. It is easy to make out Johannes on the far right because of his round glasses, which reflect a stray shaft of light. And there is his smile, open and so excessively well-actually, meaning it makes him look like an ingratiating vicar. Do not swear allegiance to anyone, the priestly smile seems to say; remember, if you don't there will be no one for you to betray.

*

When did the decay set in, the slow, inexorable disintegration that stood out as the one ever-present part of Minna's and my childhood? Johannes got his job because of his handsome looks and impeccable reputation (as people put it at the time), but later, when the war was over and her husband held in a penal institution, Mrs Kaufmann let it be known that she had no further use for him. Anyway, the farm workers seemed to despise and distrust Johannes, probably from early on, and no one was more against him than Mr Carsten, the farm manager. Johannes had of course always been there *on show*, as it were, and now he was simply too visible; just walking about, he reminded everyone of the shame and notoriety heaped on the Kaufmann family after the war. Perhaps one should make a distinction between the external and internal signs of decline. Long before he arrived on the island, he must have sensed the inner disorientation that he himself thought of as having a *spacious soul*. Even though he never completed secondary school, he was better read than almost anyone else in the neighbourhood. His first job was as a gardener's apprentice, but he dropped out and joined the merchant navy, perhaps because men in his family had earned their living at sea for as long as anyone could remember. Unlike them, Johannes did not have a family to support. Both his parents had died early, within a year of each other. He grew up in the care of an uncle, a rural doctor with a large district who was, as far as I know, quite well-to-do. Perhaps Johannes went to sea because he felt there really was nothing else for him or perhaps he followed the path of least resistance. At least, until that fateful sailing from Constanta. Time passed but he did not marry, not even once he had moved into breeder Brandt's old house. It would have been the proper thing to do, but not only that: he would also have had a wife to stand by him. Instead, he hired a woman to clean and cook, the first of many housekeepers who all had uncertain functions in the household. Some remained just housekeepers, others shared his bed and at least one of them advanced to the point where she got to do his accounts. Regardless, all of them quit within a few months and were remembered only in Carthage, usually the best place for womenfolk, Johannes felt. I remember one of the housekeepers well, perhaps because she stayed on longer than most. Her name was Anne-Louise Hegland. She was not from the island, so she came and went by the regular bus service that linked us to the mainland: four round trips daily. Mrs Hegland was a nice, straightforward woman who would surely have agreed to extend her duties a great deal if Johannes had been able to suggest what and how with any sort of delicacy. Once a month, on a Sunday, the two of them visited a Mrs Guddal, who had worked in the Kaufmann household and later became an in-patient in the Sanatorium at the far end of West Island. The clinic was housed in a large villa, almost a mansion house, which for a few years in the early 1900s had been a nunnery. West Island did not have a bridge either, so the nuns rowed back and forth across the bay in two longboats, which afterwards were left belly-up nearby, looking like beached whales. Once the bridge to the Main Island was ready, the Sanatorium became the home of a psychiatric clinic, run by a trust, with Mrs Kaufmann as one of the board members. Mrs Guddal had been employed by the Kaufmanns since the mid-thirties but had lately succumbed to a condition that was officially understood to be feeble-mindedness but which all the locals knew was kleptomania. Mrs Kaufmann had caught Guddal red-handed in the process of pilfering a cream jug from the family china collection and, once an investigation got underway in earnest, the woman turned out to have quite a treasure trove tucked away in the basement, where the servants' quarters were at that time (the basement could be reached via a separate entrance at the back of the house). Guddal's booty included jewellery, clothes and a considerable sum of money. Mrs Kaufmann gave her a stiff talking-to, Mrs Guddal claimed to be full of remorse and apparently handed everything over. She worked as a cleaning lady in various island homes afterwards, but that phase ended just as badly. I believe she stole from Johannes as well. She grew more and more confused, insisting for instance that Mr Carsten was her legal husband and other similar notions, which were always dismissed as pure nonsense up at the Mains Farm. I noted that Johannes and Mrs Hegland were exceptionally punctilious about their monthly trip to visit Mrs Guddal in the Sanatorium but could not fathom why they laid on this overdone show of respect for a woman who was, when all is said and done, no better than a thief and a liar. They drove there in Johannes's blue Dauphine. Minna and I were not allowed to come along because Mrs Guddal didn't like children, or so Mrs Hegland said. Before each visit, Hegland set aside several evenings to bake and prepare meals for the ailing lady, and if it was spring or early summer, she always took a bouquet of freshly cut flowers. And then, on the return journey from one of these Sunday excursions, Johannes proposed to Mrs Hegland. He probably tried it on because their joint trips made them look like a couple but, however he went about making his obviously distasteful proposal, it is a fact that the Sunday outings to the Sanatorium ceased from that day, and Mrs Hegland never again stepped off at the bus stop or made her way up to the Yellow Villa with a laden shopping basket. Mrs Hegland was the housekeeper who stayed for the longest time, but I also remember some of the others. One of them stood balanced on the top rung of the ladder, measuring tape in one hand, as she worked out the size of the new sitting-room curtains, one length of fabric after another. She had bought the material with money from the housekeeping kitty, but Johannes took more of an interest in the lady's long, slim legs than in the curtains. He climbed up into the oxblood-coloured studded armchair and hugged the housekeeper's thighs so hard that she lost balance and tumbled to the floor in a cloud of glittering lace. And then she, too, gave notice. On top of all the recrimination caused by Johannes's offensive behaviour towards the women who helped him in the house, there was much head-shaking about the poor little children whom he had been made responsible for, goodness knows why. Anyone could see what a rough time they were having, what with that man being the only one to look after them. Johannes alone did not grasp why people were shocked. But, then, he had anxieties of his own. He must have thought it incomprehensible that his every attempt at courtship was regarded as an indignity. It made him distrustful, and more and more of a loner. One might speculate about what would have become of him if we had not been there – my merciful gifts, as he called us. As well as the great shame of his life.

*

Supper has been eaten, plates and cutlery have been cleared away, he has brushed the crumbs on the table into his palm and thrown them into the sink as usual, and opened the pad covered in oilcloth against the edge of the table, pressing the pages down with his left arm to keep them straight and bending forward over them, the biro gripped firmly in his right hand. Every evening, he sat like this, wearing only his rough string vest, with his round, steel-rimmed glasses on his nose, shaping each letter with the patient precision necessary to thread a needle. Behind his back, beyond the dirt-streaked kitchen window, the twilight was waning. Towards the end of his life, Johannes wrote more often and took longer to pen his letters, which were practically always addressed to me, or so I believe. Even though he seemed to have jotted things down with no particular care and was more likely to write about notions drifting into his mind than things he felt were important to tell me about, his letters could also be read as an ongoing plea in his own defence, always shifting between lines of argument and requiring a range of strategies to deal with an accusation that was never explicit but, for that very reason, was always hanging over him. It was as if Johannes, because he always revisited this fragmented document of self-defence, was forced into a kind of constant retreat across space and time, only to find himself unable to reach any refuge more secure than that nook of his between the drop-leaf table and the larder door, where he sat, evening after evening, busy writing his letters to me. He would set out within arm's length everything that mattered to him then: the brandy bottle, the

38

crosswords, the lottery coupons and a free calendar handed out by the brewery he had once worked for and in which he every morning crossed out the previous day, as if time was nothing other than another day's work that had to be done; there would also be a few objects from the collection of odds and ends that he had picked up during his travels, perhaps aimlessly, but which were wonderful playthings for us children. I remember in particular a small bamboo box from Java: it had a beautiful lacquered lid with a painting of a tropical forest landscape with dense clusters of palm trees and a field with a farmer in an Asian rice hat who walked behind a plough pulled by two water buffaloes. The lacquer paints were so thick the surface bulged and so glossy the figures seemed to glow. When she was little, Minna was obsessed by the Javanese box. She would not stop scratching at the lid with the nail on her index finger and picking away at what remained of the colourful crust. Inside the box Johannes kept some essential practical objects, like the keys to the garage and the car, but there were photographs as well, not like the old family setpieces, showing his relatives posed in sober, formal clothes at neatly laid dining tables or in garden arbours, but the small, shiny Kodachrome images of our real parents from America, photos that in contrast to the other ones were in colour and also taken in places we could recognise. In some, Mr and Mrs Lehman stand together with Johannes under the Morello cherry trees in the garden or in front of the NATO villa, where we lived when we were small – or so Johannes said. We were of course especially fascinated by the NATO villa, built on a steep slope and on two floors, where part of the top floor had been extended into a large, oval terrace flagged in grey slate, which had been polished to a mellow, slightly uneven surface, and finished around the edge with a terrace railing made of semi-transparent fibreglass, a material that must have been a novelty in the early 1950s, when the house was built. Johannes's family photographs seemed to overflow their hefty frames, but the snapshots in the Javanese box were different, appealingly easy to handle, small and square and surrounded by a wide, white frame. I am in one of them, about one and a half years old, standing on sturdy legs under the willow in Johannes's garden, a big, stooping tree that, to this day, walls in a lifeless spot with its long, droopy branches, and the child who was me is looking straight at the photographer with the total expressionless seriousness of the very young (who took the picture, I wonder, my father or Johannes?), while in another picture my mother stands half turned away, her long blond hair pulled lightly together with a broad clip at the nape of her neck. Unlike her husband, Elizabeth Lehman was not of German descent: we were told that her maiden name was Westwood and that she came from an old family who had lived in New England since the eighteenth century. Frank Lehman was an adult when he moved to the USA. According to Johannes, it was my father, Frank, who had insisted that his and Elizabeth's firstborn, a daughter, should be given the rather antiquated name Wilhelmine, apparently after his paternal grandmother, though on their lips and ours, it was always Minna. My name, Andreas, has no known source; I do not know whose name I bear. My father probably had a great deal on his plate when my christening was due. Frank was a real-life war hero. At least, that is what Johannes always says when he takes the precious pictures out from the Javanese box and we lean forward over the table to see properly, straining so much we almost get neck cramps. During the Korean War, your father carried out several hundred life-or-death sorties over enemy territory, Johannes tells us. Was he the pilot? I ask, or perhaps it is Minna. No, he was the one who made the bombs drop, Johannes explains. He sat in the bomb bay at the far end of the plane and when he was told through his earphones that they were in the right position, he opened a hatch to let the bombs drop, and so we imagine this: the bombs that move across the sky, looking like small cross-stitches on a wall hanging, and then blossom into great exploding stars when they hit the ground over there in the black enemy landscape. Here he is, our heroic father, smiling as he stands next to his huge pistachio-green Studebaker, which he has parked in the middle of the drive to Johannes's house. It is in the late spring or maybe early summer of 1961, clearly a warm, sunny day. He wears a suit and tie, but the jacket is unbuttoned and the trousers casually worn, held up by a belt just below the navel, as people did then. I look in vain for my own features in my father's broad face, but it is hard to make anything out because of his merry grin. His smile has the boundless self-confidence of someone who feels it is due to him alone that the grass grows so tall and the fruit trees in the background are in such fluffy bloom. Every time I look at these pictures, even now (they are still in place in the brightly painted bamboo box), it is just as hard to comprehend what happened a little more than a year later, also on a day in early summer. Johannes had been standing on top of the folding ladder, busy spraying the plum trees that had been plagued for years by grey mould and shot hole blight. From inside the canopy of a plum tree, already almost in leaf, he spotted the pistachio Studebaker driving on the long, gravelled road that begins outside the NATO villa at the top of the slope below Bird Hill. It was so strange, Johannes said afterwards, the way the car seemed to take it easy. The dust cloud that always followed it had almost settled by the time it stopped outside the gate to the Yellow Villa. As Johannes put away his spraying kit and climbed down, my father, holding Minna and me by the hand, already stood leaning against the hood of the car. Behind his sunglasses, Mr Lehman had looked troubled, despite his smile. You see, Johannes said, he didn't just look jolly on photographs, it's a fact that Frank smiled whenever he spoke or was spoken to. There had been a regrettable accident, Mr Lehman said, or was that really what he had said? Johannes didn't remember exactly. Frank might have said it straight out but without mentioning what kind of accident. Anyway, he had to accompany Mrs Lehman to the hospital, and could Johannes possibly look after the children? It would only be for a few hours, at most. Johannes assumed that the accident had happened to my mother but admitted that it was just a guess: the car windows facing his way were closed. Still, who else could it have been? If not, why all this fuss about the children? Of course Johannes agreed to keep an eye on the children. The NATO villa was far up along the sloping road but, even so, Johannes was the Lehmans' closest neighbour. Besides, the two of us had been darting in and out of his house all the time, as he put it. It was surely Minna who did the darting; if I did, it was just as an unknowing witness following in my sister's wake. Johannes gave us a snack meal in the kitchen, a sandwich and a glass of milk, he told us (smiling at the memory of the milky froth that stuck, as always, to Minna's upper lip), and then we played in the garden until he called us to come inside because it was getting dark. By nine o'clock in the evening there had still been no sound of the Studebaker (it had become a habit of Frank's to hoot the horn as he turned off the road into our drive and then wave to us), so Johannes called the hospital and was put through to a ward. Yes, a woman by the name of Elizabeth Lehman had been admitted. Once Johannes had told the sister that he was in charge of the Lehman children and that they were anxious to know how their mother was, Frank Lehman came along to speak to him. My father's tone of voice had changed, Johannes said; it was loud and distinct but sounded colourless, almost hollow, as if from far away. They talked briefly. Frank Lehman had said that the situation was extremely serious and that they could only hope and pray. *Hope and pray*. Had he used precisely that phrase? I asked. In English? Or in Norwegian? Because he did know quite a bit of Norwegian. Johannes could not recall the language, only that Frank had sounded tense and distant, somehow *encapsulated*, that was one word he used. This seems

43

to have been the last time anyone on the island, including Johannes, spoke to Mr Lehman. The following morning, Johannes drove us to the hospital in the old Dauphine. With much less room in the back than in the Studebaker, we were squashed together and Minna held me on her lap. The girl had been excited and happy, Johannes said. We had been in the garden to pick the still slightly unripe cherries for our mother and had bought her flowers as well. But when we arrived in the ward, she was no longer there: a patient with the name Elizabeth Lehman had been discharged earlier that morning and professional confidentiality meant that the nurse could not tell us why the patient had been admitted in the first place. In response to Johannes's question, the nurse however confirmed that Mr Lehman had been with her all the time. He had brought his wife's things, apparently. What she meant by *things* was never clarified and no one knew, of course, where the Lehmans were now. Once he had got this far in the story, Johannes invariably took his glasses off and began to rub his forehead. I had no choice, I had to bring the two of you back with me, he would say with an embarrassed smile, as if found out to have done something forbidden, even shameful. Around this time, he must also have contacted the US embassy, but the officials denied all knowledge of any Lehmans, either well or suddenly taken ill, which is, as I now know, their routine for dealing with such situations. (That is, denial is the set response: diplomats will always say they know nothing until they know more, and then keep silent because of what they have learnt.) By the following morning, the police had

44

cordoned off the road to the NATO villa at the crossing with the Mains Farm Road and men in strange white suits and helmets with visors were walking along the ditches and pottering around the pump house at the Mains Farm. They had brought instruments for measuring things, and a constable on guard duty told Johannes that the entire area was, from now on, a designated crime scene and that we would learn soon enough what it was all about. *Soon enough* turned out to be at six o'clock the same evening, when two plain-clothes policemen came to the front door of the Yellow Villa and wanted to know if we had noticed any effects from the water recently. By *effects*, they meant things like feeling sick, vomiting, fever, diarrhoea. They were concerned about the possibility that something in the drinking water might be a cause of trouble as several people in the neighbourhood had shown such symptoms, some so serious that those afflicted had to seek medical help. Even so, it had taken time before people had drawn the only reasonable conclusion. Because the residential water supply had been drawn from the lake for as long as the current population had settled on the island, it must now have been poisoned somehow – and who would have the opportunity to do that except the person or persons in charge? In other words, someone at the Mains Farm. Soil samples were collected from all around the pump house and the pump itself was taken apart and examined in detail, but no plausible explanation for the sudden attacks of sickness was ever found. (A later report stated that the soil and water samples from the island contained certain perfluorinated compounds that are components

45

of firefighting foams, and because the fire and rescue services ran exercises regularly in the nearby mainland airport, the contaminants could well have built up in the still water of the lake; PFCs break down very slowly in nature and are described as persistent. It seems that, in the long term, PFCs can cause hormonal malfunctions, including reproductive ones, and foetal damage, but not the acute illness that struck so many people more or less overnight. All the report provided, if anything, was yet another argument for Mrs Kaufmann to use in her campaign against the flights across the island, so dangerous to health, and in favour of moving the nearby mainland airport to somewhere else.) Once the incident had been investigated, the only remaining issue was the presence of two orphaned Lehman children, thought by many to be the most scandalous part of the whole event, especially when they realised that Johannes was the official carer. The American bureaucrats consistently refused to confirm that Mr and Mrs Lehman ever existed, so the social services moved in and used every argument they could think of, including bribes and threats, in order to make Johannes accept that the children must be looked after by people described as *responsible* foster parents; when Johannes refused, quite a few women, some young and some not, suddenly overcame their distaste for the old Quisling and turned up to sit on his threadbare sofa and drink cups of coffee. I remember some of them: their sticky hands on the back of my neck and their eager talk about well-heeled husbands and the very good schools we would attend, and Minna making faces (I also remember that, of course):

how she rolled her eyes or pretend-strangled herself or staggered to the toilet and made vomiting noises. The police must have been involved, I suppose, perhaps they sent out an international search warrant, but throughout Johannes refused to shift from what Frank had told him that afternoon: that he and his wife had to go away but would be back shortly. However, they never got in touch with Johannes or with us, never sent as much as one single letter or card, not any kind of message, nothing.

*

I often wondered what Minna remembered about our real parents, who are almost blanks in my memory, reasonably enough, since I was the younger child. It is a source of deep regret that I never got round to asking her while there was still time. The fragments that stay with me are sequences of sights or sensations that could belong to anyone. A hint of a warm, rough and somehow oily taste on my tongue that I now tell myself might be the leather seats in the Studebaker, warm after a long day in hot sunshine. I imagine that I can also remember, with my sense of touch as much as sight, the tight pleats in a wide, white skirt (my mother's, perhaps?), a steady, bluish light from a table lamp that someone has covered with a cloth (to soothe us children to sleep?) and a threshold with a varnished surface so shiny that it reflects the much larger room on the other side of it, a room I can only guess at. Sounds of voices come from the far end of that room or perhaps from somewhere near it, where many grown-ups have gathered, and whose elegant hairdos and black-suited backs I can see mirrored in tall, dark windows. Johannes always said that our parents had never wanted to leave us for good, that they had every intention of coming back as soon as my mother was well again or as soon as circumstances permitted. He never said anything about what these circumstances might be. The content of the stories Johannes told us would change with his moods. Quite often, he said that our parents had been on board the Vickers Viscount plane that crashed when descending to land at the airport on the other side of the strait. It was late in the winter of 1963, a disaster that eye witnesses, like Simonsen and Brekke, will reminisce about to this day. Frank and Elizabeth Lehman were supposed to have been on a plane flying via the North Pole, a common route for flights from America at the time, or so Johannes said (it sounded as extraordinary every time he used the words: they flew over *the Pole*), landed briefly at Søndre Strømfjord on Greenland and went on to Copenhagen, where they boarded another plane to come here. It was in February, an evening of grey mists and hard snow showers rushing inland from the fjord, reducing the visibility to practically nil. The plane from Copenhagen came in too low, Johannes told us, and would make his flattened hand dive menacingly close to the edge of the table, then draw his shoulders up to mimic the tight gap between the low cloud cover and the island forests as the Vickers Viscount with a rough, roaring noise broke through the snowy mist but, Johannes went on, I don't know if there was something wrong with the

48

plane or if the bad weather had led to a navigational error, still, it didn't manage to climb again and instead reared up *like this*, and he put his hand up straight from the table top, and then it slammed into Bird Hill, *like this*, he said, and slapped the table so hard the glass of brandy fell onto the floor and spilled its contents, and since he had just filled it up to the brim, he had to go down on his knees to rescue the newspaper cutting he had extracted from the pile on the kitchen table. The report of the air accident had been given a big black headline and was illustrated by pictures of firemen in helmets pulling hoses across a field that was presumably the impact site, snow-covered by then. It was a terrible accident, Johannes said when he had got up from the floor, and tears were glistening in the reddish folds at the corners of his eyes, though maybe that was just the booze. But you were little at the time, you won't remember anything, thank goodness. Then what happened? Minna asked. With what? Johannes was so drunk he had to prop his body up by placing his elbow on the table before he could refill his glass. With our mum and dad? Surely they must have been buried somewhere? (Minna could be very persistent when she felt like it.) Or are they still lying up there? Instead of answering, Johannes only smiled. So, of course, we realised straight away that he had not told us the whole truth. But, if he lied to us, it was not because he wanted above all to protect us from feeling that our parents had abandoned us; rather, it was a way of dealing with a painful memory of his own that he could not handle except in this kind of over-dramatised, drink-fuelled tale. Meanwhile, the NATO villa, the house we believed had once been our home, stood high up on the ridge and easily visible to all, the broad sweep of its terrace finished with an 'American' railing, its steep, low roof and, on the facade facing the farm, windows so tall that all of the sky was mirrored in them. I can't remember if I ever met the new people who moved in; I don't know where they came from or if they, too, had children. Back then, if I took notice of anything at all, it was only what Minna wanted me to notice. I walked in her shadow. Even early on, she had begun to talk to strangers and tell them about how she and her little brother were kept in captivity by a drunken seaman and how her real parents tried to free us and secretly got in touch with her at night. They used a special code language that they tapped out in rain-letters against the roof tiles of the house and against the tin window ledges. The bit about the rain-letters she told me about when she crawled into bed with me and pressed her heavy, sticky body against mine and said, can't you hear it? *Tap-tap-tap*, that's Mum who's whispering to us. Mum had told Minna what had really happened that had forced them to escape from the island. That Mrs Kaufmann was behind it and had been plotting to get rid of the intruders. Yes, that was what they called us, the whole family, not just Mr and Mrs Lehman but us children as well. The intruders and their bastard offspring. Mr Carsten had apparently placed traps all over the forest, hoping that we would get caught in them. And the old one, Mr Kaufmann, he was behind it all. He was out from prison by then and installed in the Mains Farm, almighty and powerful even though nobody saw him. His health was not the best, Johannes said, but Minna was not to be shaken. She was convinced that Kaufmann was evil and whispered it into the back of my neck and my scalp: *evil evil evil!* Then, one day, she made up her mind: we were to walk up to the NATO villa. To find the *clues* and make them safe, that was how Minna put it. She must have really frightened me because my only memory of getting there was of how scared I was to lose touch with her. Minna always walked four or five long, determined paces ahead of me. The garden had grown wild and the thorny raspberry bushes made long scratches in our arms and legs. Minna clambered up to one of the windows and tried to cling to it, but it was too high on the wall, so we could only look inside if one of us stood on the other's shoulders. Now, I have no memory of what we saw except for some furniture I did not recognise, and that's all; the homes of strangers always look the same. But I do remember how worried I was that someone inside the house would catch sight of us, or maybe someone walking along the road would come to find out what we were up to or, even worse, someone from the Mains Farm would spot us. What really stuck in my memory afterwards was how different all that was familiar and trustworthy looked from here, high up on the hillside. The old dusty country road followed the outlines of the cultivated land as usual; the farm was the same and the fields and the dark forest. But because all of it had been displaced through 180 degrees from my usual perspective, it seemed to belong to another world. I also saw things I had never noticed before: the Mains Farm, with its apparently solid frontage (interrupted just once where the road entered), was in fact made up of several small, quite widely scattered buildings, stables and hay barns and, a little further away, the pump house and the farm manager's house, a smaller copy of the family villa, with a tiled roof and front steps leading to a veranda. Mr Carsten's car and old horse trailer looked harmless where they were parked on the shady side of the house. A large, probably ancient oak that I had not seen before grew on the far side of the farm, its tall canopy overshadowing half of the yard. Black birds perched on the oak tree's branches. So this was where they came from, all the crows I watched as they swarmed across the sky at dusk.

*

It is raining. I stand near the garden plots, next to the old incinerator bin, listening to the whiplash sounds of raindrops hitting the leaves. The tart scent of wet grass is sucked up into the smoke belching out of the bin. The smoke stings my eyes, making them water. In Johannes's large garden, this is the most sheltered corner and also, as it happens, the part closest to the road. Beyond the damp wall of the trees massed along the boundary, I hear the sounds of children's voices calling to each other, tough plastic rain-proof trousers rubbing against saddles and cycle frames and the unmistakable pings of bicycle bells. I can't make out their faces but the voices bring back the past, memories of how Minna and I set out for school together every day, and some of the boys cycled past close enough to hit my head with their satchels and then they would call out over their shoulders while pedalling hard towards the school: hey, when's your *daddy* back? This afternoon, I am wearing Johannes's old sheepskin-lined winter coat that smells of oil and mouldy cellar, and in the tall grass around me I have dumped stuff brought out from the house, things like beer crates, broken kitchen chairs, threadbare old rugs and stacks of cardboard boxes and newspapers. The fire burns with searing intensity and throws cascades of sparks up into the billowing black smoke. The boards crack loudly when I break them across my knee, a bird erupts from the silent mass of leaves and then, as I turn, there is Mrs Simonsen's pale face, outlined against the curtain of greenery on the other side of the raspberry hedge that marks the boundary between Johannes's site and theirs. She has aged since I last saw her. Her blond hair is white now and cut austerely short. The Cottage, a tiny house where we children used to play, still stands in the middle of the lawn but a glasshouse has been built next to it. Its glazed walls look lighter than the sky but are dappled with rain just now. Further away, by the front steps to the house, I catch a glimpse of Simonsen. For a moment, all three of us are immobile, like statues in a park. I fancy the Simonsens are looking at me with a kind of mournful sympathy, the way you look at the one child who never got anywhere, who was always pushed out of the way or left behind . . . and look, now he's back again! Which is probably how they felt. The electricity is off, I explain, just to say something. No water, either, I add after a short silence. A plane is flying overhead in the low clouds, slowly on its way in to land.

It suddenly becomes visible above the edge of the forest, as if catching up with the roar of its engines. A Lufthansa flight. Andreas, have you had anything to eat? Simonsen abruptly asks from his front step, where he has stayed as if glued to it and where he stays while he listens to what Ebba and I are saying, or tries to. Now and then he speaks loudly to us, as if he neither dares to come any closer nor wants to go inside in case he misses out on something important we might say. Sigrid Kaufmann is dead, you know, Ebba Simonsen tells me. Maybe you didn't know? Actually, I did know. Her death was referred to in an article I had seen, more of an obituary of her husband and written well after the loathing of the old man had finally come to seem meaningless: twenty, even thirty years too late. I would have liked to ask about Mr Carsten, if he has finally managed to die by now, but I don't dare to. Something about the farm on the far side of the field makes it still out of bounds for words. I'll phone the electricity people for you, Simonsen shouts from his post by the front door. Straight away, he adds and, relieved at having hit on the reason to get away that he has been trying to think of all the time, he raises his arm in a jolly wave before disappearing inside. He shuts the door behind him. Ebba looks at me and smiles. It could be that she, too, is struck by the distances in space and time, which might be why she can see through the grown man by the fire bin and recognise inside him the little boy wearing nothing but worn underpants who was sent out to pick raspberries from his side of the hedge while she was picking on her side. The boy's bare shoulder blades fold back like the wings of a bird when he lifts the empty bowl with both hands, as if to offer up fruit that is not there. She puts three of her raspberries in the bowl and then, jokingly, pops a fourth into his mouth. He does not move and, wide-eyed and silent, he still holds out the bowl, and she carries on picking for him until it is full, and he turns to walk back through the shoulder-high grass with the brimming bowl raised above his head to bring the raspberries to Johannes, who is up on the roof nailing something down. What separates the two of us, the inscrutable adult burning his past in the garden incinerator and the shy four-year-old, walking so carefully and uncertainly, his whole life ahead of him? On the outside, nothing much. There is something similar about the way they hold themselves when they walk, shoulders back so that the spine gets a sway curve all the way down to the tailbone. Later, when I was diagnosed with a sideways curvature of the spine, Johannes always said it was inherited and that my father had also had a problematic back.

*

They meet up in the Simonsens' house, all the past and present neighbours, some of whom even claim to have been Johannes's close friends. That they happened to turn up here at the same time is just coincidence, they tell me, but of course I realise that they have come to inspect me. They simply want to find out what kind of man I am. But despite the mutual wariness, the crowded kitchen is full of good cheer and Mrs Simonsen is kept busy brewing coffee while laying the table in the large sitting room. The talk is about the island *old-timers*, the original site owners who still cling tightly on to life. Take Skakland, for instance, the old chap who used to deliver the papers. In the seventies, he drove a battered yellow Swedish post-office van. Skakland's son delivers the papers nowadays and does the entire round, east and west of the neck of land, in one hour and eighteen minutes, or so they say. In a record time anyway, so they call him the Speedfreak. The current owner of the NATO villa, van Diesen, has also come along. He had finally decided to buy it, and then had an extension built, a tasteless monstrosity with bay windows and sliding glass doors in the style its detractors call *builder's baroque*. Sure enough, it was Klamm, boss of the construction firm, who organised the job for van Diesen. By now, Klamm seems to be at work everywhere in this country . . . it says KLAMM BUILDS in giant red capitals on the big hoardings along the drive to the airport because they are building a brand-new shopping centre with four floors of underground parking. Ads with the same text have pride of place on the cranes and on the piles of concrete blocks with protruding steel bars turning up all over the country, which these days seems to be close to suffocating on its obscene wealth. As for Master Builder Klamm, his whereabouts are unknown to everyone here. One of the rumours on the island is that Klamm has carried off his young mistress and all his financial assets to Switzerland or, alternatively, the Cayman Islands. A lead-in for someone to ask if Johannes perhaps had *left something*? It is Brekke junior, I think. My head is full of the letters, notebooks and newspaper

cuttings that *actually* are Johannes's only gift to posterity, but
the oddly expectant smile on Per-Ulrik Brekke's round face
tells me that he is after something more substantial. Johannes
was destitute when he died, I reply. What about the house?
The question comes instantly. And: what do I plan to do with
the house? The land alone must be worth a fortune. Joking
aside, are there really any doubts about my inheriting the lot?
Anything in writing? Didn't Johannes have other relatives,
somewhere on the mainland? People ask questions that are
genuinely well-meaning and I am not offended. I know as well
as they do that Johannes never formally adopted me and that
I cannot lay claim to anything. Nothing here is worth a penny,
I say. Just crap, the best idea would be to torch the lot. This
makes the whole congregation burst into hearty laughter and
then, urged on by Ebba Simonsen, everyone moves into the
sitting room, with its wide window that offers a full view of
the Mains Farm, stables, outbuildings and all. The view makes
it feel natural to start talking about the people up there: even
about the once untouchable one – Helga, the daughter. She
died last spring, Brekke says, though no one got to know until
several months later. She was cared for at home to the end.
I think it was arranged for a nurse to live in, Mrs Simonsen
says. She was the one who made it known that Helga had
passed on. Well, indirectly: we knew because the nurse simply wasn't around any more. So, Mr Carsten is the only one
left up there now. Remember the time we got the old sod well
boozed up? van Diesen reminisces suddenly, and gives Brekke
a shove. Gave him half a litre of home brew and talked him

into believing it was Stolichnaya. So what happened with the farm? I ask. Executor's sale, Brekke replies. There's no one left who can take the place over and run it as a farm, and it's good for nothing else because of the nature reserve that is all around it. Then the talk returns to where it began. Prices, money. How much might the farm be worth? What could be done with the land? And, inevitably (as a thousand times before), stories are told of Mr Carsten's grandiose plans, like constructing a horse-racing track around the entire lake, for harness racing. He's *a right one*, Brekke says, no legs fit to stand on, let alone any good for sitting on a horse.

*

In the old days, it happened sometimes that even Helga, the daughter, a girl who wasn't at all well, would be seen outside, mixing with other children. Johannes caught sight of her once near the Yellow Villa. She was cycling. It was a couple of years before the war. Her being out and about must have had something to do with the National Day on 17 May. She had dressed up, wore a white hat with a red hatband tied into a bow and a white dress, and her strong, honey-blond hair had been combed into a long, lovely plait that emerged below the wide brim of the hat and reached well down her back. She was concentrating, cycling with sudden, hard tugs on the handlebars, as if cautiously trying to avoid all the puddles. At each rough twist, her head jerked and made her jaw muscles tense and her eyes widen strangely. It was her illness showing, Johannes said, it had already settled in her face. Beneath the hem of her dress, the pedalling legs were clad in some kind of shaped metal supports and, a few paces behind her, Mr Carsten was walking with his marked limp, his eyes not for one second leaving the rear wheel of the bicycle. Once the war had ended, for a while the word was that young Miss Helga would go to school with the other children, the same school that Minna and I would later join and the only school on the island. But her first day in a classroom had not even ended when her mother told Mr Carsten to go and fetch her back home. Since that day, many decades ago, she was rarely seen. Little was said about her disability while I grew up but all the more about how she, Kaufmann's only child, had been too good to mingle with the island kids: an anxious, spoilt girl. The proof, plain for all to see, was the large black limousine that came to pick her up every day and took her to a private school on the mainland. For years, this was a familiar sight. The back seats of the limo were so wide and deep that nothing could be seen of the young woman inside. Naturally this was just the thing to pile up more distaste for her and the rest of the folk up on the Mains Farm. It was as if the gossip circled around two quite different people: one was an ill, vulnerable girl and another was the Princess, superior and untouchable. Mr Carsten, the farm manager, was also hated. Even though he was ugly and had a gammy leg, it still was somehow quite in order to detest him. Unlike Helga, he was always about, too much so, with his polio-damaged leg and partly paralysed face where half his mouth hung open in a permanent grin while, above it, a cold, grey eye stared at you. People would keep meeting him on the island roads, moving with his peculiar limp, a manner of walking that even his many dogs seemed to mimic, as if scared to be different from their master. On top of this, there was his bragging, superior way of speaking and his half-Danish accent, which was such an alien language it seemed almost archaic. One of Simonsen's tapes had recorded him boasting about something or other to a group of people whose presence one could only guess at from the odd nervous cough and restless shuffling of feet. But it was unclear exactly *what* Mr Carsten was holding forth about. This could have been because of poor sound quality or else it could have been that his harangue consisted not so much of words as of noises, often a rasping, rather painful wheeze that I assume was a self-satisfied laugh but which sounded as if he was about to suffocate. There would be a few strings of words that somehow tightened into a long, heaving inhalation, then some guttural noises, followed again by hoarse, constricted breathing through an open mouth, as if gasping for breath and failing. Since we had not the faintest idea what he was saying, we laughed, but it was frightening, too, because the speaker was so unmistakably Mr Carsten: an entire human being reduced to a collection of obscene sounds. As far as I can remember, we felt much less hostile towards the lady at the Mains Farm, the widow, Mrs Sigrid Kaufmann, even though she had lived with her old man throughout the war and ought to have been as hated, if we had been consistent. When we spotted her occasionally out and about on the island, we would shout *you old hag* after her, but our hearts wouldn't be in it. I do remember that. And also that she never turned to look at whoever was shouting. This was supposed to show that she was arrogant but was later explained by the fact that she was hard of hearing. And it seemed as if her partial deafness counteracted some of the resentment that we would otherwise have felt.

*

The Dead House: this was the children's name for the Yellow Villa. As if we, who lived in it, not only made the decay worse but were somehow part of it, perhaps even the very cause of its degradation. But what did I really know about how the talk went? Nothing was ever said outright. Still, it seems likely that most of the islanders must have thought it out of order for two small children to live with a single man who was getting on in years and was not a widower, or even divorced. Besides, the children, too, were somehow out of order. This had nothing to do with our foreign origins or anything else that we had done, or were like, only with the fact of us *being*. Minna, in particular, exasperated people. Her rudeness was almost unnatural; she was such a go-getter and seemed to have no inhibitions at all. And there was her red hair and the way she moved: her thin, skinny body was like a living scream below the tall willow in our garden, the willow that was a slowly, ponderously rustling dome of greenery in the summer, and in the winter a mass of harsh, scratchy branches that gashed the sky just as Minna's screams tore into every silence; the shrill sound of her voice could be picked up anywhere in the neighbourhood. In the rare moments of quiet, the Dead House stood there as if *truly* dead, carved out of the very silence: a jarring eyesore on the less respectable side of the road to the farm, the old fur breeder's house giving way under the pressure generated by the comparatively proper house frontages *up there*, as if, despite all Johannes's efforts to rebuild, it had been unable to defend itself against the shiny glare of the well-kept Mains Farm buildings and begun to rot and disintegrate by itself, perhaps from the ongoing struggle to keep up appearances or even to stay upright at all. I remember this: it is summer, and warm outside; the garden is filling with dense, heavy greenery, and the children move among the berry bushes as swiftly as birds' shadows. Minna wears her droopy and too low-cut green swimsuit; she is laughing, her lips swollen and blue with the juice of all the Morello cherries she has stuffed into her mouth, and she has draped a lace curtain over her head, one of the curtains put up by a former housekeeper and nowadays used by Johannes to protect the fruit. The curtain material is absurdly long: it flows from her head out over the grass like a covering of fish scales or the sloughed-off skin of a huge snake. The hut that would later be known as the Cottage, or the toy house, was then nothing more than a small shed where the Simonsen couple lived while their own house was being built. This was how people managed when the war had ended: once you had got hold of a site (Simonsen got his at about the same time Kaufmann gave Johannes the fur breeder's place), you skimped and saved, and built a little more every year until your proper house was ready for you to move in. Simonsen had shown us pictures of the Cottage barely standing upright in the snow, while what was to become their real house consisted of a pile of bricks and stacked timber over by the wooded hillock at the back of the garden. When the house was completed, the Simonsens' two eldest girls used the Cottage as their playhouse. They served their dolls tea on a plastic toy set, which they insisted was made of real china. There were hordes of children on the island in those days. I don't know where they all came from or what happened to them later in life. A girl called Emelie lived up on Bird Hill, and her neighbour was a solitary woman, whose name I cannot remember, who bred beagles. Emelie stomped about; she was not right in the head and fat for her age. I can see her now, squeezed into the far corner of the Cottage, large and greyish and long-suffering, with an imbecile smile on her face. And naked. Minna had managed to make her undress, presumably because she wanted us to play doctors, or maybe it was farm animals, because the daft girl had been ordered to stuff grass into her mouth and also to push sticks and pine cones into her *down-there*. When Emelie would not do it herself, I was told to get on with pushing these things inside her and I remember trying (I never dared to defy Minna's directives whatever they might be), but Emelie squashed her thighs together and yelled like a stuck pig, so Minna tried to muffle the screaming by pulling a sack down over Emelie's head. Minna called it a nosebag, like the ones the horses were given to eat from up at the farm. Was it this scene, or another one, which Mr Carsten watched and later briefed the social services about, and which, in the end, led to them to decide that Minna should be placed in a foster home? Or was it just (as I heard him tell Johannes) that Minna would turn up on the roadside and make rude faces and gestures at him every time he went past on his tricycle? Much later, once the old man had died and his widow, who was growing increasingly deaf, no longer bothered about the running of the farm, Mr Carsten would turn himself into the master of the Kaufmann estate, but then he came to the Yellow Villa's front door in his knee-high boots that were always caked with mud and chaff and with one corner of his mouth twisted into a crooked smile, and stood there in the doorway, addressing us in long, weird, Danish-sounding harangues that flowed out, soaked in spittle. Mr Carsten always seemed to be informed about everything that happened on the island and felt no compunction about telling whoever he met about what he had seen, and *kan de tell me, Johannes*, he might say, what sort of devilry will that lass of yours think up next time? You would like to get rid of her, wouldn't you? He would say this kind of thing in a way that sounded as if the very best thing would be for Johannes himself to see to it that not only Minna but his entire objectionable family was dispatched somewhere else, once and for all.

*

We ate oranges, crammed slivers of peel between our lips and teeth and made yellow grimaces. *Clowning* – that was Johannes's word for our antics. Once, he tried to teach Minna how to dance the tango. The record was old and scratched, and a man's voice, frail and spiky like a flower stalk, was almost drowned in the crackly music from a distant orchestra as it sang something incomprehensible deep inside the horn that seemed filled with darkness as solid as cement. Johannes counted, *One two three and four*, they walked alongside each other and then: *the cross!* Johannes said, and made his own hand into the shape of a crown for her hand to lace into, high above both their heads. Minna had put on a pair of low-heeled shoes with a red bow that had been left behind by one of the housekeepers, and he had dressed up in an old, moth-eaten tweed suit and sported a bow tie. Surprisingly, Johannes, who was usually so awkward, was moving smoothly and fluidly, so that even I who watched with childish eyes perceived a much younger man, a charmer, behind the distinctive hawk-like pro-file and the long, slicked-back hair, and as I crouched next to the gramophone, admiring them sincerely, I must have been flooded by a sudden wave of jealousy because I put my fin-ger on the old 78, slowing down the tempo of the music on purpose and *eeeeehh-EEHHH . . .* groaned the flower stalk as if suffocating slowly inside that dark cement, and STOP IT! Minna screamed, and put her hands over her ears, suddenly bright red in the face from a mixture of shame and rage.

*

We had our own inner spaces, just as we had colonised our own secret places on the island. We had a language known only to us, made up of invented words and phrases, and a collection of English words and expressions that Minna believed we had inherited from our parents, though Minna was the only one able to recall the words correctly and pronounce *gorgeous*, *ravishing* and *voluptuous* as she believed they should be pronounced. She whispered the words in my ear, her voice hot, and her cheeks grew shiny and red with excitement and her eyebrows shot up almost to where her hair began, *vo-lu-up-tuo-ooous*, and her lips parted in that self-satisfied smile of hers that stretched her mouth like a rubber band and made her look just like the Cheshire cat in the storybook that Johannes had been reading to us. We also had our own, carefully thought-out daily rituals, like the way one of us would stop the other if either of us spotted something especially noteworthy – like a strangely rounded stone, or an abandoned bird's nest on the field verge, or if Mr Carsten drove past in his Volvo pulling the rattling horse-box trailer – and if I had made a particularly interesting find, Minna would approvingly tap her temple with her index finger, then raise her arm and swing it up over her shoulder in a wide arc while pointing at me with the same index finger, and I, only too overjoyed at a chance of imitating whatever she did, soon learnt to tap my temple and gesture the same way to point at her, and then there was another thing that we did every time we had made one of these interesting finds: we would stand stock-still for a moment or two, continuing to gaze fixedly at whatever it was we thought important, then move away by taking three solemn paces backwards and say *fart on you*! before we could turn and run from the place. We observed this especially if we were in one of our *secret* places. We had a whole network of secret places, in the forest and down by the lake. The most secret of them all was the broad stony field on top of Bird Hill, which, according to Johannes, was the crash site of the plane our parents were travelling in when on their way to collect us. Though he was pissed when he told us that, Minna said. Everyone knew what bullshit Johannes would come out with when he was drunk. Our parents were living in America and could come to get us any time, or perhaps send us the plane tickets so that we could go to them. Unaware of the contradiction, Minna all the same insisted on us building a small chapel for our dead parents on the place where the plane had come down. If our dad had been sitting at the bomb-bay doors, he would surely have fallen out and landed here, she said, mixing things up even more, but why should I mind as long as I was an accepted part of her games? She pointed at a reasonably flat piece of ground and we both set about finding stones that we could move along to the spot and then added sticks and bottle tops and Minna's shawl, which she claimed had once been our mother's and then, after we had said a home-made prayer for our parents, we were taking the three backward paces prescribed in our ritual and I remember having taken the last backward step and being about to say *fart on you*, when a large, furry, reddish-grey dog with its tongue dangling from its muzzle bounded towards us out of nowhere, with Mr Carsten following just behind, groaning with the effort of dragging his paralysed leg up the hill and past the large boulders. This was the first time I had seen him up close, and the first time (I think) that either of us had been alone with him in such a distant, exposed place. Mr Carsten stood and looked at us for quite a long time, shifting his weight from one leg to the other and breathing in heavy bursts, the way he did, inhaling with a rasping, painfully tearing sound and then letting the air out in a slow puff, before he bent over to put the leash on the dog, who had been jumping at me but now went unprompted to his master's side. You young 'uns shouldn't be here, he said. This is no place for children to be running around. It's where the plane crashed, right? Minna asked, and I had to admire her courage. As for me, I just stood there, shivering like an eel. I had not been able to stop shaking ever since that big, shaggy beast had jumped at me. It was the plane my dad was in, Minna said, and, once more, I was amazed. Just a little while ago, she had denied all that, dismissing it as Johannes's drunken chatter. Meanwhile, Mr Carsten stood still and panted and did not take his eyes off Minna for a second while he put his weight first on his stiff leg and then on the other. At the time, I could not work out why he kept staring at Minna like that. Me, he did not even glance at. Yes, it was over there, he said, pointing with his walking stick at a tree, an ash that grew a little further up the hill and had partly lost its leaves. I was one of the first to arrive at the site, he said with a smile, as if this fact gave him particular satisfaction. By then, it was a roaring sea of fire up here. He was hanging there, he said, and raised his stick to point again. And: who was? (This was my question, I couldn't stop myself.) And Mr Carsten: he had been thrown out of the

68

plane, seat and all, so he was hanging still in the chair, like it was a parachute that hadn't unfolded. Mr Carsten started to laugh. *And my, how he burnt, the poor fucker, like in the fires of Hell!* His laughter looked very odd because only half his face was laughing. The other half kept staring at us, with an expression that seemed to say that he was quite terrified by what he had just said. And: you're lying! Minna screamed, and started to run. Halfway down the hill, she stopped me and said: don't believe him, he was just trying to scare us! After that, we kept on running until we reached the bottom of the slope, where the ground was ordinary, soft and just grass, and then Minna let herself fall on purpose, rolled in the grass and pressed the palm of my hand against her ribcage, all flat and bony at the time, and inside her heart leapt and splatted. Like a frog, I said, it's jumping about like a frog in a water bucket. And Minna: would you have guessed, he keeps a heart that behaves just like that! And I: who, Mr Carsten? And she: no, not Mr Carsten, you idiot, Kaufmann of course, he has this heart in a glass jar and he makes it beat by using a lot of electrical wires. And I: what, a *real* heart, a *person's* heart? And Minna tapped her index finger against her temple to show how smart I was and then raised her arm towards me in a long, challenging arc. A human heart, she said. Don't ask me whose it was.

*

I have written that we went to school together every day. But 'together' may not be the right word. Minna always walked well ahead of me, as if to show everyone that we did not belong to each other one bit. At least, not in school. The teachers, however, made no distinction between us. To them, we were both *the Lehman children*. The name tied us to each other even when nothing else did; that name, and those special, deeply unfortunate circumstances which everyone on the island knew were linked to that name. No one took any notice of other facts: for instance, that we were in different classes and did not even get together in the breaks. My classmates soon worked out that they had better avoid me like the plague, as if I were infected by whatever ailment they believed was causing Minna's problems. I grew lonely then, a loneliness that I would for a long time believe to be not so much chosen by me and somehow self-inflicted but rather the direct effect of my dependence on her. We were not just each other's sibling but we were also drawn into a strange field of energy that affected our minds every waking hour of the day, determining who we were and influencing what we did more distinctly than anyone or anything else. And, paradoxically, it seemed at the same time to suck all strength out of us. It could make me feel utterly drained simply to raise my hand at her, or nod or shake my head or try to answer the questions that she incessantly asked me. How to name this condition? I have tried to define it several times but every attempt failed. 'Dependence' is too weak a word. Perhaps I can express what I mean in much more straightforward terms: neither of us existed away from the island, outside our natural *habitat*, as it were. Or, if we exist, we were fragile and vulnerable, as easily broken and fragmented as the island slate. At least, this is how it was with Minna. As for me, I am not sure. What saved me might have been my awareness that I must always watch out for her. Constantly watching out for her served to keep my mind off other things. It made me forget that I was alive only when close to her, nowhere else, but also that it was totally impossible to live side by side with her, that (as Johannes would say later) if she had not shown the good sense to disappear, she and her freakish whims would have been the death of us one fine day.

*

Inventory, after the first five days spent on the island. The garage: Johannes's blue Dauphine is still there, and so are the old, persistent smells of sour exhaust fumes, burnt oil and dirty plastic seat covers. On free-standing shelving, ill-assorted engine parts are scattered, loose or in cardboard boxes. Closer to the floor, broader shelves hold petrol and oil cans and rags, all at hand if you wanted to check things under the bonnet. In the cool cellar, the neat log stack almost reaches the ceiling. Fixed wooden shelves are stocked with a variety of tinned foods, including cat food, even though Johannes had not had a cat for years. All this looks orderly and well made; tap the wood and it seems to be solid workmanship. No damp and nothing else that someone considering making an offer for the property could complain about. But all you need is a fleeting, treacherous reflection of light on a window pane for the solidity to slip and vanish. If you lean your hand against a wall or a

71

door frame, you get a sense of something insubstantial, as if the whole house were about to collapse. I fetch the folding ladder from the garage and climb up to undo both clasps on the attic hatch. It drops down on screeching hinges, with a noise like the shriek of a terrified animal. After slapping my arm across my eyes to keep out the chaff that billows out of the attic space, I begin to play the beam of the torch on the exposed rafters and then down over the spongy brick walls. Bit by bit, the light picks out elements of Johannes's life that I would have preferred to leave there, forgotten. Closest to the hatch, a pair of knee-high black leather boots lean against the wall, the boots that Johannes boasted about because they were part of the uniform he wore 'in service', and hung up on hooks hammered straight into the bricks are the uniform jackets: a black, lined winter jacket and a lighter, more summery grey one. The motorbike is no longer around (in the early fifties, Johannes sold it to a Harley-Davidson enthusiast) but, as a memorial of the good old days, what was left of the Steib sidecar stands almost in the middle of the dirty wooden floor. Johannes managed to haul it up into the attic with blocks and tackle attached to the roof beams, a set of lifting gear he used successfully over the years for winching all sorts of items into the attic, such as the crates of beer delivered regularly from the brewery where he once worked, and chests stuffed with clothes and books, too heavy to lift in any other way, and the cupboard-bed he slept in and the primus stove he used to heat the tinned food he ate. When he withdrew to philosophise, as he described it, he sat in the sidecar with the bottles of beer and spirits on one side of the seat, the gramophone and the chamber pot on the other. Once settled in, he could stay there several days without us noticing any signs of life other than occasional heavy thumps and blows against the ceiling above our heads, sometimes long bursts of screaming, as he fought whatever demons had been aroused by his philosophical inquiries. The older we grew, the more often he retired, and every time he seemed to stay away for longer. It was as if something unfathomable hovered over him always, something that he had to save himself from at any cost, just as a drowning man, once the floods have swept away everything he owns, climbs higher and higher up, until a swaying branch of a tree or a steeply pitched roof is all that remains to cling on to. The books he read in the sidecar are still there, stacked along the bare brick wall on pieces of torn-off cardboard meant to stop the damp from rotting them. Many are so badly affected anyway that their covers have softened until their edges are bending and the internal layers of compressed paper have almost dissolved. Johannes was unwilling to let us into the attic and we were reluctant to go up there (if for no other reason than because of the stench that filled it and also lingered in Johannes's clothes once he emerged after a few days or maybe a week away), but he was always perfectly willing to share his reading with us. The great classical historians fascinated him in particular. He could spend hours deeply absorbed in the descriptions by Tacitus of the Roman forays northwards to do battle with the Germanic tribes. He loved the writing of great explorers, the travellers' tales and memoirs, perhaps because he was reminded of his own vagabond years at sea. Before I learnt to read, I used to sit with him, leaning against his shoulder, so that I could look at the illustrations that were glued to some of the pages, often protected by a thin sheet of almost transparent paper. The pictures usually showed strange landscapes like the banks of wide rivers or the edges of desolate steppes where tiny explorers stood with their walking sticks raised to point at something, and it seemed to me (even when I was little) that the travellers were portrayed as so small in order that the wild places would appear all the more grandiose, like the river delta alive with colourful birds or the rocky desert where, in the distance, a mighty volcano rose so high there was a wide rim of snow at the very top of the cone. I remember liking the pale colours, which made earth and sky merge, and the detailed representation of the few objects that, after all, had been allowed into the foreground as if they had positively *asked* to be examined at close range: a river barge laden with exotic fruit, crewed by brown-skinned natives wearing nothing except generous loincloths, and in the middle of the boat a kind of house that, though made from skilfully woven palm leaves, looked like a real house – like *our* house. But the passages Johannes chose to read aloud to me had none of the clarity of daylight and dealt only with the mindless struggles of people and animals against the elements, or against each other:

When the burning heat of the day is followed by the
coolness of the night, which in these latitudes is always
of the same length, even then the horses and cattle
cannot enjoy repose. Enormous bats suck their blood like

vampires during their sleep, or attach themselves to their backs, causing festering wounds, in which mosquitoes, hippobosces and a host of stinging insects niche themselves. Thus the animals lead a painful life during the season when, under the fierce glow of the sun, the soil is deprived of its moisture.

Up there in the attic, sounds from the outside penetrated much more distinctly than elsewhere in the house: the metallic clatter of the aeroplanes that were flying just above us or the long summer rains that pattered against the roof tiles, causing a peculiar rustle that wrapped itself like cotton wool around Johannes's reading voice, which was quiet but deep and had an insistent, rhythmic quality. If he reached a section that he was especially keen on, he would often read it several times, as if to take in the flavour of every word. Sometimes, he read for a while to us after supper, remaining in the kitchen, where the window stood open to the warm, still summer evening. Outside, the cock pheasants patrolled the garden, letting out their hoarse two-tone screams. The pheasants always screamed like mad things when a storm closed in. Before the thunder arrived, the brow of the forest along the far side of the field would be crisply lit by the setting sun, and stand out against the bruised-looking, swollen sky above it. Johannes would not let the storm disturb him and carried on reading even when the lightning flashed so incessantly it seemed the house could go up in flames any minute, and, somehow, the words he read built a bridge over my fears. The way they arrayed themselves calmly in the right order and every sentence reached its completion made me trust that nothing was final: another sentence would always follow the one Johannes had already read, and yet another event would always come after the account we had just heard. I felt the same about the book he was reading from. Behind all the terrible things the writer told us of, like the saw-toothed crocodiles floating in the shallows of the murky river and the bloodthirsty bats clinging to the flanks of the cattle, there seemed to be *another narrator*, a sober, thoughtful person able to put the formless in its proper place and explain the incomprehensible. Eventually, the storm would pass, the birds started singing again in the garden, where everything was moist after the rain, and an uncanny white mist, a combination of light and damp, made the pale, paper-thin sky shimmer and drifted in through the open window. Johannes would have put the book away and be gazing absently, with empty eyes, as if he were in a place beyond all story-telling where words were no longer necessary because everything had already been identified and described: a place like this one, silent, full of rain-soaked sunlight. Perhaps this was why Johannes always sought the solitude he found in the attic: because the state of contemplation, spoken of by the classical philosophers whom he admired so much, is not a once-and-forever attainment but an acquisition that can be yours only through a constant, unconditional inner *struggle*, concealed from the eyes of others. ('You have power over your mind – not outside events. Realise this, and you will find strength' was a quotation from Marcus Aurelius that he loved to repeat. It sounds like an excuse for avoiding all responsibility, but perhaps Johannes's mind was such that he could exert power only if he withdrew from all that might bewilder and beguile him.) Next to the bookshelf where Johannes kept his own books there is another, larger one filled with Jan-Heinz Kaufmann's old library, a big collection of volumes that Sigrid Kaufmann had asked Johannes to look after when, after the war, her husband was taken to court, accused of having betrayed his country. She explained that if she continued to have these books at home, she would fear for her own as well as her daughter's life. I wonder if Johannes ever considered what risks he ran himself by undertaking to hold on to Kaufmann's books, or if he simply handled the issue in the same way that he dealt with all tricky or uncomfortable matters that turned up: that is, he shifted it into some place out of sight and pretended to understand none of it. And here they are, all the diaries, starting at the time Kaufmann first began to run farms on the Inner Islands, with entries in which he accounted for most things in no particular order, from purchases and inventories to notes on his various diplomatic tasks and journeys, and that were as abbreviated as telegrams in the beginning but gradually became less formal. The writings that Kaufmann had published himself stood on the bottom shelf and included a set of the leaflets under the general title *On the Nutritional Requirements of Nature and of Mankind*, the little handbooks that he gave away to everyone who joined the first colony, and then, lying on top of these books, a large volume in octavo format seemingly placed there almost as an afterthought; it was bound in moss-green speckled leather with Kaufmann's monogram (the letters JHK) set inside a beautiful frame of garlands on the front cover and the title inscribed on the yellowing title page:

NOTES ON THE SUBJECT OF
PLANT DISTRIBUTION ON THE INNER ISLANDS

by Jan-Heinz Kaufmann,
Doctor of Agronomy

I have seen that book many times. Or rather: Johannes would take it out to show it to us on certain important occasions, almost as if it were a sacrament. In an introductory section, the Inner Islands are discussed, in the first instance in geological or, more accurately, palaeological terms; the second section consists of drawings, in which a double-page spread is devoted to each plant that grows or has grown here. On the left-hand page, the reader is given a detailed description of the particular plant, its distribution and time of flowering, as well as how to identify and understand its seed pods, root systems and other such essentials; the right-hand page presents one of the author's botanical drawings, a hand-coloured and graphically precise illustration of its sepals and its petal arrays, with the number of the image shown in the right-hand corner and, below, a series of letter and number combinations that categorise every described aspect of the plant. The book contains 120 such sets of text and image, and ends with an extensive index. But it is the dedication on the inside front cover that matters most, inscribed by Kaufmann in his characteristic hand with its tall, upright and clearly delineated capital letters: *To my most highly esteemed Johannes from his Friend, the Author of this Work – JHK*. When Johannes showed us The Book, he would also draw our attention to the photograph of a team of harvest workers that was kept inside it. The note on the back states that the photo was taken in a field belonging to the Söderängen farm on a day in August 1927, by which time the first colony was in existence. The photo is pale with age and marked by having been folded on the far right and then in half. On it, a dozen or so men and women are grouped around a cart loaded with a gigantic pile of hay. The women are wearing short-sleeved cotton dresses with wide skirts, and the men baggy trousers and collarless shirts or tunics. On the far left, I can just make out Mr Carsten, since his face is in one of the fold lines and it is really only his leg, stretched out stiffly in front of his body, which gives a clue to who he is. In the centre of the picture, Jan-Heinz Kaufmann sits perched on the edge of the cart, just in front of the hillock of hay; he leans forward, his arms held straight with his hands on his knees and one booted foot resting on Johannes's right shoulder, while Johannes stands immediately below him, the grin on his face looking almost identical to his master's broad smile. Kaufmann's booted foot on Johannes's shoulder: it tells you practically all about the nature of the relationship between them, and explains why Johannes was so proud of the image that his fingers trembled when he showed it to us.

It is raining again. I stand at the edge of the forest, listening out for an aeroplane that I can hear in the distance as it approaches the island. Because the sound fuses with its echo there is no spatial definition, and it is impossible to make out from where it is coming. You sense it only as a strangely metallic bulging of the air. Then it gradually grows stronger and heightens into a dark roar that encloses the entire landscape in a cage of sound. Inside it, the birds rise from the forest canopy and climb frenetically upwards until the plane breaks through the horizon above the trees, as unexpectedly as always but hovering, moving slowly at such a low height that the extended wheels seem about to touch the tops of the trees. By now, the engine sound is a deafening, needle-sharp whine and then it is followed by a massive crash like a thunderclap that somehow compresses the air into big blocks while the heavy body of the plane, oddly independent of the sounds it creates, flies low above the lake, its wing tips rocking as if in its own sea of noise. Two boys of about twelve, maybe thirteen, stand astride their ludicrously overpriced mountain bikes to scan the plane before turning to look at me and, when they notice me watching them, they suddenly turn away. It is a sham manoeuvre, as there are in fact no tracks to the lake in that direction, not even paths, only a few landmarks to go by: one has to know before coming here just where the forest grows thin enough to make your way through. The route I have chosen opens into a narrow gully some five hundred metres behind the village school. They are building two new villas here, identical to the rest that have erupted like a rash along the island's coastline: oversized wooden monstrosities that come complete with detached garages, large enough to hold a whole fleet of vehicles. Presumably, the boys live in one of these villas. I watch as they jump on their bicycles when they reach King's Road. On this side of the island, the road runs very close to the banks of the fjord, but the building sites do not reach all the way up to the edge of the forest. The area at the back of them is a nature reserve and must not be interfered with, which means that I can move a quarter of a century back in time by taking only a few paces towards the forest. At the far end of the narrow gully, the maple that branches just a couple of metres above the ground is the very tree that Minna and I would climb as children. A little further downhill towards the lake, where the path is as overgrown with ferns as ever, I spot the now rust-eaten remains of the plough that was once used to scrape the surface of the lake free of snow before they started to cut blocks of ice. The rowing boat hauled up on the shore is the same one that has always been moored here, secured to a cut lakeside alder by a rusting chain that has no lock, so that it has to be lifted clear of the stump. A little higher up, a board is fixed to two sturdy wooden posts that have been hammered into the ground: it says NATURE RESERVE at the top, and then *Established with the support of the Sigrid Kaufmann Memorial Trust*. Below, there is a list of rules: keep your dog on a lead, observe the bans on fishing and starting fires, and so forth. That sign, or a similar one with the same admonitions, has been here for as long as I can remember. But the poster next to it is new. It is a simple map of the lake and its surroundings, with walking routes picked out in red and blue. There is some information about the history of the place and a survey of the animal and plant life in the protected area. Even though it is obviously out of order here, as elsewhere on the island, to mention Jan-Heinz Kaufmann by name, the poster text has actually been lifted word for word from his great work on the flora of the island. The locations of particular plants are exactly described after an introduction to the island's rare mix of slate, limestone and sandstone rocks, all created in the Ordovician and Silurian periods from the skeletons of sea crustaceans. Johannes was right: before, everything here was covered by the sea. This is the explanation for why the rocks crumble easily. The very presence of the lake is due to the rocks giving way and folding, which encouraged water and soil to collect, creating an unusually rich growing ground for trees and plants that otherwise would not have survived this far north. Below this, there is a list of protected plant species, illustrated by Kaufmann's own drawings. I look out over the lake, standing next to the beached boat, and think about the day when Johannes and I said our final goodbyes to Minna. It was a late morning in November and, like today, steeped in a pearly grey mist of light rain. The beach had disappeared after twenty or so strokes of the oars. I might have been out on the open sea despite the presence of the forest, the twittering of the birds and the noises of guillemots and divers from the reed beds around the cape that almost reaches the middle of the lake. I pulled the oars on board, undid the knot on the string and pulled off the wrapping paper provided by the funeral directors. Then I asked Johannes if he wanted to do it, but he shook his head and looked away, so I unscrewed the lid of the urn and scattered the ashes on the water. I intended to move decisively, strongly, but overdid it and almost fell out of the boat when it suddenly rocked beneath us. All the same, the ashes kept floating in the air for quite a while, glinting in the light like the white butterflies Minna had been telling me about the night she came into my room, sweating, with the smell of lake mud and forest on her hair and skin, and whispered: I have seen him, and then I: who do you mean? And she: Kaufmann, he's alive! And then (as if the thoughts followed each other naturally): you must kill him! This happened sometime in the early seventies, and Kaufmann was of course no longer a prisoner (originally he was jailed for twenty-one years, though, as far as I know, he served only a fraction of the sentence), but there had been few sightings of him on the island. The rumour that he harboured secret plans to start a third colony circulated but was just idle talk. In the post-war years, material changes happened with increasing speed on the Main Island: more and larger areas of land were scheduled for building, the old dirt roads were tarmacked, the school was extended with a brand-new nursery and the shopping centre now had a doctors' practice and a post office. Kaufmann alone did not change and perhaps *his island*, too, stayed much the same as it had been: at least, along the still untouched lake, quiet paths remained discernible only to him, and there he might be seen rambling, carrying his vasculum and butterfly net, and so it was the day Minna saw him. Or, anyway, it is what she said in the night when she came running into my room and threw herself on my bed, not upset so much as strangely *agitated*, as if she could hardly wait to voice all the things that were on her mind. It was June, the time of year when the night never comes, and the bog myrtle and wild sorrel on the dank water meadows fill the moist air with their astringent yet over-whelmingly powerful scent. She never told me why she had gone down to the lake at that time of night, only that she had been trying to find her way across dark, sodden ground under branches heavy with leaves, when suddenly something white rose right in front of her feet. Looking up, she saw a cloud of fluttering white wings as a swarm of butterflies lifted from the grass and whirled away over the lake, whose surface glittered with reflected light. And then he appeared on the path ahead of her, his white shirt almost emitting its own light between the black lines of his braces. Do you like the butterflies? he had asked with gentle curiosity. I've created them, you know! She had hardly recovered from the sight of him, so unexpected was it here among the massed shadows of the trees, where the air was dense and mellow with bird song. She must have laughed. He had bent over her and asked if she liked the but-terflies. And, if she did, then what did she make of the island foxes? Are there foxes on the island? she had asked, because once Johannes had told us that lack of foxes was the reason why there were so many pheasants everywhere. In the past, Johannes had said, the fox would cross the strait in the winter when he was hungry and food was scarce, but nowadays it is seldom cold enough for the water to freeze over. But of course Master Fox is around, Kaufmann says unhesitatingly, though he is tremendously wary! If you like, he says, I can show you his lair. It is only now that she tries to distinguish him from the flickering backdrop of light and darkness that surrounds him on the path. He is considerably taller than how she had imagined him, and so thin, his body still almost boyish-looking despite his age. His head is long and narrow, his forehead high and his chin also long and protruding. His build and features make his round, steel-rimmed glasses seem like some kind of equipment that he has stuck on his face to examine her more closely. And so he does: inquisitively and intently. If you'd like to? he says, and smiles again. His voice sounds slightly old-fashioned, the tone dry and precise but not at all unkind. I'll show you where they are if you come here early tomorrow morning, he said. But you must promise not to tell anyone. She promised. And then he went on his way, nearly *dancing*, old and frail as he was.

*

Odd how the island landscape changes the moment one leaves the well-trodden paths. I have been aware of this since childhood: that the island is made up of not one but several landscapes, joined so tightly that it is hard to tell where the differences begin. This is why it is impossible to wander by the lake to try to find the paths you once used – inevitably, you get lost. Is this not what happens with the words, with the stories we tell each other? Minna had gone to meet Kaufmann again at the same place by the lake at around six o'clock the following morning. Even though only a few hours had passed since they met earlier, everything seemed different. The ground was dry and soft underneath their feet, the morning air flooded with early sunlight. Kaufmann took her along paths she had never known before or, at least, did not recognise, leading away from the reed beds on the island's western shores, across the isthmus and into its interior. After walking for a good hour, they reached a meadow. Though it might not have been a meadow, Minna corrected herself later, perhaps just a grassy slope, but it might not have been so much a slope as some kind of clearing, or maybe a thinner part of the forest. I cannot tell how many times I have tried to follow Minna's vague, contradictory descriptions but it has been just as impossible to find this place as to track the unusual animals Johannes told us about when we were little, stories to make us believe that they had been here before any people had come to live here: animals a little like stoats or white martens. On the other hand, it might have been that I never found the right route into the interior. Viewed from the familiar spaces of the landscape that everyone on the island knows, the terrain to the north of the lake rises and becomes stony and barren. If you walk up high enough, you finally reach a ridge from which you can see all the way to the strait and across to the airport with its two parallel runways for landing and take-off. Perhaps only Kaufmann knew the whereabouts of that secret place. It would not surprise me. Was it just the two of you? I asked at the time. And again, Minna hesitated. Yes, she said, yes, just the two of them, the old man and herself. At another time, she told me that Mr Carsten had come by, briefly, with his dogs. (Walked by, did he, as if it were the most natural thing in the world?) But Kaufmann had been worried that the dogs would be a nuisance and sent the farm manager on his way. Then he had explained that she had better lie down so that she was quite hidden in the grass, and she had hardly done so before the foxes emerged from the forest. Three of them: two males, one female. And, she went on without drawing breath: as if he had called them! Didn't you get scared? I asked. And she: not just in that moment, no, at first I thought it was almost beautiful. It looked like the three of them doing the moves in a square dance, as the two male foxes tried to keep their distance from each other while both made up to the female. In the end, one of the males gave up and left. The female just feigned indifference and ambled off towards the forest, but the remaining male followed her as if pulled along on a string. And then something weird happened, Minna said. Both animals turned, as if to run away from each other, but neither of them moved an inch. I didn't get it at first, but the thing was, they were *stuck* to each other, well, their *bums* were! So, for a while, they didn't seem to mind, just stood there, staring in opposite directions. Then the female tried to lie down but she pulled the male with her, and at the same time they did that Kaufmann grabbed me round the waist, really hard, and whispered *they're mating, see, that's how they go about mating!* Then

I realised that the poor foxes didn't do what they wanted but simply acted out what *he* wanted. He had *power* over them, like that time when he only had to stamp his feet to make the butterflies come out of the ground. He is an evil person! Do you see, Andreas? she said, and grabbed hold of my hand so firmly that I thought my fingers would break. The aircraft with our mum and dad on board, he was the one who made it crash. What happened afterwards? I asked, mostly to escape from the pain. What happened *afterwards*? Minna said, and looked hard at me as if I was stupid not to get it. Afterwards, he wanted to do the same with me, of course, the same thing that he had made the foxes do. But there was a stone next to me on the ground and I took it and hit him with it to free myself and I ran away as fast as I could. Couldn't you have called out to Mr Carsten? I asked. Now Minna bent over me, her face so close to mine that I could smell the hot scent of resin and wild sorrel in her hair. Don't you get it, Andreas? We have to kill him! *You* have to kill him. How? I asked. And she: do what I did, find a stone and whack his head with it. Do you promise to do that, Andreas? Will you promise to kill him for my sake? And I said, I promise. I would not have been able to refuse her anything then. Besides, I needed to make her stop shaking me so roughly. And she finally let go of me.

*

I spent days drifting along the shores of the lake, keeping my eyes open for suitable places where I could carry out my sister's command, at the same time terribly worried because I suspected that Kaufmann had found out about my plans already. If he could make planes drop out of the sky and wild animals behave like trained monkeys, surely he could read the mind of a lonely child? I somehow came to identify the always glowing lamp on the stable wall with the awesome intelligence that I imagined Kaufmann to have. Without understanding why it suddenly seemed so crucially important to me that I should find out what the old man knew, I was certain that I, too, should meet him face to face at least once. But a boundary had always been recognised, a borderline between the farm *up there* on the hill and the rest of the populated parts of the island. Where exactly it went was hard to determine, unless you stood at the crossroads where the Mains Farm Road became a private drive. Then a sign told you exactly what was what: *Private Road* – and next, *No Unauthorised Access*. But there were innumerable places on the island where you could never be sure about which was the right or the wrong side; grey zones. Besides, it was not the old man that I feared most but his farm manager, Mr Carsten. Nowadays, I have much better insight into what it was about Mr Carsten that frightened me so much. At the time, people hated him but also tended to regard him as a jester, and told jokes about him that made even his fits of rage seem comical. Besides keeping horses for trotting races, Mr Carsten ran a small-scale dog kennel; the dogs would bark and howl from early morning until late at night. He exercised them once or twice a day, going about on a cycle of the kind that was known locally as a Danish bike but which was actually an older type of delivery tricycle. An elderly retriever bitch with reddish fur sat on the front platform. She had one paralysed leg, just like Mr Carsten, and the whole outfit was quite a sight as it zoomed along King's Road: Mr Carsten pedalling with only one foot, while the bitch sat with her useless leg stretched over the edge like a diva, and the rest of the pack, a dozen or more dogs of different races and sizes, either rushed ahead or followed, panting and barking, or wandered off, distracted by scent trails, sniffing in the grass on the verges. I picked my moment one afternoon, when I had seen Mr Carsten speed down the Mains Farm Road on his tricycle, and turned into the forbidden part of the road to the farm. The yard, with the ancient oak in the middle, was as I had seen it from the NATO villa, but looked if anything even bleaker and more abandoned without the noisy dogs. Mr Carsten had laid out the horse paddock on the far side of the farm manager's home, but there were no horses in it now. There was actually no trace of any animal apart from the distracted cackling in the hen house. With movements as anxiously restrained as the time Minna and I had inspected the NATO villa, I went up the steps leading to the Kaufmann villa or, to be precise, to the veranda that, beginning at the main entrance, ran the full length of the south side of the house, and putting my feet down as quietly as I could so that no one should hear the wooden boards squeak, I looked through the third window counting from the entrance, saw into the hall, filled with pale sunlight, and beyond it a kitchen or breakfast room where Kaufmann and his wife were seated at a table. This is how I came to see, for the first time, not only the master of the farm but also the mistress and his widow-to-be, Mrs Kaufmann. Before, I had only caught sight of her at a distance on some of the few occasions when she had been walking along the road on errands to the shop or the pharmacy. Then, she had always worn a coat and skirt, and a headscarf. Now, in a white blouse and with her blond hair down, she looked almost shockingly young, if you kept in mind how old she was. Her relaxed posture boosted the impression of youthfulness. She rested both elbows on the table, thoughtfully supporting her chin on the back of one of her hands. Kaufmann, too, looked calm and at ease. He was apparently speaking as he ate, and put his fork down once or twice to emphasise a point and then picked it up again with a formal, almost pedantic gesture. I could not see Helga. She might have been sitting at the far end of the table, behind the back wall of the hall, or she might not have come to the table at all that day. I cannot tell how long I hid on that veranda, incapable of grasping how two people who were so hated by just about everyone on the island could spend their time on something as trivial as eating. And then he suddenly appeared next to me, only a few metres away; I had not heard the front door open and could not even recall if I had seen him get up and leave the table. His expression as he observed me was curious but baffled and at first he did not move, except for his lips, which twitched a little as he mumbled something to himself; then, after a few uncertain steps forward, he asked, who are you? He spoke Norwegian very distinctly, his vowel sounds high-pitched and sharp, and sounded a little old-fashioned, as Minna had said, and his eyes were very light and blue. In that moment, I felt convinced that he could see right through me, past my terrified face and straight into my mind, where vague plans to murder him had been instilled by my sister. And then his stiff features softened and his eyes took on an almost pitying look. You must be Johannes's boy, he said. So, he recognised me. Wouldn't you like to come inside for a while? Even if I had wanted to, I was not determined enough to resist him. Instead, I followed him into the bright hall and then into a room that was not the one where those two had been sitting but a large drawing room. Afterwards, the only thing I remembered about it was how marvellously spacious it was compared with the poky nooks and crannies in the Yellow Villa. At one end, a long line of tall windows faced the yard and at the other, sofas and armchairs had been placed well apart around a large stone-built fireplace. A large painting, hung above the fireplace, showed a group of naked men and women sitting or half lying on smooth sea-side rocks. Below them, on the beach, a St John's Eve bonfire sent a mighty pillar of smoke straight up into the ominously darkened sky, while the reflections of the flames that licked the damp stones made the naked bodies glow with a matte, reddish sheen. Look, have some of this! I had not noticed him go out but now he was back, holding something wrapped in a red-and-white checked napkin. It was a piece of apple cake. Its moist filling stuck between his fingers as he showed it to me. At first, I didn't accept the piece of cake, but he insisted and at the same time managed somehow to pilot me through the door and back out into the yard. I walked away obediently, holding the cake as I had been told, but there was a roaring noise inside me, as if the huge St John's bonfire was in my head, and I heard Minna say, her voice seemingly part of the sound of the fire, he's trying to poison you, that's why. When I had reached the Mains Farm Road proper and felt sure no one could see me, I threw the linen napkin with the cake inside as far as I could, and watched the cloth as it flapped in a beam of sunlight before vanishing into the already yellowing ears of wheat. It pleased me that no one would see the cloth until the autumn ploughing, or perhaps in the spring, and by then, Kaufmann would be dead.

*

Minna spent most of her time with *the lads*, as the island folk used to call the older boys. A gang used to meet up on the sports ground or the supermarket parking lot, turning up on the motorbikes and home-built scooters they used to get around the island. In the evenings, the gang set out with Minna riding pillion and would drive past the Yellow Villa to annoy Johannes. Her hair, now with new bright violet and flame-red streaks, was flying in the wind. I would watch from my window, my eyes following her. She never glanced my way, or looked at anyone or anything. Not even up towards the farm, where the outside light shone as ever, throughout the bleak, blanched summer nights, as if it could not have enough of its solitary staring into the distance. Minna smoked cigarettes that she rolled herself from Tiedemann's tobacco and Rizla papers and treated Johannes worse and worse. She called him an old wanker and stole booze off him, which probably explains why the lads tolerated her.

Most of them were quite a lot older than her and surely must have found her trying with her incessant shrieking. She was their mascot, they bounced her between them, took turns to feel her up or tease her, lit her fags and urged her to drink straight from the bottle. Often, they would simply take no notice of her, but it only made her play the fool even more. I could see how badly their indifference hurt her: the emptiness behind her eyes, the persistent, silly-excited blush on her cheeks. And I suffered, too, as I kept watch over her. Even then, I could not stop myself from following her. I took care to stay a few hundred metres away so that she would not spot me unless she was looking out for me. In any case, I believe that she knew exactly where I was all the time. They say that the connection between siblings can develop into something a little like a sixth sense. Each one is always intuitively aware of where the other one is and what he or she is doing, even when neither can express this certainty in words or even recognises that it exists. This was definitely how it was with us two. During this period, Minna went out with a boy called Morten, who was, more or less, her steady boyfriend. He worked in the supermarket and that was where they met after closing time, in places where no one would see what they got up to; mostly, they went to the parking lot or a loading platform at the back of the shop. The platform jutted out close to the steep rock face that reached straight down into the fjord. There would always be a pair of large green waste bins furthest out and, between the bins, stacks of flattened and bundled cardboard boxes. I thought it would be a smart move to sneak up on them by following the lower route, a narrow, cobbled path past the jetty where the boats were moored. When I had got to the end of the path below the bridge, I could see them up at the top of the rock. To be more precise: at first, Morten was the only one I saw, standing with his pants down, partly inside a cleft in the rock. I knew it was Morten because his black padded bomber jacket was instantly recognisable: it said (S)CREW on the back in big red capitals. Below the hem of the jacket, the cheeks of his butt glowed in the dusk and even though they were bumping up and down, I still did not understand what he was doing. I thought he was pissing and had just started the climb to the top, with some insulting remark at the ready, when I caught sight of the legs that clung to his hips like shafts. I saw Minna's face. Her head had slipped a little off the piece of cardboard that they had been careful enough to spread out on the floor of the cleft, and then she caught sight of me and smiled her rubber-band smile, a kind of stretched-out grimace. I am not sure if it was directed at me or if she was just grinning in general. Not that I hung around for long enough to find out. I simply turned round and fled. Just a few days later, Morten's motorbike unexpectedly swung into the drive to the Yellow Villa and Minna jumped off to demand that Johannes should allow Morten to stay overnight with her. Johannes stood in the doorway to the cellar, looking jovial and smiling as usual, but no one could doubt that this time he was not going to give in. He cared hardly at all for whatever Minna was up to when she was out of the house (to this day, I really cannot understand how he could be so unconcerned), but if she thought she could drag her misery across the threshold of his house, she had another think coming. Minna tried every trick in the book: she burst into tears, appealed to his good will, to his broadmindedness, and showered him with abuse. Eventually Morten lost patience, started his bike and drove off. With a shrill scream, Minna leapt at Johannes, hit and kicked him, and when he tried to quieten her down, she grabbed the garden rake that was leaning against the wall of the garage, struck his head and neck with it and then went for the Dauphine that was parked in front of the garage entrance, going first for the windscreen, then the rest of the windows, and the front and rear lamps, and when he tried in desperation to stop her from destroying everything, she chased him off with the rake that by now glittered with splintered glass. I saw it all from the window in my room, suddenly feeling that everyone on the island must be aware that Minna was going berserk. I locked the door and stayed in my room for the next night and day. Something like a week later, she came to see me and was full of tearful compassion. You're not like the others, Andreas, she said in a smarmy voice that might have been all right for one of the lads or anyone else but not for me. Tell me, are you still following me around to protect me? Are you my guard? She lay down next to me and locked her fingers into mine the way she used to, raised my hand to her lips and blew on the tips of my fingers. Aren't you too weak? she said, and bit my knuckles until it hurt, so I forced myself to pull my hand from her grip. Too weak for what, against whom? I asked, expecting once more to hear her name the person she wanted me to kill. I might have made my hands into fists, in terror or in anticipation, because she whispered, *shu-ssh*, and pulled the blanket over us both. She stayed there, lying next to me, still and staring at the ceiling, as she often did for hours on end. It used to make me feel safe and I might even fall asleep with my head in her armpit. Only this time nothing was the way it used to be. Minna? I said. She sat up, with her back leaning against the wall, and began rolling a cigarette with restless hands. Do you know what? I had a letter from Mum the other day, she said. Mum wrote that we can come to live with them now. In America. This made me angry and I turned away from her. Why wouldn't she stop saying this kind of thing, when she knew that I didn't believe any of it? *Shusssh!* she said, and patted my back as if I were a small child and, when I was facing her again, she pressed her lips against mine and blew cigarette smoke straight into my mouth. Choking, I sat up straight and started coughing. Minna laughed and slapped my back, but the next second she inhaled deeply and immediately blew more smoke into my mouth, and because I was still coughing, I could not stop myself from drawing the pungent smoke deep into my lungs. I felt dizzy, and next her warm, wet tongue slipped in between my lips. Baby bro, she mumbled contentedly, and nibbled at one of my earlobes. You're a big boy now. I felt her hand sneaking in under my pyjamas to caress my penis. It was small and limp, and, *such a tiny prick*, she said. There was no escape to be had by lying on my front, her hand found its way in under, pulling and relaxing alternately until my face was hot and flushed. I let her carry on since this was clearly a punishment that I had to endure because I had been spying on her and Morten. Then, a little later, I realised that she had begun to think of something else. She was twisting and tugging at my still limp cock, as if fiddling with the limbs of a doll, but gave up in the end, slumped back onto the bed and gazed at me, her eyes clear and wide open. Do you want to come along with me and Morten next time? she asked. Morten says it is all right with him. We're going for a drive on his bike. If you like, we could meet up behind the shop at eight tomorrow night. There was something about the too affable look on her face that should have warned me of a trap. I did not creep along the beach path round the back this time, but walked all the way along King's Road, head held high, as if I had a proper errand like everybody else. Minna and Morten were waiting for me on the loading platform, and the motorbike was parked there, just as we had agreed. They were smiling, Morten was smoking a cigarette, and Minna waved as she called my name. A lot of flattened cardboard boxes had been piled up on the tarmac in front of them. I couldn't think what they were for or why there was such an odd smell everywhere but, whatever, they had been waiting for me and I had no time to stop and think. Smiling idiotically, I started running towards them. Morten had got the bike engine running already and was settled behind the handlebars, and Minna was about to climb up behind him. *Hurry up, Andreas!* she shouted. In that instant, Morten threw his glowing fag on the cardboard, and the petrol it had been soaked in caught fire and flared up all around me. The last I saw of them was their crouched bodies as Morten drove his bike through the fire. Then, as they turned into King's Road, the word on the back of his jacket, (S)CREW, went out of sight and the flames rose around me like a huge wall. The heat was so intense it scorched my face and hands. Smoke, humiliation and fear made my eyes fill with tears. The flames died down when the cardboard had been reduced to ashes, but something else was still on fire, something thick and oily, with a smell that was sharp and stale at the same time. I do not remember any more after that, except that a person who was not Johannes walked me back to the Yellow Villa. That night, I was awake, alone in my bed and waiting for Minna to come in and lie down beside me, take my hand and rub my knuckles against her cheek to show that she was sorry and regretted what she had done. But Minna did not come. Later, my head was swimming again and I ran to the toilet to vomit it all up: the black, stinging smoke and the taste of her mouth against mine and the smell of her moist skin, and the more I vomited, the more clearly I understood that throwing up would never rid me of the things I wanted to get out of my system. Like the aviation fuel dumped on the island, the poison that had filtered into everyone's wells, the herbicides, the forest killer substances that make up Agent Orange. You can never free yourself of what has become part of your body.

*

For days afterwards, I behaved like a wounded animal, dragging myself back to what used to be our safe places on the shore of the lake. I took Johannes's binoculars with me, and a book about bird spotting and a notepad where I entered every observation I made as precisely as I could. *Time, place, species. 5 May. 3.45 p.m. Red-throated diver, in reeds at Näsudden.* To record bird sounds I brought a simple tape recorder that I had borrowed from Simonsen. The diver sounded spooky, like the unearthly call of a ghost in the silence, the bittern like a very small bass tuba. I taped the lot, noting the time and place as well as the duration and strength of the sound. And then, suddenly: the tremendous weariness, paralysing everything, whenever I heard the high-pitched whine that warned of yet another aircraft coming close, the clatter of birds' wings slapping against the water as all the species I had fancied myself observing secretly flew up and became visible to all comers, just in order to escape the grotesque metallic bird that flew so low beneath the clouds and from which I tried to distance myself by pressing my hands against my ears as hard as I possibly could. And that was how it began or, rather, how it ended: now I wrote down everything, not only what I cared to observe but also what I did *not* want to see. *6 May. 8.45 p.m. Minna with M outside Brekke's grocery store.* I had stood some fifty metres away, hidden around the corner, and felt like throwing pebbles at the pair of lovers to force Minna to pay attention to me, even though I knew exactly how that would end and what kind of attention I would receive. Instead, I stole both her packets of tobacco and cigarette papers, hiding the loot in a hollow under a tree stump near the two mooring posts for the rowing boat. I kept other things of hers under that tree stump: a comb, a pair of nail scissors and a can of hair spray, and a pair of earrings shaped like stalactites that one of the lads must have given her, and I also stored a small selection of foodstuffs such as tinned fruit and chocolate wafers that I had brought as traveller's fare, and there I would lie on the shore next to the boat and pretend that I was looking out for the bittern, while hoping that she would come walking beneath the trees along the path and call out to me: Andreas? are you there? have you seen my . . . ? And then I would show her everything I had and things would be like they used to be between us, so we would sit together, splashing with our feet in the water, and peel oranges and eat the KitKats and talk or, at least, Minna would talk, spinning another one of her improbable stories that would form a roof over both our heads; it would be like an arching, sheltering, colour-flecked fantasy cover that I could crawl under for safety and, at least for a while, forget myself and all about me that was altogether too obvious and bulky or hurt too much. I was so preoccupied by preparing this escape route of mine that I heard nothing until a twig broke just behind me and I turned to see him come walking, just twenty metres away. Him: Kaufmann. Fully kit-ted out: he carried a rucksack and a lunch bag, held a gigantic butterfly net and, hanging from a lanyard around his neck, an odd-looking object (I later realised that it was a magnifying box used to examine insects). Oddly enough, all I felt was astonishment. Only a few weeks earlier, when I had dared to walk to the main house on the farm and he had caught me on the veranda, only to invite me in and offer me some scraps off their table, I had felt an almost nauseating disgust: I remembered how everything about him had seemed repulsive, from his long-fingered hands with their well-kept nails and liver spots to his elaborate, polished manner of speech. Out here in the open air, he looked frail and vulnerable, lanky and skinny in his thin, white cotton clothes, his long neck protruding like a beanstalk from the carefully buttoned shirt collar; an impression that was made stronger by the way he held his head to the side all the time, as if secretly listening out for something, and how sharp his shoulder blades looked (as I noted when I later saw him from behind), the shell-like forewings of an insect about to take off. He walked like an insect, too, with probing, cautious steps, as if with twitching antennae. That I had suddenly found a long-sought opportunity was clear to me at once. Not to kill him. Whatever Minna had said, the idea remained utterly abstract to me. What I wanted was my sister's attention again. If I hit him on the head with a stone, Minna could not ignore me any longer, she simply would have *no choice*. And my head was so full of the beautiful vision of what this would mean to me that I totally missed my chance. When I came back to my senses, the woodland path lay in front of me, shimmering with sun and shadow, and not a sound to indicate where he had gone could be heard from anywhere. But, from that day onwards, I waited for him with a new, ambitious eagerness. It didn't take long to work out that he had certain routines, so fixed one might have set one's watch by them. Not that he walked the same way every day, but he regularly followed favourite paths and visited and investigated certain selected sites. With great effort, because of his stiff back and inflexible joints, he would crawl about, lifting stones and peering at the ground under the root plates of fallen trees. Once, I even saw him surrounded by white butterflies, just as in Minna's story. True, these ones seemed to be quite ordinary cabbage whites. I realised that he must have charted the entire forest in minute detail and kept areas of terrain under constant surveillance. The next time he passed by, I was prepared. I had understood that his near vision was poor, and that he found it especially hard to keep his balance when light and dark made shifting patterns against the shadowy depths of the forest, and so I had borrowed a strong rope from Johannes and stretched it across a path. I hid in the clump of ferns a few metres away, clutching a rough block of stone that must have weighed more than a kilogram. I had found the stone behind another tall bunch of ferns and carefully scraped all the moss and soil off it, and tested it against tree trunks and other likely surfaces to make sure that it would not slip out of my hand. But when the time came for me to strike, it still felt shapeless and heavy and slippery and the arm that held it had gone strangely limp and unwilling. The day was humid and sultry and the sun was hidden behind a slight haze that down by the lake made the light white and opaque. There was not a breath of wind. Where I lay curled up behind the wet ferns with the stone in my hand, the entire forest seemed to be roaring even though no sound was heard. Kaufmann was making his way with, if anything, steps more uncertain than ever, and when he stumbled on the rope, he went forward with his whole body, as if felled by the blow of an axe. And it was as if he already knew what would happen: he was very still, made no attempt to get up or even to move a little, and all the things he had brought (butterfly net, lunch box, magnifying device) were scattered around him. Perhaps that was why I stalled for a moment. Or perhaps there was another reason. He was lying on his front, both liver-spotted hands stretched out like claws, and I remember the strange *smell* that hung in the air around him, a smell I had never noticed before despite the many times he had passed by me less than a metre away. The smell was dankly thick and oily, as if from some kind of fuel, but at the same time more astringent and piercing, and when I finally bent down over the apparently paralysed old man, the smell overwhelmed me and almost made me faint. But I struck him all the same, or tried to. I hit his head first and then (when he still refused to defend himself) the rest of his body, his neck and upper arms and shoulder blades, then his back and legs. The later the blows, the more aimless and feeble they grew. As if I hit out mostly to alert him and make him get up. Because it was so weird, the way he did not resist, did not twist or twitch, not even when the stone struck his head. He just lay there on the ground, flat on his belly. In the end, I could not bear to keep hitting him. The stone fell from my hand.

Somehow, I managed to straighten up and run away, faint from the smell rising from his body and from the dawning insight into what I had attempted.

*

And, predictably, what I feared most happened soon enough: Mr Carsten came to see us. It was around half past six. The strong evening sun made the upstairs windows look scratched and dusty. Downstairs, the doorbell rang its mechanical *ding-dong*. I heard Johannes walk to the door, watchful as always on the rare occasions when someone rang the front doorbell. As for me, I stayed in my room, sitting with the hand that had held the bloody stone squeezed between my knees, which would not stop shaking. No need for me to hear Mr Carsten's voice to imagine him standing there with his muddy boots far apart and his false half-smile and his *kan de tell me now, Johannes* and *do de not think there's some'at wrong wi that lass* and *so I want to know wat de are going to do aboot it . . . ?* But Minna was nowhere to be seen. Not that night, or the next, as I recall. And although it would be several months before Mr Carsten acted on his threat and Minna was placed in a foster home, I cannot remember a single time when she let on, even with one word, that it was I who had wielded the stone that almost killed Kaufmann. Or that it was she who had commanded me to do the deed. The consequence was, of course, that I had to keep carrying the bloody stone. I still do.

Only one route reaches the farm from around the back: it goes across the high ridge at the northern end of the lake. The vegetation there is quite different from the low-lying meadows near the lake. Fir trees dominate the forest that forms a tall wall around the mossy outcrops of rock, and the paths dwindle and disappear. You have to make your own way between the boulders and climb down while holding on to supports like exposed roots and branches that slip treacherously in your grip. Once up on the ridge, it becomes obvious that the view of the farm from the Yellow Villa (that is, what I always saw as I grew up) shows no more than a frontage, with the main house and the long barn fused into a close, compact facade. Seen from the interior of the island, the farm lies open and quite unprotected. There is an expanse of rough meadow between the farmyard and the edge of the forest where, after the winter rains and the frost, the grass has been folded over into tufty ramparts. Kaufmann's house stands at the far end of the uncut meadow. The building was designed as a romantic take on the simple, rustic style that was popular at the turn of the nineteenth century: two storeys high, it has a tall hipped roof which ends in a small domed turret topped by a spire and weathervane. There is a first-floor balcony and a veranda of white-painted wood that runs along the southern side of the house. In the past, a pergola covered the way to the servants' entrance at cellar level, but Mrs Kaufmann let the last of the staff go after her husband's death and then had the doorway blocked off. A garage with a turf roof has been built to the side behind the house and then comes a row of stable blocks, one – the last in the row – with direct access to the paddock laid out by Mr Carsten just before Kaufmann's death. The pump-house ruin is located on the opposite side of the meadow, another old carriage shed stands next to it and, a little further up the slope, is the farm manager's cottage, a miniature version of the main farmhouse but without the turret and the spire, the balcony and the long veranda. A horse trailer has been parked behind the house, and a yellowy-brown Volvo 240 with mud splashes on its bumpers. The many new, criss-crossing tyre tracks in the rain-soaked mud in front of the farm manager's house make it likely that he is at home. Although something, perhaps simply my old fear, stops me from approaching any further, I scan the villa through the binoculars several times. Presumably, the new owners have not moved in yet since there are still curtains and potted plants in the windows and the outlines of seating can be seen through the sun's reflections in the window panes. A door slams on the other side of one of the outbuildings and a dog barks, a sharp, excited yelp that lingers in the damp air. Soon afterwards, Mr Carsten limps into sight, pushing a wheelbarrow that contains a garden fork, a spade and two rattling galvanised buckets. I cannot remember when I last saw him at close range. Possibly that time, ten years ago, when he turned up unexpectedly at my flat in Carl Berners Square in Oslo, dressed in a suit and a fedora hat, although he was unshaven and drunk, and the suit looked as if he had been sleeping in it. He tried on his most ingratiating smile and asked for my sister, but I fended him off and kept him outside the door. Since that encounter, he has aged visibly. In the past, he could move forward quite quickly despite his paralysed leg. Now, one shoulder and half his upper body slip markedly sideways with every step, which means that, every so often, he has to come to a halt and lift his stiff leg clear so that he can get going again. As he proceeds towards the potato patch with his waggling, swayback gait, he reminds me of Johannes telling Minna and me about the Chilotes and their mythical *invunche*, boys schooled from birth to be the guardians of their native islands: these boys had one leg crushed and tied to their back to stop them from running away, and all their bodily orifices, from mouth to anus, sewn up so that nothing of the knowledge stored inside them could be leaked to strangers or enemies. The wind is growing stronger and drives the rain in long, pale curtains between the main house and the stables and barns. I have advanced quite far into the yard, before the dog catches my scent and comes running towards me, barking all the time. Mr Carsten shouts at the dog and swears at it while he extracts a lead from a bulging pocket in his coat and manages to attach it to the dog's harness. He has clearly not been expecting any visitors but pulls himself together with admirable cool. *So*, here he is, our little mongrel, the bastard boy! Back to the island to disturb a dead man's sleep, right? So, how are things, *laddie*? There is something about his chesty, rough voice with its obvious Danish inflections and drawling vowels that in an instant takes me right back: those powerful *ding-dong* notes from the ground floor that rang out through the house, the creaking treads as Johannes went downstairs to open the door, the *kan de tell me now, Johannes*, the draught through the opened door and their low voices reaching the *laddie* who sat with his bloodied hands gripped between his knees. But Mr Carsten seems not to feel that his choice of words is anywhere near as meaningful as I do. While he limps away, crooked and with his neck bent, to find somewhere to tether the dog, who pads around him anxiously and gets more and more entangled in the lead, I hear him complaining in the familiar fed-up, whining tone he always resorts to when he does a run-through of the state of things in general, while swaying on and off the dead leg as if not only that leg alone but everything that he has been burdened with during a whole life is hurting him now. People, he says, addressing the dog, are running in and out of here all the time. *Private Property*, it says. Can't they read? (How many times have I heard him utter just these words?) Coming along here, asking for the mistress. Helga, too, has passed away by now. No one to take on the farm, the lot of it has gone now, executive sale it was. He turns away, spits in the direction of the wind. The few lumpy little potatoes he has managed to dig up must be the first this year and, down there in the bottom of the bucket, they look like tiny, crumpled faces. Rather like his, in fact. Well, how long will you be staying here? I ask. Until the new owners come along to take over. The talk is, they'll start up fur farming again. There's equipment left from old Brandt's time, peace be with him! That last phrase is uttered in a low voice; he is still turning to the dog, which is lying down in the flattened grass, its head just visible. The silence bursts open and through the rain-soaked ocean of air above us sails, with almost unreal slowness, yet another terrible steel body, a clashing, screaming nightmare that prevents any single sensible thought. Johannes is dead, I say, but you must know that? Then, at last, he looks at me with what I at first take to be a satisfied smile but then see expresses pure anxiety. It is as if his rigid, lifeless face cannot produce anything except comical grimaces and half-smiles. *So wat?* he says. The words sound as if spat from his mouth. I wait until the plane has sunk below the ridge and the roar that it pulls behind it has stopped echoing. I have come to give you these, I say, and try to offer him a handful of copied receipts that I found underneath the pile of newspapers. *Received from Johannes Lindalen for services (various) – the sum of 1000 (one thousand) kroner, signed C. Gerhardsen.* The bundle is made up almost exclusively of receipts for payments to Mr Carsten, every time for relatively modest sums: seven hundred to one thousand kroner, at most (on two occasions) fifteen hundred kroner, but made in close succession, some with only a couple of days between them. What is all that? he says, without more than a quick glance at the papers I try to present to him. Receipts for blood money? I suggest. Did Johannes pay you to get Minna off the island? I have no idea whether this is true or not. I am assuming that there might be a link because the receipts were made and signed the autumn Minna was forced to move. I don't understand what you're on about, Mr Carsten says, suddenly busy again with his fork and his bucket in the potato patch. And where is her birth certificate kept? Whose? he says. Minna's, I say. By now, he no longer looks alarmed, only scornful. Listen, you little motherfucker, he finally says (or, more like it: he *croaks*), I never gave a fuck about what happened to Johannes's little bastards and I don't want to know now either! It strikes me how much he has shrunk during all the years that have passed, as if he has always been on his way back down into the sour soil where his muddy boots are planted now. I despise him boundlessly. Not that he notices. Now he even attempts a more conciliatory tone. Johannes is dead all right, he says, so tell me, what's the point of digging up all the old things now? We are all just as deep in it, all supping from the same bowl, isn't that what people say? he says, and swings the garden fork in the air. And that means you as well, *laddie*. Behind the dull film of rain, his face looks almost normal: one half of it crunched up as if squinting through the rain, while the other, healthy half carries on watching me with an open, clear and soberly appraising eye. He speaks with no hint of deference, but then he never did, however loyal to his masters and superiors he has pretended to be over the years. A mongrel, a bastard child, those were the names he called me. Perhaps we never change in the eyes of our enemies. I turn my back on the shrunken old man in the potato patch and walk down to the Yellow Villa, my head pushed forward against the rain. I have just put the key into the lock on the cellar door when the most awful noise hits me. It comes from inside the house. It sounds as if a horde of people are incessantly talking across each other. I pull the door open and run upstairs. The voices go on talking, in bursts between interruptions of something like raucous, evil laughter. I stand in the doorway to what was once my room, staring at the long draperies of static sweeping across the lit TV screen. Now and then, coinciding with moments when the TV noise shifts into almost-human voices, the flicker stops and freezes into something that is vaguely reminiscent of a body or a wall or a landscape, before it rapidly dissolves into empty flashing again. And the television was not the only device Johannes left switched on when the electricity was cut off. All the lamps in the sitting room are on. And in the kitchen, on the shelf above the sink, the radio is muttering away. When everything is switched off again, I curl up opposite the blank screen with my back to the wall and my knees pulled up against my chest. For some reason, my whole body is shaking.

*

The attic is the only place in the house where I can really feel at ease, just like Johannes. Now that the electricity is back on, I have carried several of the old radiators up there. They stand in line, smelling sourly of dust and red-hot metal bars. I also dragged Johannes's portable Brennenstuhl lamp into the attic and hung the wound-up flex on a hook on the wall behind the sidecar, which I have emptied of old rubbish so that I can sit in it myself, reclining on the torn faux-leather seat. Lately, I have spent much of the day seriously examining Kaufmann's own writings, not only the diaries but also the books from his library, which Sigrid Kaufmann after the war insisted that Johannes should come and collect from the farm. A series of faded red Baedeker guides interest me in particular; Johannes had put them on one of the shelves closest to the floor. One of these books is a guide to the German Baltic coast, another to *Tirol, Vorarlberg, Westliches Salzburg und Hochkärnten*, a third to Southern Bavaria and a fourth to the Black Forest. The fifth and last is simply called *Baedekers Generalgouvernement*. Glued to the inside of the cover, a map expands to show the occupied inner regions of Poland, with all the Polish towns and rivers named in German. Inside the book is a twice-folded receipt from *Deutsche Buchhandlung Alfred Fritzsche, Adolf-Hitler-Platz 23, Krakau*. The bill came to fourteen zlotys, and the sum is followed by the stamped word *Bezahlt* next to an unreadable signature. Kaufmann must have bought the book himself when visiting Krakow. And he has clearly read it attentively. In one chapter, entitled '*Landschaft, Mensch und Wirtschaft*' ('Landscape, People and Industries') and written by a Dr Ernst R. Fugmann of the Institut für Deutsche Ostarbeit (Institute for German Development in the East) in Krakow, there is a long account of the Polish agricultural and animal farming sector, in which certain passages have been marked in the margin with long, strong lines in pencil:

> *The Yield.* Thus, it follows that it is impossible to overemphasise the erroneousness of assuming that Poland as a whole is a highly productive agricultural region [. . .] Even though practically all of the land in the General Governorate, if cultivated in the proper manner, could produce greater yields corresponding to at least half as much again of today's yields and with similar increases

of animal, notably cattle farming, the age-old affliction has still deeper roots in so far as the current subdivision of the farm holdings and arable land, and the almost fatalistic state of mind of small-scale farmers steeped in docility, predispose improvements in land use to succeed only if established on a wider basis of dedicated and extensive education provided by the German Agricultural Authority, with its advice and schooling applied to every aspect of agricultural matters. Overpopulation, which in the region of the General Governorate has been estimated to be approximately 4.5 million = 47% of the rural population, and which consists of a massed labour force that is not only free and unrestricted but which might actually constitute an obstacle to increased farming yields, has in this context come to be of particular concern to the Reich.

The receipt is not dated but, if the book was published in 1943 as stated on the inside page, then Kaufmann's field studies on the modernisation of Polish agriculture cannot have taken place any earlier than that. I turn to his diaries from 1943, and it is not long before I come across a note from *Warschau 13 juni*:

– arriving by train from Posen, lodge at Hotel Bristol –

He presumably stayed there because the Baedeker guide to Warsaw said the Bristol was one of the better hotels in the city and rated its restaurant as *good for Germans*. After the four-day stay in Warsaw, which goes without comment, the diary lists the names of hotels and dates he stayed there during his almost four-week-long travels through, to begin with, south-east Poland and then what is present-day Ukraine: to Radom, Częstochowa and Krakow, where Kaufmann is 'detained' for a day and a night because of 'overload on the rail services'; finally, he goes to Lublin and Lemberg (Lviv), where the entry on 7 July states that his outward journey ends. During those weeks on the move, Kaufmann makes detours to villages and small towns, where he meets with people whom he describes in the diary as 'functionaries' and who are likely to have been senior party officials. Kaufmann seems to have examined everything along the way with the greatest interest. In his notebook, one page is devoted to a drawing of an old-fashioned harvester and another to a mill powered by water released from locks further upstream. In a hand-drawn column next to the drawing, the water volumes and pressures at each lock gate are exactly recorded. Where did he want his studies to take him? Johannes said that Kaufmann was often away from the island during the war years but, for some reason, I had come to believe it was due to his workload at the ministry. Johannes told us children of only one journey: that is, when Kaufmann went to Berlin in November 1942 in order to persuade Hitler to increase the total German export quota for crop seeds, a great diplomatic achievement and very significant in a country with shortages of almost everything. I do not have to look far to find the episode in a diary. The visit to Berlin takes up two separate, page-long sets of notes in Kaufmann's characteristic hand with its tall, upright capitals:

22.11 We arrive in B in bad weather. Disturbances within atmospheric strata led to a rough plane journey, fog on arrival. Radio contact with B interrupted several times.
23.11 To see the trade secretary at the legation. We have a three-hour meeting at the German Ministry of Foreign Affairs. During the meeting, a message from the Chancellery to say that I am expected there. Earlier message states that the Führer has informed himself of my report but that he was not present in Berlin at the time of our negotiations. The visit appears to have been arranged at very short notice. We are taken in a motorcade to Voßstraße, where I am escorted by a private secretary to an inner suite of chambers where the Führer is in conversation with three gentlemen. He comports himself in these situations with an unassuming ease that is remarkable, and moves with a light step that one might have thought was that of a considerably younger man. Also, how frank and modest he seems. Our talk lasts for almost twenty minutes. Now and then, he interjects a humorous comment or serves himself from the dish of cakes provided for us. Since I did not have time to prepare a more detailed exposition, I have to speak from memory, but H. allows himself to be distracted only on a few occasions, when one of the other gentlemen in the room addresses him in a whisper about some matter of state.

In his diary, Kaufmann's tone as he narrates the story of the meeting is straightforward and unguarded. It sounds as if the possibility of a German defeat never occurred to him and as if he regards this ultimate victory as a historical necessity; meanwhile, all efforts in support of this end, including his own, are natural stages of preparing humanity for the better life that awaits after the end of the war. 'Those who travel *from the east* into the Reich already have an impression of the General Governorate that is much determined by a sense of coming home, while for those who travel *from the Reich* eastwards, it is like a first greeting from the world to their east,' so Governor General Hans Frank writes in his Preface to *Baedekers Generalgouvernement*. Kaufmann came from the west. What did he take note of when he arrived? Did he see in all the old family farms, with their overgrown forest clearings and undrainable meadows and fields, so many mirror images of the poverty on the islands of his youth? Or did he see possibilities, ideas for innovation? A world freed from the overpopulation that Dr Fugmann insisted was an obstacle to effective cultivation of the rich soil, with its potential to yield good harvests? In his meagre diary notes, there are no answers to questions about what Kaufmann actually thought about the population policies of the Nazi Party, about the extermination of Europe's Jews (I assume this process is the cause of the recurring train delays he records) or the raids by German SS units in eastern Poland and Ukraine, which laid waste to whole villages and towns in exactly the areas he travelled through towards the end of his journey. Kaufmann seems to have kept his eyes open for practical details only; at least, that is the kind of thing he writes up in his diaries. However, it is also clear from the notes that, in parallel with his extensive travelling, he was utterly absorbed by another idea, the project initiated in the first year of the war, which had become known on the islands (perhaps rather misleadingly) as the 'second colony'. His plan was to offer children from crowded, dirty homes in the inner cities the opportunity to come and stay in the countryside, with access to milk and fruit and fresh vegetables. To that end, Kaufmann had already arranged to reopen the old West Island phalanstery, the communal lodgings shut down and locked in the early thirties. It was there and in the Sanatorium that he would welcome every summer hundreds of children, who would all have to show themselves as 'deserving' by working on his farms. What I wonder about is if there might not have been some kind of link between the travelling he undertook and his charitable project, which on the face of it seems quite unselfish; a link that is not at all obvious when all you go by is what enters into his diaries. Though one thing I do know: Kaufmann saw the need for *reciprocity*, as he puts it in his notes. At the end of August 1943, he arranged for a group of functionaries (that word again), whom he had met on his journey, to make an official visit to the Inner Islands. The programme included a tour of the children's colony. I know from Johannes how the visit turned out in practice, because he was told to collect the guests from the mainland and take them to West Island, not an easy job since not all the visitors were steady enough on their feet for a trip on the wobbly cable ferry that, even in the 1940s, was the only connection to the outlying islands. Once arrived, refreshment would be laid on. Photographs would be taken. To round off the excursion, there would be a grand banquet at the Mains Farm. Rumour had it that Vidkun Quisling, the Minister President of the pro-Nazi government, and Jonas Lie, his Minister of Police, were among the guests, something Johannes persistently and vehemently denied. After all, the story was that Kaufmann never let a German across the bridge. Though that is non-sense. As everyone knows. Simonsen and Brekke have told of how a company of prisoners from Grini, all sentenced to hard labour, were drafted in to shore up the barracks on West Island and lay water and sewage pipes to the island. But perhaps it is more useful to get a grip on why Kaufmann should be so keen to prove his debt of gratitude to the German industrialists and party officials, rather than harp on the purity of his motives? Could it be that he saw in the colony *his own* version of the thousand-year Reich, where blond, bare-legged children and their rumbustious play took over in the old Sanatorium area? Or was it to distract attention from what must not be seen: the physically enfeebled, terminally ill daughter who lived upstairs? Asking Johannes about this kind of thing was pointless, and his jovial expression never changed. In front of us children, he preferred to return to his memories of that amazing day and evening. And it really was a magical evening to Minna and me, half asleep with our heads resting on the kitchen table. The Mains Farm Road was lit by real torches all the way from King's Road up to the farm, Johannes told us.

There was no wind that evening and the torches flared with tall, bright and smokeless flames. At the top of the slope, the entire farm was illuminated. Throughout the night until the morning, you could hear the foreign visitors call out and laugh in voices as clear as glass. It was almost as if you could pick up every word they said, Johannes would tell us, and every time I had a vision of the farm about to cast off from its moorings and move away into the night, like a gigantic steamship about to cross the Atlantic.

*

I must have fallen asleep in the sidecar when someone, a man, shouts my name at the top of his voice. The rough call is followed by the sound of breaking glass and a loud thump on the ground floor, as if a heavy object has fallen over. On my way downstairs, lit by the Brennenstuhl lamp, I hear more window panes break, then the crunching of gravel underfoot and stamping footsteps of someone running outside near the house. The gun: odd that I did not think about it sooner. It is an old hunting rifle with a revolving cylinder. I know Johannes used to keep it somewhere on the first floor. I put the lamp down, fumble across the dark landing into the bedroom and, in the end, find the worn leather case with the gun in a corner of the further of Johannes's two wardrobes. There is a telescopic sight in the case and a magazine with cartridges in a zipped pocket. I feed a cartridge into the cylinder and walk downstairs without putting on any lights. The window next to the front door is broken and there is a stone on the floor in the hall, and plenty of splintered glass. In the cellar, the boiler-room window has been smashed by someone using the wooden table and the paint-splashed stool that used to stand along the garage wall. I stop, gun in hand, and try to work out where the intruders are hiding outside. Now, all is quiet apart from the clock on the wall, slowly ticking off the seconds. Even the noises of rain and wind whipping against the house have ceased. After waiting a few minutes, I unlock the cellar door and step outside. The rain is drifting away and the darkness of the night is about to dissolve, but it is still dark under the trees. Rainwater running off leaves and branches drips into the soft moss below. The two front windows, which face the road, have lights in them: the lamps in the sitting room and in Johannes's old room are on, an easy-to-read sign, for all to see, that the house is lived in again. The light is enough to show that the vandals collected quite a few objects heavy enough to break windows and pulled out several of the edging stones along the drive, and also took the lid off the waste bin by the gate. But I cannot find the energy to walk all around the house to inspect the damage, not now. With rainwater trickling down the back of my neck, I make my way to the fence to look for any tracks that my night-time visitors might have made in the sodden mud along the road. At the raspberry hedge, I stumble over the incinerator bin. It, too, has been knocked over. I am not sure if this is yet another example of their meaningless destructiveness or if they went through the contents to check whatever was left of what I tried to burn. Down by King's

Road, a car can be heard changing down through the gears and then quickly back up again. Next, the same car is driven full throttle on skidding tyres up the Back Lane. At this time of the day, it cannot be anyone except the newspaper delivery man, Skakland's son – the Speedfreak, as they call him. I walk down to the gate to wait for him. A letterbox snaps shut a little further along the road, then the car revs up again. Brakes are suddenly slammed on. Next, the engine is revved up again. The beams of the headlamps sweep over the fruit trees, where I stand, gun in hand. The car stops at my gate. Skakland is rooting about among the piles of newspaper inside the lit car, then looks up and shows me the finger. I watch as the rear lights gleam when he brakes abruptly over by the crossroads, where the road turns off towards the Mains Farm. But Skakland does not drive up there.

*

Kaufmann died in January 1973, just over half a year after the incident down by the lake. The islanders spoke for a long time about the severe illness that tormented him during the last few years of his life. It was cancer and was said to have caused such awful pain that he could hardly bear to move during the final months. So this was the man I had encountered on the lakeside paths: someone tired and ageing, who unmistakably found it difficult to make out the ground in front of him but who defied his pain because of his deep realisation that no part of all that he regarded as sacrosanct would ever be lost. Not a day too soon, people were saying, inevitably, when the announcement of his death was finally made. As for me, I spent the autumn after my bumbling attack in a haze of guilt and fear. I was frightened that Minna would tell the lads what I had done. Or that someone, Mr Carsten, for instance, had seen me do the deed with his own eyes. Or that Kaufmann had put some kind of curse on me. Meanwhile, I was seen as a good, reliable boy, my sister's opposite in every way. I helped Johannes sterilise jam jars and juice bottles and prepare jam and pickles. I walked on my own all the way to Langmark's timber yard with the measurements for the boards Johannes needed for the shelving that was part of his refurbishment of the kitchen in the Yellow Villa. He had been measuring and pondering all summer long, and had finally decided to tear down the clumsy old kitchen cupboards left from the days of the fur farmer, and instead build new ones: modern, wall-mounted cupboards with sliding doors. They would be wider at the top and narrow towards the base so that one at last could stand straight in here. When he turned his hand to carpentry, Johannes proved capable of much greater concentration than usual. He was fast and efficient, and the tools seemed made to fit his hands, which never wavered. I helped him estimate and measure and then position the boards and hold them in place. But all I could think about meanwhile was that phone call, which I knew had to come one day and would mean Johannes turning to me with that special, quiet but reproachful expression of his, which also made him look troubled, almost sad. I would never have believed this, not from you, he would say. An old, ill, defenceless man! And then, one day, it finally happened: that much-feared telephone call from the Mains Farm. It was on a Sunday in early January, the first mild day since Christmas. Above the forest, which overnight had shed its coat of frost for the first time in months, the sky hung black and as heavy as lead. Johannes left to walk to the farm without a word to me. I do not know if he knew, but it *seemed* as if he did. I watched his back from my window. The car from the funeral directors overtook him as it slowly drove up the Mains Farm Road. Several hours passed when nothing happened up there as far as I could see, but I did not dare leave my vantage point. Eventually, a small group of dark figures gathered around the parked hearse. Johannes must have been among them but the distance was too great for me to make out individuals. Mr Carsten's limp I did recognise, though. After a while, the black hearse detached itself from the tight cluster of people and slowly started off down the road. It crawled along but no one followed it. Everyone must have seen it but no one opened a window or stepped outside or stopped to watch it at the end of their drive. Such was the end of Kaufmann's reign on the island: the sky over the forest was darkened by big, black clouds, heavy with unreleased rain, and not one human in sight, as if the islanders to a man and woman had decided by common agreement to turn their backs on him.

*

Minna went to a foster home in the autumn of the year Kaufmann died. The official version was that she had been accepted at a special school on the mainland and the new lodgings would make it easier for her to attend. Everyone knew that it was some kind of punishment and that, when all was said and done, it was Johannes who was being punished. He had been made responsible for a task and had failed to bring her up properly. (Later, I realised that handing me over to the authorities had also been considered but, at the last minute, it was agreed that I was too young, so I was allowed to stay with Johannes.) Afterwards, my longing for Minna was like a fever or a shameful itch that would not go away, not ever. I could not sleep in my own bed at night and instead went to lie down in hers, breathing in what was left of her scent in the sheets until Johannes came and hauled me out of bed in the morning. For the first time in my life, I went to school alone. On the way, I avoided splashing in the puddles, just because it was something we had done together. Or, at least, this was how I felt then. There were places in the interior of the island where I longed to be, *our* places, but which were now forbidden territory after what she had made me do to the old man. This was how Kaufmann's power continued to grow after his death, as a direct outcome of Minna's absence. The winter, when it arrived, helped a little. There is always something special about the winters on the island. The snow obscures the usual boundaries between the islanders and the grounds they own. People who usually would take no notice of each other can be seen walking together out on the ice or chatting on the seashore.

In the ice-free channels, the water steams and smokes in the wake of the ferries. Sometimes, a dense, damp fog drifts in from the outer reaches of the fjord and all flights are cancelled. They have a special word for that pale, thick sea mist, *the whitey*, which at worst could stay put for weeks. After a few days of the whitey, the trees are glazed with frost and, with no aeroplanes overhead, the silence is so intense that space seems about to explode. At night, the damp cold casts a sheen over the sky and the snow, a matte, reddish glow as if a fire were burning somewhere in the interior of the island. During whitey nights, Johannes kept wandering restlessly from room to room. He did not say anything but it was obvious that Minna's transfer to the foster home had made him feel ill at ease. He became almost manically dependent on his books and his bottles. Because it was too cold and draughty to sit in the attic, he carried the radiators down to the sitting room and holed up on the ox-leather sofa while the red heat from the radiator shone on his cheeks and forehead, making his skin look more than ever like the smooth, fine-textured skin of a child. Early that spring, something happened that no one could have predicted. Mr Carsten began to drop in at the Yellow Villa for some reason. Then, one day, Minna suddenly came back. At the time, it never occurred to me that these two things, Mr Carsten's visits and Minna's return, were related in any way. When Mr Carsten pressed the front doorbell, all Johannes said was that they did a bit of betting on the races together. But I would have noticed if they had done that, seen them bending over the racing papers or discussing odds going up or down the way folk did over at Brekke's. And I did not see anything of the sort. Mr Carsten never stepped inside and the fact that he rang the bell *down there* was significant in itself. People who knew Johannes would call out their hellos from somewhere in the garden before coming in through the cellar door or across the terrace. The fateful *ding-dong* ring of the front doorbell was something I associated with Mr Carsten and him alone, with his staring gaze and stroke-affected half-smile. The times Mr Carsten came, I never dared to go downstairs. I shut myself in my room and kept an eye on the activities of the two unlikely chums from my window. Mostly, they wandered off into the garden, as if to be alone, unobserved while they spoke. After a quarter of an hour, maybe twenty minutes, Mr Carsten would leave without another word, dragging his stiff leg through the garden while Johannes stood and looked after him, as if Mr Carsten's message had left him deep in thought. Do you think Johannes ran up gambling debts? I asked Simonsen the other day. It was the payments from Johannes to Mr Carsten that I had in mind. Simonsen said he didn't know of any such thing, but he did not think so. On the other hand, he believed that, back then, Mr Carsten had a fifty per cent stake in a harness-racing horse, which he and the co-owner raced over on Bjerke from time to time, so he might well have tried to persuade Johannes to invest in that horse. Or in some other horse. Simonsen couldn't say; after all, Mr Carsten wasn't exactly the chatty type. However, he was pretty sure that Kaufmann had not taken kindly to Mr Carsten busying himself with sidelines that had nothing to do with his proper job, but that he had lacked the energy to confront his farm manager, whose interest in horses finally got the upper hand. Even so, it was only when Kaufmann was in his grave that Mrs Kaufmann called Mr Carsten to the house and told him that was that. What, Mr Carsten was sacked? I said. Yes, he was. Of course, then there was *the other story* as well, Simonsen said in a lower voice. He looked anxiously over his shoulder, as if he seriously suspected that somebody was lurking behind the raspberry hedge to eavesdrop on us. At one point, Mr Carsten and his partner were at daggers drawn about the horse, and Mr Carsten tried to push his mate down a staircase. It got to be a court case afterwards, Simonsen said, but there was no proof of anything. Apart from the actual embezzlement. And what about Kaufmann, I asked, did he have any knowledge of what Mr Carsten was up to? Who can tell what Kaufmann knew or didn't? Simonsen said. Towards the end the old boy lived in a world of his own. And then there was this thing with Minna. That autumn, she had got a job in the supermarket where her boyfriend Morten used to work. Officially, this was why she came back to the island. First she worked in the store room, later at the tills. She detested all of it. On her very first day back, I went to see her in the shop, and she sat there as if caged, wearing some kind of green uniform and keying numbers into the till. She did not even look at me. There were highlights in her hair and dark shadow on her eyelids. The skin on her hands was dry and flaking, her nails chewed to bits. She had changed a lot during the months she had been away from us. Her cheeky chatter had gone, and so had her frenetic activity (her teacher had called it an attention deficit). She was glum and withdrawn most of the time, would not respond if you tried to make contact, only rejected you, with one corner of her mouth pulled down in an ugly grimace. I stood in the doorway to her room, watching as she unpacked her things. Nothing of what she had brought was from the past. There were lots of skirts and dresses, and rings, earrings and other jewellery kept in special boxes on her bedside table. She claimed that these things had been given to her by her foster parents but I felt quite sure they had been stolen and, besides, what was all this talk about foster parents supposed to mean? Had she been adopted again? Did I and Johannes not provide her with family enough? But she did not answer that question either, just nodded towards the door, which meant that I was to get out of her room. She dressed up and went out every evening. To me, it seemed unbelievable that Minna should wear a tight skirt and high-heeled shoes: Minna, who had been running barefoot wherever she went, not even putting on shoes to run along the seashore with its high drifts of sharp-edged seashells, or across the stubble on the fields. I watched her turn right, towards the school and the shop, and assumed that she was off to meet the lads again. Unless she was going to take the bus to the mainland. It was impossible to know. I followed, keeping about two hundred metres behind her, and saw her take the shortcut across the football field, walk down to the shop and then turn right to join King's Road and right again onto the Mains Farm Road. She had walked in a circle in order to arrive unseen at the farm by the road on the other side of the house. I could hardly believe my eyes, seeing her in that weird outfit, strolling towards the Mains Farm. Later, I settled by my window, looking for her and waiting. At about six in the morning, I heard her open the front door and, carrying her shoes, tiptoe upstairs and into the bathroom. I went in and stood in the doorway. Through the window, the reddish light of dawn fell on her naked upper body as she bent over the edge of the wash-hand basin, her long spine protruding under her grey, somehow porous skin. She seemed frail and vulnerable, like a captive and utterly defenceless animal. Why did you go up there? I asked. She was splashing water over her face and did not look up. After all, he isn't there any more, I tried. Who? she asked. *Kaufmann!* I shouted, because it was such an effort just to make his name pass my lips. But then it's OK for me to go there, if he isn't there, she said, and there was a hint of a smile around her lips in the mirror. You must have wanted to go there, I insisted, 'cause if you didn't, you wouldn't have. Her face disappeared from the mirror again. How's one to know what one wants? she said, as she scooped water over the back of her neck. Things happen, she said. She fumbled for a towel. *What* is it that happens? I asked. And she: how do I know? What happens, happens. And that was all. I did not get a thing. She went to bed, but I stayed up. The next day, I tried a new strategy. I asked her if she would like to go to the lake with me. She looked reluctant but agreed after a while. Perhaps she had a bad conscience and felt that she had better humour me, at least once. I led the way, small and dying to talk with her, and she followed, plodding, absent-minded. In the end, we stand by the lake on precisely the spot where we have stood together so many times before, and Minna shows only too clearly that the situation makes her nervous. She lights one cigarette after another and laughs when I walk around slapping the bushes with a branch as if to call forth memories of the dying Kaufmann. He created them himself, Minna says. Which them? I say. The butterflies, she says. I stare at her, with the broken-off branch dangling from my hand. What the fuck are you talking about? I ask. Butterflies are attracted by this scent that the females secrete. If you play tricks with these scents, you can make the males of one species seek out females from another one and, with a bit of luck, they could mate and produce a completely new butterfly species. He told me this. He said it was quite easy to do, Minna says and drags on her cigarette one last time before dropping it on the ground and pressing it down with her heel. And what about the foxes? I ask. Was it the same way with them? The foxes, now, she says, I made all that up. I stare at her. And then, without understanding why, I start to cry. I'm sorry, she says. It wasn't him, it wasn't Kaufmann. Then she turns and walks away, and a little further into the forest she starts running, as if she cannot get away from there quickly enough.

*

I make notes: this is the fifteenth evening since I arrived, the tenth since I started on the inventory. I have continued to go through Johannes's old papers. I have sorted his piled-up receipts and accounts ledgers into separate stacks around me. On the top shelf of the wardrobe in the hall, there are six or more old shoeboxes, all stuffed with paperwork and cuttings. He seems not to have thrown away a single thing in his life. In the main, the papers are perfectly innocent. Like the invoice for a new oil pump, or the order of tin for new downpipes; or a newspaper subscription, cancelled soon afterwards. The receipts that still confuse me are the ones I tried to ask Mr Carsten about. All are marked *Received from Johannes Lindalen for services (various)* in irregularly formed letters; next, the sum in numbers and in letters and, below, Mr Carsten's signature. Generally speaking, none of the sums is very large, even for the time, but for Johannes they must have been significant. Was it a matter of paying off old gambling debts or, as Simonsen thought, part of a deal to own one of Mr Carsten's racehorses? I check through the dates again: two are from August and October 1973 respectively, two from March 1974 and another one (for 1,500 kroner) from May the same year. But in May 1974, Minna returned to the island and got a job in the supermarket down by King's Road. It cannot be a coincidence that the payments were made just then, I tell myself, in the period immediately after Kaufmann's death. There must be a connection. Could it have been that Carsten knew that I had attacked and hurt Kaufmann and demanded money from Johannes in return for his silence? I had of course met Mr Kaufmann on the farm only a few weeks before I tried to murder him down by the lake and, at the time of that visit, Kaufmann had clearly recognised me. You must be Johannes's boy, he had said. Later, he might easily have said the same thing to Mr Carsten. It was Johannes's boy, he might have said, that boy was the one who attacked me. Mr Carsten had waited until after Kaufmann's death, then come to see Johannes and told him, if you don't pay me, I'll make sure the whole island knows it was your little bastard who killed the old man. Then Minna had to serve as a kind of hostage; that is to say, she was placed somewhere away from the island and out of Johannes's reach until the debt was paid. At least, this scenario explains why Johannes behaved so oddly when Mr Carsten called at the front door and why Mr Carsten never stepped inside like other visitors. Instead, the two of them talked standing in the doorway or pottering about in the garden like two restless pheasants. Still, it is not all that likely. Why, in that case, would Minna have walked up to the farm of her own volition once she was back home? Where did all those clothes come from, the ones Minna wore every time she went to the farm? I am sitting in the sidecar pondering this when, once more, I hear people stomping about outside the house. *Fucking Nazi!* two of them shout at the same time, almost as if on cue. Then they start throwing stones again; it makes a sound like a minor rock-fall when the stones hit the wall. I clamber back down the attic steps, crawl on all fours in the hall so as not to be seen through the windows, move from room to room, turning the lights off, and then get the gun out from the wardrobe in the bedroom. That the whole house has gone dark seems to have surprised the attackers. There is a brief silence and then I hear footsteps again, now in the cellar corridor, where voices speak quickly, anxiously. *They have got into the house.* As I throw myself almost recklessly down the stairs, a voice calls out, *he's coming! he's coming!* Unthinkingly, I raise the gun and shoot into the dark. The recoil of the rifle almost knocks me over. A whistling sound just above my head; it must be the ricochet. Heavy objects, chairs or tables, fall over in the dark, then the sounds of running again. Holding on to the rifle, I follow in the dark and keep bumping against the walls like a drunk. The cellar door is still locked, so they must have climbed in through the window. I turn the key in the lock and kick the door open. They are of course all over me in an instant: most have the agile bodies of half-grown boys, but at least one of them is older, heavily built, and seems enormously tough. He is the one who clings to my back and tries to twist the rifle barrel from my hands while the others are in full flight. We wrestle in the dark in front of the garage door. Finally, I manage to get a grip around his neck and meet his frightened, staring eyes. I recognise him: the thick nose and half-open mouth belong to Skakland junior, the newspaper delivery driver who showed me the finger the other day. That he and his mates have dared to enter my house fires me up. Enraged, I try to force the mindless creep to the ground. He seems about to give in for a moment, but then he unexpectedly twists his body and bites my hand. I scream and let go and just have time to feel something greasy and sticky slide across my arm before he hauls himself upright and stands there, heavy and panting, right next to me. And I briefly look him straight in his young face: it looks wild; his forehead and cheeks are painted with broad, black lines. War paint. Then he, too, runs away, and I am left in front of the garage with the stinging pain in the back of my hand.

*

A first for this visit to the island: a morning without rain. The dawn sky arches over the forest like a bowl of pale blue enamel but the trees are still black and threatening on the horizon. I walk around the house to inspect the damage. All the ground-floor windows have been knocked in, including the ones in the hall; even the milky glass in the high, narrow window by the front door has been shattered. At the back of the house, the glass has been broken in the two windows that lead to the terrace, as well as the other sitting-room windows and the single one in the small space that was Johannes's television room. When they ran out of edging stones from the drive, the lads moved on to throwing hefty logs. I pick up quite a few of these lying scattered around the rooms. On the hall floor and everywhere in the cellar, there are trails of soil and mud and dead leaves from last night's break-in. I measure up the windows and set out for Langmark's, the carpenter's workshop-cum-timber yard, which I know is still in the old place, by Horse Strait. During that long, hot, insect-humming summer when Johannes refurbished the kitchen, it was to Langmark's I went with the measurements; I was to see the boss himself, and waited by the planer among the sweet-smelling slivers of wood while Langmark, whom I remember as a slight but strong and sinewy man, always walking about with an unlit cigarette stuck behind his ear, measured up, cut and planed the planks. When he had finished, I loaded the planks on Johannes's wheelbarrow and wheeled it back home. It took many turns, and I remember, too, how the sun burnt my sweaty boy's back like a hot iron. This time, a man I have never seen before serves behind the folding counter in the carpentry shop's office. He is middle-aged, with a round, flabby face disfigured by a bulging tumour on the left cheek. The swelling is about the size of a golf ball, almost black at the base and somehow infiltrated by a network of thin blood vessels. The man looks at me with an expression that is at the same time dismissive and anxious, which could be something to do with his tumour or possibly with the rifle, which I have put down on the counter next to a piece of paper with notes of what I need. At the top of that list: sheets of board to stop the rain from coming in through the broken windows. His first reaction is to ask if I have contacted the house insurers. Fair enough, so how can I explain to him that Johannes never took out house insurance, just as he never signed agreements of any kind? His distrust of the world went too deep. I had better cover up the whole bloody mess for the duration, is all I say. They'll do it again anyway. He eyes the gun. Seems to me it's you who'd do anything, he says next. You've always been like that in your family. Utter fury at this fatuous assertion makes my knees suddenly start to shake. Our family! What's that supposed to mean? And from him! I ask him what he would do if his kids vandalised other people's property. Punish them, naturally, he replies. But my

kids weren't involved, he adds hurriedly. They'd never do anything of the sort. He is lying, of course. As everyone on the
island has done, always. Lying is deeply ingrained here, like
blight. I place the order and he promises that the cut boards
will be delivered in a few hours, so I cross King's Road, take a
shortcut over the meadows and start walking along the path
up to Bird Hill. Minna and I often took this way home in the
summer when we had been swimming off the Horse Strait
beach. You got back to the farm and the Yellow Villa faster
than by any other route, even if it was steep and you had to
clamber a bit. It was up there, at the top of Bird Hill, that Mr
Carsten told us about the plane crash and how the passengers
had hung like burning torches in the trees, still strapped into
torn-off seats. I lie down flat on my front in the grass, lift the
binoculars and, after sweeping past the Yellow Villa, focus on
the farm. In the old days, the yard used to be crowded with
people, with cars parked wherever there was a space, while
old tractors and ploughs used for clearing snow were lined up
against the stable wall. Now the yard lies completely empty
and bare, apart from Mr Carsten's Volvo, parked in front of
the farm manager's house next to the trailer that has been
standing in the same spot for as long as I can remember. At
the far end, beyond the stables, no horse is to be seen behind
the white-painted fence around the paddock that Mr Carsten
laid out just before Kaufmann's death, nor is there any trace
of the man himself. Even the dog's long running lead lies slack
and abandoned in the grass near where it is usually tethered. I
take aim with the rifle to find out what I could hope to shoot

from up here. But it is meaningless to take aim without any visible target. I turn the binoculars towards the Yellow Villa and, inevitably, they are back. The children: now, in a loose cluster of four or five, rambling in an apparently desultory way along the verge of the field. Some of them look no older than schoolboys, others are already lanky teenagers, but all of them have stuck grass and twigs in their hair and painted their faces black and green. I should have thought of it: the procession – tomorrow is Procession Day. That explains why old Skakland's son had paint all over his face. I cannot tell if the boys are on their way to the house, but it does not matter. The van from Langmark's has been bumping along the Mains Farm Road and overtakes the boys before they reach the drive. It drives all the way to Johannes's garage and two men in blue overalls climb out. I hurry on down to meet them.

*

From now on, I take no risks. I bring the rifle with me when I sit in the sidecar and leave the attic hatch open to make sure at least to hear, and preferably see, any intruders in good time. Thus prepared, I carry on reading Kaufmann's diaries. The man's transformation from a brittle-boned aesthete into an assured, adroit politician and diplomat is remark-able and I cannot stop marvelling at it. Here he is, with the protective carapace of a dark suit in place, standing with his guests on the long wooden veranda of the Mains Farm house. Next to him, his wife Sigrid, who smiles discreetly towards the photographer and leans a little against her husband; the couple are surrounded by a skilfully arranged group of thirty or so mainly older men, some stiff and awkward, others visibly pleased and relaxed, holding cigars or glasses of brandy and water. The photograph was kept in the 1943 guestbook, another item that Sigrid Kaufmann thought it wise to leave with Johannes. A seating plan for that notorious dinner was sketched out on adjacent pages in the guestbook. There were ninety-odd guests to be found seats at three separate tables placed around the table of honour. However, neither guest list nor seating plan gives any clue as to whether Vidkun Quisling was present or not. (It could be because he was the kind of prominent guest who always arrives late and without warning, if at all.) It is also impossible to work out from the guest list alone who joined the guided tour of the islands that preceded the dinner. Not even the photographs taken on the long veranda can be used to find out who went and who did not, since the pictures could just as easily have been taken before as after the tour. Several books have been written about the so-called 'second colony', most of them by people whose long wartime summers were transformed thanks to Kaufmann. When we were little, Johannes read aloud to us from one of these books, called *Memoirs of a Wartime Child*. It was written by Steinar Brage, about whom I know nothing except that much later he presented a TV quiz show called *Jeopardy*, in which Brekke's grandson went on to participate for several years. It could be that since Brage had not tried to atone for his presence in the colony by adding his voice to the standard hate demonstrations against *that Nazi* Kaufmann, Johannes felt more sympathetic towards him than most of the others. Steinar Brage seems to have only happy memories of his time on the Inner Islands and speaks about the friendships between the boys and the work on the land with childish, enthusiastic eagerness. He describes at length the foreign delegation that came for a visit in 1943 and illustrates the passage with a large group photograph that must have been taken in the park on West Island, just below the Sanatorium and with the jetty and the sea as a backdrop. The caption is 'The Vaccination' and the text comments on the visit:

On the morning of the day before the vaccination, we had been forewarned that the colony could expect some very special guests coming on a visit and so we were not allowed to go swimming as we normally would. That afternoon, a group of people came strolling along from the jetty where the ferry moored. They all looked tremendously elegant. Most of them were men but there were also ladies present, wearing plumed hats and long white gloves. We were told to line up on the lawn and they asked us questions. They spoke German and, as soon as a question had been put, an interpreter stepped forward to translate it. We had to say how old we were and if we 'enjoyed it there'. I recall being asked what I liked best and answering that I liked Old Abraham best. We had four goats – one of them, the ram, looked like a very old man and we thought he should be named Old Abraham

– it made quite a few people laugh, although others shook their heads and looked uncomfortable. I think the interpreter did not translate just that part.

The photograph: the first row is formed by ten or so young boys who seem to find it really hard to keep their restless bodies still; behind them stand several older children, boys *and* girls, and the latter all stare into the camera with earnest faces. The boys are dressed in shorts and shirts, some wear little kerchiefs tied around their necks; the girls have their hair in plaits and are wearing dresses and neatly ironed aprons with large patch pockets. I have seen that photo many times and it always struck me as dull and nondescript because it is so blatantly prearranged. This time, I scrutinise it much more attentively but honestly cannot explain why. Perhaps it is because of the man I met down at the joinery earlier today, the chap with the cheek tumour: I cannot recall having met him before in my life but, all the same, he felt at liberty to opine about how I and my family *always* behaved. Could one of the man's relatives, perhaps even Langmark himself, of whom I have only vague memories (that cigarette behind his ear!), have been among the children who are smiling obediently at the camera on the photographer's command? In that moment, I see him. Not Langmark, but Frank Lehman, my father! He is in the upper row, furthest to the left, half a head shorter than the two boys next to him but with his face fully in the picture, above the shoulders of the blond girl in front of him. At first, I cannot believe that it is really *him*. I ask myself if this is not some kind of optical illusion. After all, I have been spending years absorbed in efforts to find my father, and even travelled to the USA in search of him. Could it not be that I have started to read his features into the faces of strangers? I run downstairs to the kitchen to get the Javanese box with the photographs of our parents and also the cuttings about the plane crash, which Johannes stored at the bottom of the pile of newspapers as if they were relics of some kind. When I compare the boy in the group photo with the man in the small, white-framed Kodak snapshots taken more than twenty years later, the similarities between them stand out, not only the wide, somewhat flat face with slightly protruding ears but the posture, the easy assurance of the boy in the upper row, who is relatively short but *stands tall* with his straight back and broad shoulders. But why was he there at all? As early as that, with the war still going on? Only *Norwegian* children were supposed to be recruited to the colony. On the other hand, if that boy really *is* Frank, it would explain a lot. Like this: the matter of why an American, as he was, would ever think of settling on this distant island. Or why he spoke reasonably good Norwegian, as Johannes always claimed. Frank must have learnt the language somewhere. It would also explain that actual or imaginary third visit Johannes told us about, when our father and mother planned to be reunited with the two of us, the two bastard kids, as Mr Carsten had it, a journey that was interrupted by a fatal accident. No one who has been orphaned, or just been uncertain of where or even *who* his (or her) parents are, can fail to understand my mixed feelings of terror and awe as I unfolded the newspaper pages that Johannes had put aside. Two large photographs share the double-page spread. To the left, a picture of a group of agitated, gesticulating men, some wearing helmets and holding thick hoses. The picture to the right only shows a field of grey ash with a sprinkling of either snow or fire-retardant foam, with some indeterminate things sticking out, perhaps parts of the wrecked plane, or just crushed or scorched vegetation. The headline running above both photographs is dramatically black:

Twenty-Seven People Lose Their Lives in Aeroplane Accident on the Inner Islands

The plane, believed to have been a four-engined Vickers Viscount, was on its way from Copenhagen. The weather was poor at the time of the accident. For some reason, the plane had come in to land at too low an angle; the pilot made a last-minute correction to the course, but the plane reared up in the air and then fell straight out of the sky – 'like a stone', according to one eye-witness. It immediately caught fire. The reporter had taken note of these and other particulars. Burning people hung from the trees, he notes. This was of course what Mr Carsten had said to Minna and me. Had Mr Carsten really been at the site as it happened and seen everything, or had he read the same *Dagbladet* article that Johannes had read and saved? In other words, had he lied to our faces? On the other hand: if our parents *had not been* on the plane, why would Johannes have taken the trouble to show us the fragile newspaper pages so often and instruct us about all the repulsive details? In the first place, why would he have bothered to say that our parents had been on their way to collect us? Was it because he could not bear to live with a huge *lie*, as he would say when he was drunk? Or simply because he could not resist the temptation to tell a good story that could be presented in suitably dramatic ways to a young and receptive audience? The pile of newspapers contained other items of interest as well, articles describing the clearing up after the accident, work that Johannes claimed to have participated in; discussions of the damage caused by the impact to the forest and the land; reports about Sigrid Kaufmann, who took the accident as the starting point for what would become her lifelong campaign against the flight paths across the Inner Islands. Johannes had saved several illustrated pieces about her: she stands near the lake and speaks about the necessity of protecting the unique bird populations, a need that could only be met by reducing the inhumanly high noise levels. It is the first time I have seen her in print; she is eyeing the camera with an alarmed but defiant gaze, as if it were a feared opponent whose Medusa-like stare she feels has to be met full on. Out there on the islands, quite a few people still believe that Mrs Kaufmann herself made that Viscount fall out of the sky. Sheer willpower, you see: exactly how Kaufmann himself had once made white butterflies rise out of the ground or foxes mate. Johannes never peddled such superstitions, but Minna said that this kind of thing did the rounds *out there*. All just to prevent our parents from getting back on the island? (Having failed with poisoned drinking water pumped up from the forest lake, they had another go.) True, it could be that my head was full of such beliefs at the time, even though I would never have expressed them in so many words. But the small boy at the end of the row in the group photo from the West Island, the boy with the flattish face and protruding ears who I feel is so familiar, his presence instantly denies all that. He must have been allowed to join the colony because he was under Kaufmann's protection. If not, he would never have been let in. But, if so, why force him to go away when, twenty years later, he had moved to the island? It made no logical sense. And if, as a grown man with wife and children, he came back because he had spent some years here as a wartime child evacuee, then it stands to reason that his return would be known to quite a few locals. Like Johannes, for instance. After all, he had driven all the new children to West Island from the station at Holmen. Nonetheless, Johannes had never suggested, not by a single word, that our father had ever been to the island before or that he was somebody other than who he claimed to be: an American employed on some mysterious military task who had brought his family with him to stay in the NATO villa for a limited time. But why did people insist on secrecy if the truth was out there for anyone to see, for instance in Steinar Brage's book? Exhausted, I put it all down – books, newspaper cuttings and notepads. At this point, it strikes me that I have spent hours in the attic without any interruptions at all. The vandals, whoever they are, have kept away all night. Rifle in hand, I patrol the empty house, then open the cellar door and go outside. The rain has stopped and the sky cleared. A slender crescent moon hangs high above the garden, spreading a pale, waxy light that makes the trees look as if they have no shadows. Perhaps that is why the boys did not bother to turn up tonight: the moonlight makes it too easy to be seen. Presumably, I am fully visible where I stand at the far end of Johannes's garden, staring up towards the farm. Up there, behind the dark stable block, Mr Carsten is waiting for me. If anybody around here knows the answers to all these questions, he does.

*

After just a few hours' sleep, I am up and about again at dawn. The crescent moon, like a splinter of bone, hangs in the transparent sky that is as fragile and improbably thin as glass and has a faintly turquoise streak running through its blueness. To the south, what is left of last night's storm, a saddle of dark clouds, has settled above the forest. The air is warm and moist after yesterday's rain and redolent of damp bark and bare soil, the tart scent of spring. The annual procession has not yet set out but the rhythmic, heavy and strangely thrilling sound of drums is carried along in the wind. From the school, where they traditionally set up the children's play area and the frankfurter stall, come the clanging tones from the brass players ,who are trying to blow new life into their instruments. But nobody comes along the road. Not a trace of the boys who were hanging around outside yesterday. Up on the hill, the farm looks empty too, silent, shut down. Though that is how it has always been on Procession Days, perhaps the only time in the year when the islanders definitely turn their backs on the people up there. I am not sure when this custom began: perhaps in the early fifties, perhaps earlier still. One version I have heard is that three youngish men got together after an outstandingly boozy celebration on 17 May and concocted a plan for evicting the old man from the island once and for all. One of them, an assistant in a menswear shop on the mainland, contributed a shop mannequin; they dressed it in hat and coat, a collarless linen shirt and wide trousers with braces, placed the effigy in a wheelbarrow, disguised themselves with leafy branches, painted their faces with military camouflage paint and set out down King's Road with the Kaufmann doll's long legs splayed over the edge of the barrow. A crowd gathered behind them, people they had run into on the way, mostly returning from other National Day parties with no idea of what was going on, and there were children too, of course (even then, the island was full of children), and by the time they reached the barrier, or *the cross* as it came to be called (back then, the public road ended with a barrier), the 'procession' was already several hundred strong. Everyone shouted and clapped delightedly when the wheelbarrow was upended and the effigy tumbled down into the clay and gravel patch at the edge of the field where Mr Carsten took the rubbish bins out for collection twice a week. Just a prank: a trifle distasteful, perhaps, but harmless enough. Besides, the war was history and Kaufmann had already served his sentence. But Sigrid Kaufmann saw the matter in a different light. Not only her husband but her entire family had been humiliated in full public view, and on National Day. She notified the police and demanded damages. Inevitably, this caused the spectacle to be repeated a few weeks later: the procession followed exactly the same route and stopped at the same spot for the ceremonial dumping, which took place to, if anything, even greater acclaim from an even bigger crowd. Only this time the doll wore a lady's wig and a brown checked tweed skirt just like Mrs Kaufmann's, out on her rare errands down the Mains Farm Road. The event lapsed for a few years because it was thought an undignified rival to the proper festivities on National Day. Still, some islanders stubbornly carried on. For the sake of the children, they would usually say by way of explanation. It was moved to a couple of weeks earlier in the year and turned into a dressing-up party. I have memories of Procession Day from when I was little: all happy images of small girls in fanciful princess-style tulle creations with angel's wings stitched onto the back, and boys with black face paint and saucepan helmets with fir-branch plumes. But what happiness lasts forever? Once the wealthy upstarts on the island had redrawn the processional route so that it passed their newly bought or built villas, it was not long before the so-called Friends of the Sports Club had trained the entire football team to march along, wearing the club's training kit. And once the football team was in the procession, all the other societies had to join as well to show willing: the bridge players, and the Rotarians and the members of the music society, of course. The musicians were those same elderly male amateurs who played at the National Day events and for parties at Christmas and New Year: flautists and bass players and drummers, who could be heard above the children's banging on saucepan lids, pinging on shrill cowbells and piping on whistles. Their playing formed a thick blanket of turgid, heavy marching tunes, uninterrupted but for the occasional roar of highly tuned engines when some super-expensive car simply had to be revved up on the island's only straight stretch of road across the isthmus, between the sailing club and the supermarket. In just a few years, the carnival spirit had faded and the jolly procession had been transformed into a dull exercise in self-promotion. Which explains why it was such a scandal when, one year, something really *happened*. This was when Minna came running at full tilt from the Mains Farm, pursued at a gallop by one of Mr Carsten's horses. The horse was not the white one, not *my* horse, who always stood dreaming in the paddock below the lamp on the wall. (I knew that the horse was dreaming because its dream was at its side. The horse's dream was the enamelled bathtub next to the wooden fence around the meadow. The horse and the dream had exactly the same colour, both white in the pale, strangely floating dimness of a summer's night.) The animal Minna had released was a harness-racing roan, one of the horses Mr Carsten took all over the country in the trailer. The screams of the terrified parents at the front of the crowd who were desperately trying to get their dressed-up children out of the way only served to madden the horse; meanwhile, the brass band at the rear, deafened by their own blaring, had not yet grasped that anything untoward was going on but noted the noise and tootled even more loudly to be heard above it. Next, Mr Carsten himself came down the hill on his Danish bike. A much younger Mr Carsten than today's old man but just as stiff-legged, his face more than normally distorted by sheer rage. Mr Carsten hardly had time to show up before the near-panic turned into something else. Those who had not seen Minna running down the Mains Farm Road naturally jumped to the conclusion that it was Mr Carsten's fault that the horse was out of control and so, while some of the men tried to catch it, others jumped on Mr Carsten and pulled him down off the bike, despite his furious resistance, and dumped him in a ditch. I observed that even some of the musicians threw their instruments away and ran to join those who were beating him up. It was so strange. Even though the majority of the crowd at this point knew next to nothing of how the procession had come about, the hatred and distrust of the people in the Mains Farm seem to have been widely felt, and as intense as ever. As if hatred has a life of its own, quite apart from the people it targets. It is that sort of hatred, indeterminate and unfocused, which makes normally laid-back youths come out at night to throw stones at the Yellow Villa. No one knows where the resentment comes from, only that it is still there, more alive than anything else on the island. I shut and bar those windows that can be barred, grab the rifle and go outside, turning off into the Mains Farm Road. The farmhouse window panes reflect the clear part of the sky in the same way as the forest is reflected on the surface of the lake on a quiet day. I approach the farm slowly, holding the hand with the rifle well away from my body. I assume that Mr Carsten would stay indoors on a day like this, but the dog has not yet started to bark and the yard ahead of me is as abandoned as it seemed to be the other day when I scanned it from the top of Bird Hill. The Volvo and the horse trailer are parked exactly where they were then and the dog's long running lead is lying in the same loops on the muddy ground on the manager's side of the yard. It looks as if no one has lived here for decades. It worries me. Where can Mr Carsten have gone? Were it not for the Volvo still standing there, I would have thought that he had left the farm and probably the island for good. Is he hiding? I step up onto the small veranda of his house and use the flat of my hand to bang several times on the upper part of the door in case he has become hard of hearing with the passing years. Nothing. I push the door handle down. The door is not locked. I have an uncomfortable feeling that he is skulking somewhere, watching me but out of my sight. Before entering, I call out his name again and again. Inside: a narrow hallway smelling sourly of wood rot, sweaty feet and damp woollen clothes. On the short wall under a fuse-box, there is a wooden key board, decorated with an ornate, old-fashioned pattern of flowers and leaves. A big bunch of keys dangles from one of the hooks on the board, a pair of bright red ear protectors from another. It seems he can hear, or he would hardly need the protectors. In the next room, an unmade bed stands in one corner. The sheets are dirty, almost as if he has been sleeping with his boots on. A tray on the table next to the bed holds jars and packets of medicines and, next to it, there is a bundle of well-read porn mags, the busty women on the covers greasy with thumbprints. I lift the bundle – nothing underneath. There is a kitchen alcove in another corner. The sink is stacked high with unwashed plates and mugs; a saucepan with porridge has been left on the cooker. Along the wall, a basin, a mirror spotted with fly shit and, on a nearby hook, a cloth of an indeterminate greyish-green colour. I have brought the receipts that I showed him the other day in my rucksack, and now I put the bundle on the kitchen table with a half-full ashtray on top to stop them from blowing about in the draught from the door. Then I return to the hall. Because none of the keys is marked, I shove the whole bunch into my jacket pocket and start out towards the main farmhouse. Over and over, I tell myself that I am here for Minna's sake. If I do not dare to go to places where she went, there is no point in my coming up here at all. But the closer I get to the house, the steeper the ground under my feet seems to become, as if I were clambering up a hillside and not just a modest slope. The eerie feeling of being watched is growing stronger all the time. But it might be simply the drumbeat from the school, the memory of Procession Days in the past, and the way the farm was always forbidden territory for us children. And also the insight that I have crossed to the *wrong* side now: I am on the inner, the perverse side of the island, a place that my very *nature* rebels against. The space I am in makes me feel so flustered that just to stay upright, I have to grab hold of the banister next to the steps up to the entrance. The floor of the long veranda is covered with dried, wind-blown leaves and pine needles. Nobody has swept it for many years. I pick keys at random to try in the lock, and one of the larger ones slides in and turns smoothly. I keep the handle down for a while by pressing it against me, very clearly aware that the moment I step inside there will be no way back. And then I step inside.

*

I stop in the hall. It is the place where I stood after coming to look for the old man because Minna had told me to kill him, and he talked to me, knew whose boy I was and gave me a slice of apple cake that I thought was poisoned and threw away. My child's eyes perceived the house as huge, as large as a mansion or a small castle. Now, the hall I am in seems rather narrow and crowded with perfectly ordinary furniture: a wardrobe in one corner and, in another, a small wooden table with slightly splayed, turned legs. A mirror hangs above the table and I can see myself reflected in it, with the entrance door behind me. This figure, a man holding a rifle, with binoculars around his neck and the broad shoulder straps of his rucksack against a sheepskin-lined coat (it was Johannes's) – he doesn't look like me. But I don't know who I look like. Next to the staircase to the first floor, something cold and white shimmers in the dull light. I reach out and my hand touches a broad metal edge, below which a dark space seems to open up. It makes sense only after I have taken a step back: I am standing in the entrance to a lift with wide metal doors that have been left open. The cabin is empty. It stands to reason: how else could the wheelchair-bound Helga have moved between floors? I follow the passage to the left of the hall. It shares one of its walls with the long veranda outside. A collection of old pieces of household equipment has been lined up along the opposite wall. It is like a craft museum: a spinning wheel, a linen-heckling block, a butter churn, hooped like a beer barrel. Above these things, the wall has been hung with tapestries of abstract landscape motifs in deep, muted colours. So the executors have not even gone through the personal property yet. It is so strange. I know that Helga died childless, but surely someone in the family could or would have a claim to inherit some of these objects? The hall passage ends in a gable room, which I guess was used as a drawing or sitting room. The windows at the far end face the yard, offering a view of the stables and the farm manager's house over to the left. Anyone who stood here would have been able to keep tabs on everything that happened on the farm or on the road leading up to it from the crossroads at the Yellow Villa. Halfway into the room I turn round and find myself standing in front of a painting of a St John's Eve bonfire, the same painting that I saw as a child. Then, as now, it hangs above the stone fireplace. But I do not recognise anything about the rest of the room. Did Kaufmann really invite me to come all this way into the house, or did I see the painting somewhere else in the house? I stare at the naked bodies of the men and women against the background of the rocks and at the flames that flare from the bonfire on the beach, rising so high they might be sucked up into the darkened sky. Perhaps it is the way with kitsch art that everything about it seems unreal in every sense; the seated or half-recumbent bodies around the fire are unreal, with their bulging, muscular limbs, portrayed in the same way as the rounded shapes of the rocks. Even so, the painting radiates heat powerfully, as if the landscape is warmed not only by the flames but also by the rocks and the bodies, glowing red with reflected light from the fire. And suddenly, not only the painting but also the house that encases it strike me as both very close and very distant. Everything around me I have seen before, and was imprinted on my memory when I was a child. But now I see the rooms as if in a mirror, with all perspectives wrenched inside out. I also felt this earlier, as I approached the house: as if the gaze of the entire island was fixed on me. I find my way along the passage to the hall and walk up the wide, curved staircase to the first floor. This was Helga's part of the house. From the landing, similar to the hall on the ground floor, doors open into three rooms: a bedroom, a small, pantry-style kitchen and, on the left, a larger room that looks like a workroom or studio. It contains a loom with a long cutting table next to it. Yarns and lengths of fabric in different materials are set out on wide shelves above the table, which served as a low workbench, suitable for a person seated in a wheelchair. Tapestries similar to those on the ground floor have been put up on the opposite wall: fields in olive green and petroleum blue, broken up by long vertical or horizontal lines creating stylised landscapes: a rock face, the line of a beach or a forest. They must be Helga's work. I wander about in the upstairs rooms, all of which are almost pedantically orderly. The windows in the bedroom are the only ones offering the same view as those in the downstairs drawing room. The studio windows face the interior of the island, the forest and the lake. I wonder if this was for purely practical reasons, if the yarns and fabrics Helga worked with should not be exposed to strong sunlight or if Helga preferred her work to be done in obscurity, out of sight. In any case, it must have demanded an intense physical effort from a person who towards the end of her life barely had the muscular strength to move her arms at all. I look more closely at the loom, and underneath it I spot coils of electrical cables which supply a rotary switch on a panel attached to the edge of the workbench, suggesting that at least some of the heavier aspects of weaving, such as moving the batten or the actual shedding, have been made possible independent of muscular strength. Even so, nothing on this floor fits the islanders' usual image of Helga Kaufmann as the spoiled, languishing and almost ethereal daughter of the local landowners. But then, no one really knew much about her, apart from her being so enfeebled from birth by muscle atrophy that she could not go to school with the other children and also had to spend long periods abroad because the climate up here in the north, at least in the winter, was thought unfavourable for a person suffering from her condition. Was all that part of some kind of play-acting? With the exception of the loom powered by electricity and the absence of thresholds between them, there is nothing to indicate that these rooms were inhabited by an invalid. On the contrary, the way the entire studio has been furnished gives an impression of energy and vitality. The small photographs pinned to the short wall at the end of the workbench all show Helga engaged in a variety of outdoor activities. In one of them, she stands with her sunglasses pushed up on her forehead, leaning on a pair of ski poles jammed into the snow in front of her and smiling with an expression at the same time intrepid and mildly sarcastic. She does not look like her father: her build is stronger and her face broader, especially across the jaw. Only one feature brings him to mind: the physical tension, the hint of a grimace that always lingers. Kaufmann himself, as I suddenly recall, walked about marked by unceasing pain, as if every step cost him endless effort. I wonder when these pictures of Helga were taken. Probably sometime in the late 1930s. In another photo, the whole family stands together in lush parkland. It must be over on West Island. I feel sure that the white-limed walls of the hospital pavilions are in the background, and also the walled road down to the jetty. All three are dressed in light, bright summer clothes, with Kaufmann in a white suit with narrow lapels and a flower (a carnation?) on the lapel, Sigrid Kaufmann in a wide-brimmed hat that shadows her face and makes her smile look fleeting and vague. Helga is standing between them, leaning sideways, with her arm around her mother's shoulders and the upper part of her body slightly angled backwards as if, in that instant, something down by the jetty had caught her attention. The twist of her body means that you get a glimpse of her long blond hair as it flows from under her hat down the back of her coat. The picture cuts her off at waist height so the callipers on her legs do not show, but still, she is standing up and definitely does not look like a sickly girl. This photo must have been taken around the same time as the group photo included in *Memoirs of a Wartime Child*, when Kaufmann was at the peak of his career. He was Secretary of State in the Department of Trade and had just contributed successfully to the negotiation of a trade agreement with the government in Berlin. Almost one hundred employees were working on his farms on the Inner Islands and, in addition, he operated on a grand scale as a philanthropist by playing host to large groups of poor city children every summer. He could even allow himself to house a complete wild-card child like my father among his charges. It does not take long before I find photos of Frank, too. He and Helga look as if they were really very close. You see them together in many of the pictures pinned on the wall above the workbench. They could be siblings: she, the elder one, the more mature, more stable and rooted; he, the younger one, short by nature and, at the age of ten or eleven (he could scarcely have been any older), rather slightly built and easily distracted, always into something else – a child at play. In one of the photos, which must have been enlarged from its original size, he is standing in the middle of a field, with the ears of wheat reaching to his waist, and holding what looks like a willow flute in his hand. His torso is bare and something about the way he is posed and seen a little from below, with his face in half-profile so that his neck and the line of his shoulders are in close-up, is reminiscent of Leni Riefenstahl's images of young athletes. The angle of the perspective is such that only the sky is seen above the ripening wheat: a sky that is wide open, with a few light, white clouds that look about to melt into the greater whole. On the wall next to that photograph, several landscape studies have been pinned up, probably to serve as inspiration for Helga's textiles. The lake: a pale, shining surface, sliced down the middle by a long line of forest. Flights of birds. The even plough furrows on a field. In another, a field of wheat is shown, this time with the familiar gable view of the Yellow Villa at one end. On the drive, a large grey van is parked, the same old van that usually stood next to the garage when we were little. Its cab smelt of dust and rusty metal and mouldy fabric-covered seats. Johannes had stopped driving it ages ago but was unwilling to sell it. He had used it during the occupation years to take provisions to the farm. Because it was wartime, fuel was scarce, and Kaufmann alone was allowed extra rations. Once a week, Johannes went across to the mainland. I imagine that, in the picture, he is just back from one of these trips, which is why he has not yet had time to get the van parked off the drive. Perhaps he has just been up at the farm to unload. They must have known each other very well, he and young Frank. It could even be that Johannes had lifted him up into the driver's seat and allowed him to hold the outsized steering wheel, the way I loved doing when I was a small boy. This kind of thing could explain the friendliness between Johannes and the family up in the NATO villa, their special relationship, which so many islanders would declare afterwards they simply did not understand. They were so close, Frank even left his two children in Johannes's care when he had to drive his wife to the hospital. I remember how Johannes used to praise Frank's good Norwegian, and how sometimes, sitting in his nook of an evening, he would amuse himself and us by imitating Frank and speaking with a pretend American accent. Minna found it only moderately funny and would get cross after a while, because she insisted on speaking *her own* English, the language she said she and her mother had used, and which excluded Johannes and me. She could keep at it for several days, walking around and muttering to herself. Was it Helga who taught young Frank Norwegian during the many days of leisure they spent together? I imagine that he is chosen to push her in the wheelchair while she guides him around the island, shows him the secret paths to the lake, points out the different water birds and their breeding sites but also instils in him how crucial it is for him to be cautious when he is with people he does not know and how he must avoid visiting places where his presence might arouse suspicion. Even so, it is a mystery that he was able to stay on the island unnoticed for such a long time. In those days, only the Mains Farm had more than a dozen permanent employees, though the numbers multiplied during the harvest season. And yet no one on the island ever remarked on this boy who not only looked like a stranger but could hardly speak the language! Naturally, those who met him must have thought him the right sort of German. But still, it does not explain everything, including why he chose to return to the island so many years later, bringing his own wife and children. Next, I have a look at what was presumably Helga's bedroom: it contains a broad bed with a colourful coverlet stretched over it, fitted wardrobes along the opposite wall, a mirror placed half a metre lower than normal, to suit a handicapped person, and a small writing desk of white wood with a set of drawers fitted inside a cabinet on the right-hand side. The drawers are all locked. I go back to the studio, pick up a screwdriver and a hammer and, by forcing the screwdriver in between the uppermost drawer and the top of the cabinet, I manage to break the lock. I scrutinise the contents: desktop files, folders, stiff envelopes full of bills and bank statements, insurance agreements, contracts and various invoices. Two fat brown envelopes turn out to contain a lot of small black-and-white photographs, all taken several years before the war and seemingly intended to document the routine work of the farm. They show farmers carrying out everyday tasks like milking, harnessing horses to a plough, cutting and stacking hay (in the picture, this is done by women) or threshing with long flails. Another, larger envelope is also stuffed with black-and-white photographs, but these are from later dates and taken with a much better camera. There are twenty or so landscape images: rods of light shining between tree trunks, boulders overgrown with shimmering moss, a mountainside viewed through falling rain, with distinctive zones of woodland fading into each other like thin veils, one behind the other. At the bottom of that envelope, I find a picture in the same format but of a quite different kind: yet another group photograph of the whole family together – Mr and Mrs Kaufmann and Helga herself. Here, she is much older than in the ones I have seen so far, but apart from being seated in a wheelchair (a plaid is hiding her legs), Helga looks surprisingly unchanged. Her hair is still long, if perhaps a shade thinner where it is spread over the collar of her slightly low-cut lacy blouse, and her head is heavier, more sculptural, with the wide jaw if anything even more prominent. But, to me, what is truly remarkable about this photograph is that both my parents are included and that it must have been taken about the same time as those in the Javanese box. So much about my parents seems almost identical to what I have seen before: the expressions on their faces, their postures, even the clothes they wear. As in the Javanese box photo, Frank, short but broad-shouldered, stands with a slight forward stoop, as if he is forcing his grin on the camera, and Elizabeth's blond hair is piled up on her head in one of those bouffant styles that everyone fancied in the sixties. Frank has put one arm around his wife's shoulder, pulling her a little closer, presumably to make more room for the hosts and their daughter; Mr Kaufmann himself, with his slender, frail bones that have grown thinner over the years, his hair is also thinner and combed across his skull, but he is smiling, too; and then Sigrid Kaufmann, standing furthest to the right, her hand resting on her daughter's shoulder, without a smile, unlike the others, but at least also without the alarmed distrust that marked her on the photo taken down by the sea. An eye-catching detail makes this photo different from the rest: pale, yellowy discolouration running along all four edges, as if it has been framed but then removed from the frame and left to end up here, at the bottom of a locked desk drawer – as if it has been treated with reverence and then become disfavoured. And it is at this point that I am struck by the obvious conclusion, a thought that has previously been unthinkable: of course, they are *related*, my father and Kaufmann. I stand absolutely still, holding the photograph and, at that moment, it seems to me as if all five of them, including Helga, stare at me with challenging expressions. As if *this* is the moment I have journeyed towards all my life. Without knowing, however, when it might happen or whether it ever would.

*

As I found out long ago, in areas such as Saxony, the Black Forest and Bavaria, there were many Jewish families with the name Lehman because, at some point in the Middle Ages or later, they had found it politically useful to change their original Jewish names – Löw or Loeb. If my father had belonged to such a family, was he related to Kaufmann by blood or by marriage? I have consulted the Norwegian *Dictionary of National Biography*, and read its entry on Kaufmann so many times that by now I should be able to recite it by heart, but it is utterly unhelpful. Perhaps the question must be put another way. For what reason would a probably Jewish boy turn up in a Norwegian children's colony during the German occupation of the country? 'Hiding in plain sight'? Almost all the photos in Helga's collection that include Frank (or Franz, as the members of the household must have called him) show him either in the company of Helga or alone, which means that a family member took the photographs. The one exception is the group photo from West Island in Steinar Brage's book about the second colony. 'The Vaccination' was the title of the chapter in which that photo was included. After paying serious attention to Kaufmann's diaries, one soon realises that, as far as the children were concerned, the vaccination programme was hardly a matter of innocent inoculations. But if Brage, the author of *Memoirs of a Wartime Child*, was troubled at all by the treatments children were subjected to in the Sanatorium, he does not deal with that in his book. Despite the misery that dominated most of the country, or perhaps because of it, his summers on the Inner Islands are remembered as times of unclouded happiness:

We were asked to help with cutting and stacking the hay, and with the work on the farm in other ways. But these were no crushing tasks for us, all young, healthy boys. True, some were unused to drinking fresh milk and came out in a rash. But, apart from a few cases of nettle fever, I cannot recall any one of us falling seriously ill. In the afternoons, we divided into teams and played various ball games or had swimming races across Horse Strait. We fell asleep early in the evenings, tired out by the sun and the work and the long swims in the salty sea.

Did Franz Lehman, too, remember his stay on the island as a happy time? Did he return with his wife and two children because he wanted to see his benefactor again and thank him? To me, the whole story remains enigmatic. As does how and why, after spending the war years in the colony, he should have ended up in the USA. Kaufmann can hardly have helped him with that. Perhaps Franz Lehman had family or more distant relatives in the States who were able to help him to emigrate after the end of the war. What happened afterwards is easier to establish. Although I never met my father when I went to the United States, and still do not even know if he is alive or dead, I have unearthed plenty of evidence of the ambition and decisiveness he showed as an immigrant. After cutting short his medical studies at Brown University in Rhode Island, his first aim was to be recruited to the US Marines. Although he was not accepted, he continued to work in the armed forces. His first job was with the air force, in a section that was to become Aerospace Medicine. At first, he was stationed at the large Wright Patterson Base in Ohio, but he was later transferred to Brooks Air Force Base in San Antonio. Following the move to Texas, he volunteered for service in the Korean War. In other words, everything Johannes had told us about Frank Lehman was true: he had completed at least two tours to Korea with the USAF and, during the last of these (it ended in spring 1953), served at the air force base in Suwon, to the south of Seoul. I have no idea of the extent to which his military career affected his civilian life and work, but he changed tack after the war and moved to Pascagoula in Mississippi.

By this time, he was already married to the woman who was to be our mother, Elizabeth (née Westwood), and they settled down in Ocean Springs, outside Biloxi. Their address at 2973 Saratoga Drive is the last one I have been able to find. The house is a simple wood-and-brick bungalow on a narrow tree-lined street but does have a double garage and a wide driveway. When I went to see it on a hot, humid morning in July 1988, the house had already changed owner three times, but a neighbour two houses along the street, a man called Donald Shapiro, claimed to remember Frank and his young wife very well. Mr Shapiro used to play tennis with Frank on Sundays, and Frank won almost all the time thanks to his terrifying forehand drive. When I asked Shapiro if he knew where the Lehmans had moved to after Ocean Springs, he just shook his head. Frank had been working on some kind of research project at the Marines' base in Pascagoula, something to do with pressure equilibration inside advanced diving suits. That was all Frank had ever said. Plenty of hush-hush in the forces, Shapiro said, putting one finger across his lips and smiling cagily. This meant that I could tell Minna, in one of the many letters I wrote to her during my rambling trip around the States, that she had been right: our dad *had* been a spy, as likely as not. I meant it to sound like a joke but was partly serious because, after his stay in Ocean Springs in between Biloxi and Pascagoula, the trail left by Frank Lehman stops. I have been unable to find out anything about what he did during the few years before he and Elizabeth turn up in the NATO villa on the Inner Islands. What drove him and his wife, who both seemed to be nicely settled in the USA, to move back to the distant place where he had spent several years as a wartime refugee? And why go away again just a few years later, especially in circumstances so urgent and chaotic that they went off without their two children? Did they really intend to leave us for good, or is it true that Frank and Elizabeth Lehman were on board that plane from Copenhagen that crashed so tragically in February 1963? I can still recall Minna and myself running into Mr Carsten on Bird Hill, and what he said about my father: how he was strapped into his seat as he and other passengers were hurled out of the burning fuselage. During the years before my journey to America, I was quite convinced that this part of the story was an invention and that Mr Carsten's only motive for telling us all that was that he needed to give vent to the inexplicable hatred he felt against our parents. And then, in April 1988, with just a few months to go before leaving for the States, I was gripped by an unexpected and quite unreasonable hope. As one outcome of my digging into every kind of archive, I had come across an article in the Danish newspaper *Ekstra Bladet*, published the week after the accident on the Inner Islands. The piece was about a Mr and Mrs *Leyman*, who had booked tickets for that very plane but missed its departure from Copenhagen because of bad weather delaying the first leg of their long flight from Los Angeles. The *Ekstra Bladet* reporter had been lucky enough to run into the stranded American couple in the transit hall at Kastrup Copenhagen and chatted to them for long enough to get sufficient material for one of those *weren't-they-lucky-after-all* sagas so much loved by newspaper readers everywhere:

The Hand of God Helped Them!
A Miracle Saved Them from the Fatal Plane Crash!

There it is again: the name. True, *Lehman* is not the same as *Leyman*. There was no picture showing the couple because the page was dominated by a dramatic shot of the burning fuselage and the emergency fire crews trying to put the fire out, standing in a sea of ash. It would have been reasonable to ask myself why my parents, if they were so keen to collect us, did not continue their journey by another plane or, at least, by ferry and train? But I clung to the new strand of hope. After a lot of hassle, I got hold of the reporter, and he managed to locate an old notebook with a telephone number entered ten years earlier. The number turned out to belong to an address in Daly City, south of San Francisco. I took a taxi from the airport and was so sure I had found the right place that I even told the taxi not to wait, paid the driver and carried my case up to the front door of a Victorian-type house in blue-painted wood, one of a whole line of equally stylish houses along a steep street. A woman came to the door. She looked as if she might be of Asian origin. At first, she seemed not to understand what I was saying, but after I had repeated Leyman and Lehman a few more times, she went off to get a younger woman to talk to me. She said that her father, whose property it was, had been living in a private nursing home for the last three years. She was positive that he had never set foot in any Scandinavian country: the family's only relative living outside the USA or China was a sister who had married some twenty years earlier and moved to Peru. I told Minna all this in the long letter I wrote to her from San Francisco the same evening.

Throughout my fruitless hunt for our parents, I wrote her letters and added pictures taken at the many places I visited, from the Marines' base in Pascagoula to the bungalow in Ocean Springs and the lovely blue wooden house on the sloping street in Daly City. Writing to Minna had become an obsession. My search was not real unless I knew that we were carrying it out together. The basic reason was, I think, that our past had no tangible existence beyond us two or, at least, beyond those enigmatic little photographs, glowing in Kodak shades of turquoise and red and pistachio green inside their white frames, which were kept by Johannes inside his magic Javanese bamboo box, and which connected us at a deeper level than anything else we were able to create or even understand on our own. When I came home, I tried to meet up with Minna a few times but did not succeed. I snooped around and eventually found out that Minna had 'settled down', as people used to say, and was living in a collective on Markveien, in the Grünerløkka district of Oslo, with a partner, a Chilean refugee whom she spoke of as Chico or Chicuelo. Since the left-wing daily *The Class Struggle* had moved out there, she had been working in the Duplotrykk building over in Bryn. But whenever I called at the flat on Markveien, it was always crammed with people whose jobs were as nebulous as their relationships to my sister, and Minna hardly let on that she knew me. When I asked why she didn't want to see more pictures from the States, all she said was, did I have the slightest idea of the evil-doings of that murderous country and how its secret service treated democratic agencies worldwide? Her manners had changed not one iota; she was simply Minna. So instead I went to the island. I can understand now what a comical figure I must have been in Johannes's eyes when I arrived with my rucksack packed with address books and maps and slides. I remember that he brewed coffee and that we drank it sitting at the kitchen table in the nook where he liked to be. He looked over the pictures I showed him and hummed, sounding quite interested. Outside on the Mains Farm Road, Mr Carsten and a couple of farm labourers were trying to transport a digger up to the farm. The digger was mounted on a truck that was far too wide for the narrow road, so the whole crew had come to a halt out in the field, and while the driver revved the engine, Mr Carsten stood some twenty metres up the road, trying to measure the width and issuing instructions with both arms raised. This would have been a perfect opportunity for Johannes to confess what he had kept silent about for a lifetime: why Frank had returned to Kaufmann and the island, and why they had actually stayed here in the NATO villa up the road. The material I had ferreted out covered what Frank and Elizabeth Lehman had done for almost a decade. Johannes must have realised that he was the only one who could fill me in about those essential times: *before* and *after*.

There's something I couldn't tell you about until now, he might have said. He could have explained that Frank Lehman had been on the island before the war as well. As a wartime refugee. That Kaufmann had taken care of the boy. Even though he was a Jewish child. Nothing could have been more natural than telling me this. For one thing, it would have supported what Johannes always said about Kaufmann: that, despite the accusations thrown at him, he was innocent of being a Nazi sympathiser. But Johannes said nothing, only smiled benignly, as usual. Why did he not speak? Could it be that saying something would have meant telling me the *whole* story, that he could not explain why Frank Lehman had come back to the island all these years later, with wife and children in tow, without also going into what lay behind the scandalous poisoning attempt that had made the two of them leave again in such a frenzied hurry, while we – the children – stayed behind.

*

It was Johannes who transported the children out to the colony. He picked them up at Holmen station and drove them in the grey van across the bridge and all the way to Horse Strait, where they had to board the cable ferry that was still running between the Main Island and West Island. Once on West Island, they were housed in the reopened phalanstery or in one of the two wings of the Sanatorium. After the war, there was much talk about how the stormtroopers of the Hird had come to the island and about the role of the Hirdmen in organising the children's colony. But that was not true: if there had been any paramilitaries on the islands, which I doubt, they were not in contact with Kaufmann and the people on the Mains Farm. The children who came to stay in the summer colony were recruited through sports clubs and other charitable organisations that were permitted during the occupation. Steinar Brage was one such child. His father, who worked as treasurer in an orienteering club over on Nordstrand, was far from being a Nazi collaborator, at least if one goes by his son's memoirs. What Brage fails to mention in his book is that many adults came to stay on the islands in the war years, in addition to the summer children. These 'volunteers', as Kaufmann calls them, were in the main young men and possibly also some of early middle age. Johannes must have gone to meet them too, either at Holmen station or possibly at the bus terminal down by the bridge. Every year, at the beginning of June, the volunteers were given a rather special reception. It is all there in the shopping lists from Kaufmann's notebooks: exactly how many sandwiches with ham and egg and smoked salmon were ordered from Brekke's grocery store, and the precise number of crates of beer and Farris mineral water. It gives you visions of long tables laid in the shade of the trees, platters of sandwiches covered by white linen cloths to keep the wasps off, while nurses from the Sanatorium, dressed in white, walk about ticking the new arrivals' names off the lists. Then each man must sign a form stating that he consents of his own free will to the medical examination and subsequent treatment. The official verbiage does not make it clear exactly what kind of treatment is in store, and most of the new volunteers probably do not give it a second thought. If they worry about anything, it is more likely to be what their families and friends will think about this place and whether those who come to work here will be thought of as collaborators, since their employer is the old boy up at the Mains Farm (then again, most of them know no more about Kaufmann than his name). I can see them now, waiting to be called, restlessly striding around in the flickering shadows under the trees, overdoing an upright posture as guilty people always do and keeping as far away from the tempting spread as they feel propriety demands. And then, one by one, their names are called. A set of basement rooms has been especially equipped for them: their weight and height is measured and they provide blood and urine samples. Next they are asked to strip to the waist and step into a screened-off area to be X-rayed. Because they will be living at close quarters in lodgings and barracks, it is important to make sure that they are not afflicted by any infectious diseases, tuberculosis especially. At the X-ray stage of the examination, they are also subjected to a small dose of ionising radiation. The dosage is related to the weight of each volunteer as well as to his age and blood screening data, and eventually to other medical information recorded in his case notes, which are updated annually. The book collection that Sigrid Kaufmann left with Johannes after the end of the war includes handbooks in radiology and nuclear medicine, as well as several volumes of what were then standard textbooks in biological medicine, such as *Über die Natur der Genmutation und der Genstruktur* ('On the Characteristics of Genetic Mutation and the Structure of Genes') by N. W. Timoféeff-Ressovsky, K. G. Zimmer and M. Delbrück (1935). This work had been of particular interest to Kaufmann, who had underlined a great deal and made many notes in the margins. Delbrück and his colleagues hypothesised that ionising radiation could trigger chromosomal changes that might in turn become stable mutations. It is easy to understand why this idea would fascinate an agronomist like Kaufmann, who for decades had experimented with the artificial creation of hardier and more nutritious cereal crops. The development of human tissues is not fixed for all time by the genetic material in our cells. Genes and gene expression can be made to change. If so, it should surely be possible to direct such changes along predetermined lines. It follows that it is worth looking for cures for inherited conditions and malfunctions, even if these are usually classified as incurable, as in the case of the debilitating muscular atrophy that Kaufmann's daughter Helga suffered from. Of course, Kaufmann's notes are much less wide-ranging than this. He confines himself to factual records of *the volunteers*, such as information about their family relationships, marital status, number and gender of their children, if any, and whether they or any of their close relatives have symptoms of a known heritable condition. Their blood values and the exact radiation dose and its time of administration fill column after column. As far as I can judge, the doses were relatively small, but everyone was subjected to radiation. There were no exceptions. Most important of all: many of the names recur in the records, year after year. These are trustworthy men, experienced and faithful harvest labourers who return and each time submit to this thorough health check uncomplainingly and, above all, without questioning the routine. Going through the lists of names in Kaufmann's diaries, my first impulse was to find out where these people live now and how they live – if, indeed, they are still alive. And, if they are *not*, to find out when they died and what was the cause of death. People, when all is said and done, are not like fruit flies or gut bacteria, with cell cycles that take minutes or hours. The changes in human tissues that Kaufmann wanted to observe might have taken years, perhaps generations to appear – and then might well have been impossible to analyse in clinical terms. So Kaufmann's first premise when he started his experiments must have been that the present conditions would effectively never change: the war and the occupation and his own peculiar feudal control over his farm labourers would last forever. (It matters much less that Delbrück and his colleagues had not actually got a grip on how to manipulate human genetic change and that experimentation along their lines was hopeless by definition. If Delbrück had not existed, Kaufmann would have found some other theory to suit his purpose.) How widespread such interventions were – that is, if it was one series of experiments only, or if there were several centres of research in addition to the old Sanatorium and, above all, if the colony children were also experimental subjects – to such questions I have no answers. The fact that I have not found any case histories of children among

Kaufmann's papers is not sufficient proof that such trials were not carried out: the case notes might have been destroyed or stored somewhere else. If it were to be shown that the children were experimented on, something that is suggested by Steinar Brage's remark that everyone had to be 'vaccinated', the reasonable assumption would be that young Franz was part of it. Might it not be the explanation as to why Kaufmann wanted to see this particular relative on the island? If, indeed, the plan behind his insane project was to investigate possible cures for Helga's muscular atrophy, Kaufmann is likely to have been greatly interested in how a child distantly related to his own would respond to the radiation. (Spinal muscular atrophy is inherited as an autosomal recessive trait, which means that to show the full set of symptoms, both one's parents, though apparently normal, have to be carriers of the gene.) However, the greatest mystery of all is how a project of this size and complexity could continue for several years without any information leaking out. Which raises the question of *who* knew, and later chose or, possibly, was forced to keep it secret. Johannes must of course have known from the start. After all, he picked up and drove the children and the adult volunteers. Sigrid Kaufmann would hardly have dared to leave all this information with him if she had not been certain of his loyal silence. But what about Mr Carsten? Before and during the war, more than a hundred workers were employed in farming on the Inner Islands. If the lists are correct, many of these men must have been experimental subjects over several years. Even if Mr Carsten was not directly involved in what was going on in the Sanatorium, there must have been many occasions for him to chat to people in the seasonal as well as the permanent workforce who had undergone the treatment. He, like most others, might well have had no idea what it was supposed to be in aid of, but would nonetheless have had his suspicions. As long as Kaufmann was alive, Mr Carsten had no choice other than to keep mum, but how did he react once Kaufmann had died? I still remember how he came and rang the bell that evening, standing, legs astride under his massive bulk, at the front door that no one entered. There I sat in my room, my blood-stained hands squeezed between my knees, imagining that he had come like an Angel of Judgement, ready to demand retribution for my evil deed. But I was a child and children always believe that they are the centre of the world. I now suppose that Mr Carsten's visit had nothing whatsoever to do with Kaufmann. Indeed, Kaufmann's passing must have been a great liberation for Mr Carsten. At a stroke, he was free to devote himself to the horses which had always been his first passion. If only the money was there, he would have wanted to do it full-time. Maybe he had thought of a plan to buy up the widow's and her daughter's holdings in the farm. I remember how intently I watched the two men strolling in the garden: the slightly built, bent figure of Johannes, the large bulk of Mr Carsten, though somehow sagging beneath his broad shoulders. In the innocent eyes of a child, it could look as if they were playing a kind of game in which you had to take turns to touch the tree trunks with one or both palms while alternating between talking to the other and wandering about, deep in your own thoughts. Now I have come to the conclusion that Mr Carsten raised the matter of the Sanatorium experiments with Johannes. He might well have felt that it was every citizen's duty to speak up about the past, especially when Kaufmann was no longer with them. It would have helped to make up for all the injustices endured in the war. I imagine that Mr Carsten tried to be conciliatory at first. Much time has passed since then, he might have said, and besides, conditions were quite unusually precarious during the occupation. Yes, of course, Johannes knew that as well as anyone. But once the old boy had passed on, these things could no longer be kept under wraps. That's how it always goes. Mr Carsten might have gone on to say that people were talking about how many of the wartime farm workers had fallen ill later in life. Cancer in most cases. And how would it look, Johannes, if all the men you drove down to collect at the bridge went and died, the lot of them? Perhaps just two, three years after the end of the war and, worse, died in the most dreadful agony? And them being ordinary folk like you and me, Johannes: reliable, decent people whose one aim had been to land a good job. And if that kind of story started doing the rounds now, it would be the very devil to deal with, wouldn't it? Now, when it is all forgotten, or as near as damn it? And Johannes would have walked away a little, staring at the ground. And Mr Carsten let him alone for a while. Only to add this, slowly and with great emphasis on every word: *And then there is this matter of that girl of yours, Wilhelmine*. Mr Carsten had the grim cunning of the underdog, and knew all he needed about Johannes's weak spots and how best to attack them: *There's no telling how much that girl has figured out. Who knows what she might take into her head to come out with? What if I think up a way to get her off the island so we finally get some peace and quiet? Though maybe you could see your way to contributing a little to her upkeep?* When I hear him say this, it dawns on me that the decay of the islanders has been an outcome not so much of the inbreeding – of folks being all just as deep in it, as Mr Carsten had tried to persuade me earlier – but rather because everyone has been so self-regarding that keeping silent, refusing to admit anything, has finally blocked off every possible way out. Or it could be that silence has become unavoidable simply because everyone has lost the ability to speak, since, if what one knows was put into words, the consequence would be to concede one's passive complicity in what happened and so declare oneself guilty of condoning it going on, without ever speaking up or even making an effort to leak information, and that prospect is just too much to cope with. So much better to let Kaufmann bear all responsibility, he wasn't quite right in the head, after all. As for exactly what Minna might have known or seen, and what, if anything, Mr Carsten had feared would be made public knowledge, I have no idea. She never told me anything, except for childish stories, like the one about the white butterflies which she had seen rise in front of Kaufmann's feet at night. But, whatever, it is obvious that Mr Carsten saw Minna as a walking, talking scandal, a source of mischief that would get out of control unless he put his mind to it. And that he is the new master of the island becomes clear to all when, later, Minna returns from the mainland. Before, she had made her way to the farm on the sly, along secret routes. Now she walks along the Mains Farm Road with her head held high, wearing clothes she has acquired from God knows where and full in the sight of everyone, including Johannes, who can do nothing other than what he and the rest of the islanders have always done: that is, look the other way and say nothing. And, up in the farmyard, Mr Carsten stands, waiting for her. He has got what he wanted. No need for him to come down to us any longer.

*

It has surely been less than an hour since I first set foot in the Kaufmann villa, but here they come: all thumping percussion and hooting horns and trumpets. The procession is on the move. I crouch by the window and observe them through the binoculars. At first, the outside world is just light and rain-soaked air. Then I see the Yellow Villa, which looks as if it is about to collapse under the weight of dense garden greenery. A long line of parked cars stretches all the way from Brekke's place to the Simonsens' greenhouse. People who have come to watch are lined up several rows deep along the roadside. While some are already busy packing and unpacking cool bags and rucksacks to get at Thermoses and sandwich boxes, others stand around smoking or just stand, arms chummily around each other's shoulders, as if to make sure of not falling over backwards into the overflowing ditches. A group of children lead the procession; they leap and tumble playfully, as children will, but most of the participants proceed at a solemn, measured pace along the road. Several men of substance walk behind the banner of the local Rotary Club. The orchestra comes next: a tightly organised troop of mostly middle-aged or older men and women in red and navy uniforms. Their instruments are swinging this way and that, and the valves of the trumpets and the bells of the tubas are gleaming in the sunlight. The music swoops in the air as if freed from the musicians. Sometimes it rises in waves, a heavy swell that reaches the farm, retreats in the next moment, driven back by an invisible wind, only to return with even greater intensity. The piercing, sharp notes from the flutes rise against the sonorous background of the brass, which grows denser and cracks deep down in the bass range, while all is reined in by the dark, rhythmic beating of the drums. *Boom-pa-pa-pa! Boom-pa-pa-pa! Boom . . . !* From where I am in the farmhouse, high above the crowd, I can hear everything: the laughter and merry shouting of families with children, the beat of the drums and the drawn-out, silvery blasts of the horns. A group of jolly, noisy fathers have taken after their children and made themselves up as warriors, with paint-smeared faces and pheasant feathers stuck in their hair. A horde of disoriented dogs follow, unsure if they are to hang back, or run ahead and bark, or form a rearguard, like sheep-dogs, to drive the straying flock. I ask myself how Helga, stuck in the upper floor of the farmhouse, might have felt as she watched, year after year, the cavalcade pass by at its majestic-ally slow pace. If, on an impulse, someone had broken out of the column to 'have a go', as people used to say, she would not have been able to get away. She was in exile up here, unable to leave, always at home to visitors. Perhaps that was exactly what *he* thought, the young Franz Lehman who had been brought to the farm by her father. Did he seek her out to court her, thrill and even energise her with his infectious, boyish manner and apparently inexhaustible vitality? If they were really related, however distantly, she would surely have been curious to know if anyone in his family had been afflicted as she was – after all, her father said that her condition was inherited. They might have mulled over certain ideas, as they hid behind the tangled wild raspberry bushes or in the deepening dusk down by the lake, while he was carving willow flutes for her: one idea was that this illness was, in a way, greater than themselves, than any one ailing person, and had left its shameful stain on the hearts of the family, an imprint that went deeper than the individual's race, nationality and beliefs and must therefore be concealed, or one would be seen to be vulnerable and, if one's vulnerability became common knowledge, someone might leave the set processional route and start to walk up to the farm, as people had done so many times before. It had to happen, because the herd has no intelligence and acts purely on instinct, which means that it is unfailingly drawn towards the part of one's body that is hardest to defend. I stand at the window and watch as the procession proper marches past, and then its tail of chatting parents and playing children. All are contained within the rhythmic drumming that lies like an acoustic lid over the island, compressing all other sounds under its weight. And suddenly it occurs to me that the music and human noise are not so much surrounding the procession as camouflaging it, that these things help to rein it in and give it shape, and, by doing this, mask the burning hatred that the islanders feel and have felt for countless years but that by now is barely distinguishable from their usual ill will. That is why all the noises and the shrieking children sound so distant and muted. It is as if they are all moving through time as well as space: throughout the years, the procession has followed precisely this route, slowing down and walking more heavily until it finally reaches the crossroads and, drawing on its last ounce of strength, turns off the road that leads to the Mains Farm. At this moment, I spot him: the man from behind the counter in Langmark's with the gross facial swelling that marks him out. Unlike the other onlookers, he is not watching the procession, as it moves down the slope to King's Road in a tangle of waving club banners, but is staring straight at the farm. Instinctively, I make myself smaller, even though reason tells me he cannot see me. The *boom-boom-boom* echoes of the drums fade and are swallowed up into the roar of yet another plane, grandly indifferent to whatever is happening down on the ground, processions or whatever else, as it trails its enormous boom behind it through the stagnant midday heat and then slips slowly out of sight behind the forest on the far side of the NATO villa.

*

Because I do not know when, or even from which direction Mr Carsten is going to enter, I have shut and blocked all the doors to the house. I lifted the heavy marble top off the table under the hall mirror and upended it against the front door with its upper edge pressing from below on the door handle. In the drawing room, I hauled the massive oak desk across the room to obstruct the terrace door. In past years, there was a yard door that led into the basement. That back entrance was sheltered by the leafy walls of a pergola and wide cement steps took you down to a strong wooden door. It was intended for use by the farm workers who were housed in basement rooms. I remember that there was no doorbell but instead an old-fashioned iron clapper covered in flaking green paint. Only a few years after Kaufmann's death, Sigrid Kaufmann had the cellar door bricked up and the pergola removed, which made that side of the house look almost obscenely bare. Where the steps had once taken you to the cellar door with its green-painted iron clapper, no grass grew, or anything else for that matter. The stairwell was filled in and all that remained of it was an absurd-looking remnant of the iron handrail that protruded a few centimetres above the flattened soil. However, though the door is no more, the cellar might still be in use. I get Johannes's torch from my rucksack and direct the beam behind the stairs to the first floor. There is a space one and a half metres wide between the outer wall and the bottom of the stairs. A narrow door leads into some kind of storage area. The door is locked, but there is a trapdoor set into the floor in front of it. I grab hold of the two recessed handles on the trapdoor and the wood creaks as it comes up with a grating noise of unoiled hinges. The cement steps below are coated with a thick, crumbly layer of apparently undisturbed stone dust. I make sure that the heavy lid is securely propped up against the wall before starting to walk down the steps, moving slowly with the torch in one hand. The cellar floor is also made of cement, which makes sense if this was the area previously used to house the servants. Also, like the steps, a layer of grit covers the floor. It makes a crunching noise under the soles of my shoes. I hold the torch above my head: the cellar seems to have been partitioned into small rooms or pens that open into long, narrow corridors. Some of the partition walls are made of bricks and mortar but others look provisional, knocked together from unhewn planks or sheets of board. Even so, all the rooms, or pens, once had proper doors, although by now most of them have only holes to show where the barrels of the locks had been. There is a kitchen area in an alcove at the far end of the corridor. It is furnished with a long table, large enough for a dozen or so seated people, and, along the long wall, a sink fitted into a metal-covered workbench, with tins and empty plastic containers stacked next to it. I try the tap but no water comes. Along the walls on both sides of the kitchen alcove, hospital beds are lined up in rows or tipped upright. These are old-style cots from the 1940s or 50s, with head and foot ends of white-painted metal. The whole place has a worn, institutional look, something like an old-fashioned medical station in a military camp. Somehow, I do not dare enter any of the pens and instead go to lie down on one of the cots in the corridor to try to imagine what this place might have been like when people were living here. The solid walls surrounded proper rooms, perhaps whole apartments (the wooden partitions that turn the rooms into pens, as well as the hospital kit, were obviously added later). At least half a dozen families could have lived here, some perhaps permanently but others temporarily, when casual labourers joined the settled workforce at sowing and harvesting times. This must have been where Franz, as a refugee, was placed to avoid any unwanted suspicions, though I imagine that doors were left open and, at that time, stairwells and thresholds had not yet become markers of the impassable boundaries. The farm must have been full of children: the workers had families and others would have come to play. The air is filling with their light, shrill voices. And I remember my childhood summers: the dusty gravel roads and harsh scent from the verges where wild carrot and celery grew; the fields and pastures scattered with red clover; the strange, chalky heat that seemed to radiate from the bare shale rock surfaces, which split into flakes, sharp as needles if you scratched your skin with one of them; the unvarying pulse beat of the tractors and harvesters working on fields that darkened afterwards, as if scorched by the August heat; air as dense as syrup and clouds of wheat chaff and pow-dery soil so massive that behind them the sun, though still high in the sky, had shrunk to a thin disc, pale and emery-brown. In this unreal, dusky half-light, I see my father standing in a field of wheat that has not yet been cut. His torso is bare and he holds a bow in one hand. The bow is made of willow that he has cut and bent into shape himself. I see Helga, sitting on a tree stump at the edge of the field. Her eyes are following his movements. She has draped her full skirt across her thighs so that her callipers won't show. Lots of twigs and needles are caught in the folds of the cloth. When she speaks, her broad jaw is constantly moving from side to side, almost like a puppet's. But she smiles at him and calls out to him in German, launching her questions out over the field. *Wo in Deutschland hast du deine Familie? – Wie heisst deine Mutter? – Wie ist sie gekleidet? Seht sie schön aus? – Sagst mir etwas auf Norwegisch – Nei, denne veien må du ikke ta.* He carries her home on his back. She is the bigger and stronger of the two, and is very aware of it. She pretends to protest, noisily thumping his shoulder blades and upper arms with her large, helpless fists. When the harvest workers hear Helga's light, happily bubbling laughter, they turn to look. Perched high up on the tractor seat, Mr Carsten, too, removes his cap and wipes the sweat off his forehead when he catches sight of the two of them dancing around in the wheat, the lad so small beneath the hefty girl that she is the only one to be seen, her half-paralysed body turning left, then right, then round again like the hands on a crazy clock face. Deep inside the sun-scorched dusk, horses pull haywains piled high with dried meadow grasses towards the barns. Swallows are twittering as the evening cools. A rough scraping noise as the lid of a well slips and hits the ground; water rushes briskly from a hosepipe against a bare rock face. From the farm kitchen on the hill: lengthening echoes of rattling pots and pans. Cows moo, geese chatter. And then, suddenly, it is dark. August darkness enfolds everything like a thick padded cloth. But inside its black folds: a glittering chain of flaring torches. The torches are placed some fifty metres apart on both sides of the Mains Farm Road, across King's Road and all the way down to the jetty at Horse Strait. I never let a single German cross by the bridge, Kaufmann assured everyone on the island. Instead, they came by boat. The old longboats that the nuns once used to get to and from West Island have been repaired and painted. The boats, too, are lit by torches placed fore and aft. Long before the boats touch land, the torches, glowing points in the dark, loom into view and their reflections in the still water make it look as if covered in molten crude oil. Johannes is waiting with the old horse-drawn carriage down by the beach. There is no moonlight; perhaps the moon has not yet risen. Only the creaking of the rowlocks and the splashing sounds as the blades of the oars cut the surface are heard through the black night, against a background of the guests' excited voices and the clanking of bottles and glasses passed from hand to hand. Then the journey up to the Mains Farm begins. The hill-top farmhouse is illuminated and shadows of people can be seen moving past the windows. Some guests have been shown around the island earlier today and were also taken to West Island to visit the phalanstery, where hundreds of healthy blond children smiled at the foreign dignitaries. Now I see Helga stand in her room upstairs and pull on her evening out-fit: first a white vest over her already tanned shoulders and then a cream silk dress that she buttons with rough, hurried movements. In the room next to hers, the boy is putting on his best trousers and tightening his braces. They have already been ordered to come downstairs. The boy arrives on his short, stumbling legs and is escorted into the hall and then into the drawing room and along to the open fireplace. Over it hangs the painting of the St John's Eve bonfire. Kaufmann puts his arm protectively around the boy's shoulders and introduces him to the guests at the table of honour. Quisling dominates. By now, his heavy face has dissolved into a big grin; he has obviously already treated himself to several glasses of something stimulating. I would very much like to introduce my nephew Franz, *zum Besuch aus Deutschland*. I try to imagine Mr Kaufmann's voice and his long, slender fingers that make strange sweeping gestures in the air while he speaks. Even in German, he expresses himself in soft, polished and slightly solemn turns of phrase, just as when he spoke to me that evening I called. As the guest of honour, Mr Quisling must have stood up at once and reached out his hand across the laid table to greet the newcomer. The boy would probably not have taken the offered hand and instead looked down at the floor, but Kaufmann will already have placed his fingers under the boy's chin and resolutely lifted his face up while announcing: now, this boy will sing for us! And so the boy sang Schumann's Wanderlied '*Wohlauf! noch getrunken den funkelnden Wein*' and, after the song was finished, Quisling rose to lead a standing ovation, so overwhelming that it felt as if the ceiling would lift, and the boy stood there, his cheeks red with shame, while the host (who had also remained standing) smiled, with moisture gathering in the corner of one eye, his pale cheeks flushed. Then one of the servants shepherded the boy along the corridor as if he could not get away quickly enough from the presence of the guests. But Mr Carsten: he would have seen everything, that goes without saying. Watched, as Kaufmann played his duplicitous game: the way he made everyone see what wasn't there. Was that how it happened? Lying on the cot in the dark cellar, I become certain that this was exactly what happened.

*

Mr Carsten is back. Minutes ago, he seemed wiped off the face of the Earth but suddenly he has materialised in the middle of the yard, looking towards the road, with the dog at his side and his feet planted wide apart, as self-importantly as ever. He must be feeling safe now. For one more year, the procession has marched past without incident and the farm is just a farm again, as shut off from its surroundings as ever, while once more the usual grumbling stinginess rules on the island. It is late afternoon now: cars are crawling, side by side, in the queue on the only slip road to the bridge; school children are walking home, a steady stream of them with rucksacks on their backs are coming down King's Road; a shop assistant in his Kiwi supermarket uniform is out on the new empty parking lot shoving one abandoned shopping trolley into another until he has got a stack of at least fifty of them, and then, with back-breaking effort, he is pushing it along, swaying and bending his upper body, until the whole lot are chained up at the shop entrance. The parking area at the back of the supermarket, connected to King's Road by a wide tarmacked ramp, the place where Minna and Morten used to hang out, is covered by rubbish left behind after the big procession: burst balloons, torn banners and placards, empty plastic cups and pizza boxes. I remember how, in the weeks and months after Minna had been exiled from the island, I used to drift around the shop, so anaesthetised by my anguish that only the details I saw in close-up have stuck in my mind: the cracks in the cement of the ramp and the painfully rough-looking black lumps of tarmac around the base of the iron fence, almost eaten up with rust, that guarded the edge of the rock face rising straight out of the fjord. Then, I believed her exile would last forever. But just eight months later, as if by some miracle, Minna was back home. The same Minna – and, simultaneously, another person. I watched her stand in front of the mirror in the hall, trying on clothes that were not hers: tight skirts with plastic belts in baby pink or pale blue and clingy sweaters over bras that made her breasts look cone-shaped. And when I asked, where did you get all these clothes from? all she said was, the people I stayed with gave them to me. I knew she was lying but only asked, are you going out to meet the lads? and, *the lads?* was all she said and then she laughed, a long, snorting laugh through her nose as if she couldn't think what I was on about, so I asked, where are you off to, then? and she said, get lost, you little toad, it's none of your business. I followed her, as I had followed her ever since I could use my

191

legs for walking, always unconvinced that her assurances were the truth and that she could manage for a second without me. I saw her cross the school yard, it was a shortcut for the benefit of anyone who was watching her, and then take the long way round past the supermarket and onto King's Road, then up the Mains Farm Road towards the farm, where Mr Carsten stood waiting for her, feet apart, stiff-necked, with the dog at his side. In fact, his posture then will have been precisely the same as now; he has probably stood like that all his life, patiently waiting for something which would, at last, make up for the injustice inflicted on him. Which is what is about to happen now. I use the binoculars to see what he is observing on the road. It is late in the afternoon and the last shreds of the morning cloudbanks have vanished behind the tree tops. The fields and the overgrown areas round the houses, the farm road and the rain-swollen ditches, everything is merging in a haze of moisture and sun-dappled greenery. I note that the cars left along the field verge have driven away and that only two vans are still there, parked on either side of the drive to the Yellow Villa as if guarding it. They look a little like the vans that turned up when the water board men came along to inspect the pipework. Half a dozen older boys are hanging out down there, wandering aimlessly along the road, as if they had been part of the procession but dropped out and are left without any idea of what to do next. Every one of them has smeared his face with something I cannot make out, possibly paint but it might just as well be soot or mud, and they all carry heavy rucksacks or shoulder bags. Then the boys turn round in unison, leap at the fence, climb it with practised speed and, crouching under the weight on their backs, run towards the Yellow Villa. Some of them try to take cover behind the trees, but this is nothing but a sham diversion: I can already see the backs of two of the boys on the terrace and, less than a minute later, the upstairs windows open and some of the gang are leaning on the sills, waving energetically at those who are still in the garden. It is hard to tell which emotion causes me most pain: humiliation or fury. Or the realisation that they must have kept me under constant surveillance. For how else could they have known when to get inside the house? Why show themselves and their intentions off so shamelessly? As if breaking into somebody's home was the most natural thing in the world. Despite it all, I cannot help being fascinated. There is something hypnotic about watching complete strangers as they invade your own space, and especially when they display the calm, untroubled familiarity of people who are reclaiming what is properly theirs. But this is not only about the right to ownership. Soon, furniture is hauled outside and piled up on the terrace: first, the oxblood-coloured armchair, the one with studs, and two elegant chintz-covered chairs that used to stand at what Johannes called the 'smoking table' (a round table on a solid pedestal, with a sheet of glass on top protecting a lacy, crocheted tablecloth). Next, the sitting-room sofa, which is toppled over the terrace balustrade and hits the garage drive with an ear-shattering bang. Half an hour later, the kitchen and bedroom furnishings have also been carried out and thrown over the balustrade, including Johannes's bed and bedside table, the clothes left in his wardrobe and the ancient TV set. Now they start on the contents of the garage. Two of the boys empty out the boxes and crates full of spare parts that Johannes had kept back from cars and buses he had worked on over the years and had not had the heart to get rid of afterwards. Cutlery and broken glasses, everything ends up in a shambolic pile on the drive. To make the carnage worse, one of the young men comes along with an axe and sets about thrashing everything that comes his way. Chair legs break, table tops are chopped to pieces and odd bits of wood are turned into kindling. The destruction is barely complete when almost the entire gang, once more as if on command, head for the road. Only three boys stay behind. While two of them stand guard, the third one writes something with spray paint on the cement wall by the garage door. FUCKING NAZI, it says in large letters. He adds a carelessly drawn swastika. I direct the binoculars at Mr Carsten, who, like me, has been watching the vandals at work but presumably without batting an eyelid. The dog is the first to make a move. It slowly, almost hesitatingly, leaves Mr Carsten's side and sets off across the yard with its nose close to the ground. Next, Mr Carsten himself turns and starts walking with the exaggerated swinging or swaying movements forced on him by his stiff leg. It is only when he is halfway to the farm manager's house that he stops and looks towards the drawing-room windows where I am hiding. The moment is brief but quite long enough to let me know that we have been watching the same thing and that he has been aware that I am up here.

*

So, Minna returned to us. All the same, it felt like a total stranger had moved into our home. What are you going up there for? I had asked her. She had been lying on her bed with her legs drawn up and the ashtray balanced on her stomach, staring at nothing, lazily or indifferently, while she dragged on her thin roll-up cigarette. After all, he's dead now, I said, but she only carried on nonchalantly puffing out smoke. I can go there, can't I? she said after a while. I mean, now that he's no longer around. What's wrong with you! I yelled at her. And then, to Johannes: What's wrong with her? As ever, there was no point in asking him. I remember that last time, when she emerged from her room wearing a dress in cream silk that was far too large for her and so low-cut that half her chest was on show, and with a skirt so full she had to grab a bunch of the material to stop the hem from dragging on the ground. She had put on earrings set with blue sapphires and outsized high-heeled shoes that forced her to walk with her legs wide apart to keep her balance. It was touch and go whether she would fall over when she stood in front of the mirror to put on makeup. But Johannes said nothing, not even then. He sat in the kitchen and kept his mouth shut, silent as he had been all his life when something looked like trouble for him or others. From the window in my room, I saw Minna walk up the Mains Farm Road: a small, bandy-legged figure, tarted up in the clothes of a stranger. Of course, Mr Carsten was standing in the yard, looking out for her, although he probably did not stay there for the time it took her to reach the top of the road. For him, it must have been enough to know that, once again, he had persuaded her to come to him. He started walking slowly towards the paddock. The dog, on its long leash, ran barking towards its master and then towards the girl, as if it wanted its jerky, anxious movements to show the kind of bond that must already have formed between them, and while Mr Carsten was dragging his heavy dead leg behind him, he might well have stopped to have a few words with the men at work in the yard (that year, to make room for a new water tank, the large oak that had grown there since time immemorial had been felled and the yard turned into a huge pit, with a digger standing next to a ridge of excavated soil so tall it almost obscured the view of the main house behind it), a diversion that took just long enough for him to assure himself with a glance over his shoulder that she had not given up but had followed him across the yard. And then there they stood, perhaps twenty metres apart, he with his legs splayed in an attempt to hide his limp and a smile on his face that seemed to grow more awkward the broader it became, while she pretended to be cool, at ease and not breathless in the slightest, even though she had covered the last bit almost at a run, in the borrowed finery too, which looked even more outlandish here, among all the muck and horse shit; and: what was it you wanted to show me? she asked, and perhaps he felt he need do no more than glance at the main house, perhaps at the drawing-room windows where, surely, Mrs Kaufmann stood, her hand pulling back a corner of the curtain, or perhaps at the first floor where Miss Helga was taking in the view. It goes without saying that both women must have wondered what the manager wanted with that pathetic wisp of a girl. Or Mr Carsten's plan might just have been to show Minna off in front of the two old harpies, as he called them, and use her presence on the farm to demonstrate to them and everybody else that now, after Kaufmann's death, he had become to all the world the man he felt he had always been, in charge of the management and administration of all he surveyed: the real master of the island. For me, that night of intolerable waiting was like an open wound. I stayed awake, sitting at my window as the hours passed, but Minna never came home. Only pale sea mist came. As the darkness of the night began to thin out, the whitey rolled in and wrapped itself round the island like a duvet. I went outside then and watched as the parched field verges disappeared in the mist and saw the long shadows of the telephone poles lean in over the crossroads. It felt like an open invitation to sneak up the hill but, even though no one would have seen me in the fog, I did not dare to take even a single step. I waited outside the Yellow Villa until the dawn light cut through the misty air. Throughout the night and early morning, there had been no sound from the farm apart from the loud cawing of the crows as they erupted from the trees. By then, it was over and done with. At about six in the morning, the sharp blue light of a police patrol car slashed through the thinning whitey. Johannes and I stood together under the trees in our garden and observed the car turn right at the crossroads and drive up to the farm buildings at a slow, almost relaxed pace. It was just over an hour before it came back down the road, this time with the blue light turned off. Not long afterwards, the talk on the island was all about how Mrs Kaufmann had *had it up to here* with Mr Carsten and reported him to the police. Exactly why Mr Carsten had been arrested was unclear, though rumour had it that he was guilty of embezzlement. His tasks were taken over by another farm manager called van Martens, a Dutchman who, unlike his predecessor, had so little to say for himself that few islanders could remember ever having seen him by the time he left. Six months later, the local papers claimed that Mr Carsten's crime had been more serious than thought at first. The police suspected him of having caused the sudden death of the retired sulky trotting driver Manfred Weiler. Just before his death, Weiler and Mr Carsten had jointly owned a horse called Boxer that was trained for trotting, or harness racing. It had died recently and Weiler had been saying in public that Mr Carsten had poisoned the horse, intending to pocket his part of the insurance payout. This allegation was proved, Weiler argued, by the fact that Mr Carsten had not wanted the prize-winning animal to be kept in Weiler's stable and instead insisted on stabling the horse on the Inner Islands, on a farm belonging to Mr Carsten's previous employer. According to Weiler, the poisoning had been done in stealth, over quite a long time. One evening, the two of them met in Weiler's flat in the city. The idea was to settle their dispute, but the confrontation led to a violent quarrel that ended with Mr Carsten pushing Weiler down the stairs. As a matter of fact, none of the neighbours had actually seen Mr Carsten push Weiler but they had heard them argue. One witness also claimed that Weiler had been screaming the way you would if 'you felt death was near', just as the tabloids reported. When the police arrived, they found Weiler at the foot of the stairs with the back of his head smashed in, and Mr Carsten upstairs. He appeared confused and did not resist arrest, which may explain his relatively mild sentence. As for Boxer, it seems that early in the morning, as the fog was dispersing, Sigrid Kaufmann had seen the horse lying dead at the far end of the paddock. After trying in vain to rouse Mr Carsten (he did not answer on the farm manager's telephone), she had contacted the police because she feared that some intruder might have got into the estate illegally to kill the animal and possibly Mr Carsten too. Where Mr Carsten actually was at that point in time was not stated; he might not even have been on the island. However, one thing is certain: Minna's disappearance during the night before the discovery of the dead horse was never connected with the accusations of manslaughter and embezzlement which were later made against Mr Carsten, with the result, so Simonsen said, that the old farm manager spent several years in prison. I did not make any such connection either. At least, not until one evening (it must have been in the autumn after my return from the USA) when the doorbell rang in the apartment on Trondheimsveien, in Oslo, where I rented a room. My land-lady knocked energetically on my door and shouted *visitor!* When I came into the hall, Mr Carsten was waiting for me. He had changed a great deal and was no longer the powerfully built farm manager I had known but an almost emaciated man, with what hair he had left cut very close to his skull. Also, he was unusually soberly dressed in a tailored if slightly less than clean suit in a blue-and-white striped material, and held with both hands an old-fashioned fedora hat whose top and brim were dripping wet from the rain. Seeing him after all these years, and in this state, surprised me so much that I could not think what to say. My confusion must have made him feel he had better introduce himself: Carsten Gerhardsen, he said, and held out his hand. Then he told me that he was now employed in his former post as manager on the Mains Farm on the island. I did not ask how come he had been given his old job back after so many years in jail, or why he had left in the first place. I knew or thought I knew something about the circumstances from reading the reports in the papers. With a politeness that matched mine, as I refrained from referring to his alleged crimes, he asked me if I knew where my sister was and, if so, how he could possibly get in touch with her. Would you have an address, or perhaps a telephone number? he said. Today, I cannot recall what I said to make it clear that there was no way I could be persuaded to give out that information. All I know is that our encounter dragged on and must have been painful for him as well. Finally, he asked me to be kind enough to pass on a gift from him to Minna, and pulled a long, thin envelope from the inside pocket of his jacket. He handed it over to me, smiled again, his strange half-smile that used to frighten me but now looked simply anxious or even awkward, put his hat on and left, going back into the rain.

After the morning when the police were called in to investigate a possible break-in on the farm and to search for Mr Carsten, many years passed before I met Minna again. I ought to be more precise: I knew where she lived and a little about what she was doing but that was more or less all. She had consistently turned down all my attempts to contact her. At the time, I had a job in the Deichmann Library, where I was tasked with registering and classifying newly acquired books and deregistering the ones sent away to be scrapped. I wrote to Minna in my spare time: long, detailed letters about how Johannes was and about neighbours and mates from school and what had been happening out there on the islands. It was a little absurd, given that she had made her lack of interest in our past so very clear, but I felt that if she shared, at least in writing, everything that happened to me, it was a way to hold on to her. I wrote to her about my travels in the USA for the same reason and sent her at least one letter from each stage of my journey. I wrote to her from the emergency clinic the day when Johannes tripped on the stairs, fell and broke the neck of his femur. It was Mrs Simonsen who found him that time, too. He had been lying on the floor at the bottom of the stairs, too weak to reach the telephone extension I had had installed for him not long before. That summer, I stood in for Johannes, who still moved around on crutches, doing local voluntary jobs. I wrote to Minna to let her know what we were up to. The hull of an old ship had been found in the muddy bottom layer in Horse Strait. It took several days to haul it up on land. An antiquarian and a marine archaeologist joined the enterprise to make sure that the hull did not dry out, which would have ruined it, but on closer inspection the wreck turned out to be uninteresting: an old barge from the days when coal was shipped regularly to the Inner Islands. That year, or perhaps it was the next one, I told Minna that Carl-Anton Brekke, grocer Brekke's grandson, had been on TV for a season's run of *Jeopardy*, the programme presented by Steinar Brage. And that during the winter, Morten Skov's youngest boy had dug a cave in the wall of snow along the road down by South Meadow, but the council's new snowploughs were too wide for the narrow roads on the island; it was only afterwards that people spotted the bloodstained snow and the remains of the lantern the boy had placed outside the cave as a 'warning'. I have no idea what Minna did during all this time. After her death, I signed for her personal belongings and found among them several of my American letters, unopened. There is of course no way of telling if she had read the letters I did not find or simply thrown them away. When I had tried to get in touch with Minna again, she had a more or less steady male Chilean partner, Javier Montéz or possibly Martinéz, though everybody seems to have called him Chico or Chicuelo. Chicuelo means 'small boy', but at 190-odd centimetres Javier was unusually tall for a Latin American. His skin was mottled with scars, possibly smallpox pits, which he tried to hide beneath a big, black beard. When I realised that Minna would not return my phone calls or answer my letters,

I thought at first it was because of Chicuelo. I told myself that he might be jealous, or maybe that Minna's stories had made her boyfriend distrust or even despise me. Later on, I thought of another explanation: if Minna had agreed to talk to me, even for just a few minutes, she would have had to accept that the evil of the past was still part of her, much as she wanted to leave it behind, and that it not only still existed but could be named and touched and, above all, shared. And the only one to share such things with – the only one from whom she could have the slightest hope of understanding – was me. This, I think, was the first time I grasped that meeting with me would have caused her an almost physical pain. But, in the end, she did all the same. One day, when I came home from work, there was a message for me on the answering machine. Minna asked me to meet her by the clock on Jernbanetorget at four in the afternoon of the next day. I caught sight of her from quite far away, smoking as she paced up and down near the tram stop. She was wearing a large, wide skirt in a colourful red-and-ochre pattern, a thick grey wool coat and a long scarf, wound so many turns around her neck and face that only the narrow slits of her eyes showed below her fringe. But she looked as I remembered her, only older, her body a little heavier now. How's Chicuelo? I asked, mostly to say anything at all. She looked me over with critically appraising eyes, as if she doubted every word I said and was fully prepared to defend herself in case I should, against all expectation, try to touch her or come close to her in any other way. She had a part-time job at Duplotrykk over on Bryn, where *The Class*

Struggle was printed. I knew that on weekends she sold copies of the paper from various pitches: I had seen her at Youngstorget, outside the parliament building and down by the river. But I could not tell her that in case she thought that I was still following her about. In fact, as I realised in that moment, there was nothing I could ask her without giving away that I knew more about her than she had agreed to tell me. Anyway, there would have been no point in asking her anything much. As soon as I tried to open my mouth, her eyes impatiently scanned the street for her tram, and when it finally arrived, she just stepped on board without so much as a word to me. I had hesitated for too long. When I finally decided to get on board, dozens of passengers had already had time to push past me and we ended up far apart, with me standing in the aisle and Minna seated several rows further back. I have a letter for you, I shouted above the heads of the passengers who separated us. From Mr Carsten, I added. He gave it to me. She sat there, apparently unmoved, staring out through the window. I manoeuvred closer to her and leaned over her shoulder. You hang on to it, was all she said. He turned up at my place, I said, the doorbell rang and, imagine, Mr Carsten stood outside, he wore a suit, and a tie and a hat as well. I don't want to listen to this, she said, and stood up, pushed through to the exit and left. This was how it began, the last time we spent together. We met in trams. Sometimes she did not come. Sometimes she boarded the tram at an earlier stop. If I caught a glimpse of her through a window, I had to leap on board at the last minute. Sometimes she would be accompanied by Chicuelo, and then I did not even approach her. On several occasions, I noticed that she had been drinking. Once she was so intoxicated that she could hardly stay upright. *You vile creep*, she shouted as soon as she saw me. And when I tried to calm her, she hit me in the face with her fists and howled loudly enough for the whole carriage to hear: *fucking stop following me about!* One of the other passengers, probably someone who often used the same tram as her and had drawn his own (mistaken) conclusions, threatened to kill me if I didn't *immediately stop pestering the lady and get off the tram*, and, when I refused, he and two other righteous citizens shoved me towards the exit and threw me out. Enough to make anyone give up. But, then, I had watched over my sister for many years, through days and nights, and would never give up. Now, least of all.

*

After meeting in trams over some time, the tension between us eased a little. Perhaps she had a bad conscience. Do you remember the sucking-hole? I asked her one day when we got seats next to each other for a change. By then, it had become clear to me that the only way to make her speak to me was to start talking about something quite random, whatever happened to come to mind, a stray memory or thought. I always envied her such a lot, she said one day, oh, what's her name, the girl whose mum bred beagles? Anniken? I suggested. I was so envious of her for her swimsuit, she had a two-piece, a red one, and all I had was that ugly green one-piece job. It was so loose, it drooped at the crotch. And who would've bought me a new swimsuit? Would *he*? No way, he probably thought the floppy crotch was just fine so he could ogle me whenever. After going swimming, he always wanted me to get under the shower so he could rub soap all over me. Filthy old sod that he was. *Was?* I asked, because I assumed that she was talking about Johannes. And then: why are you always so hard on him? That last question was one I repeated many times. But in her mind, she was back on Horse Strait beach, eyeing Anniken, the daughter of the woman who bred beagles. And she said, what kind of mechanism makes one sad, silly little girl sick with longing for something another sad, silly little girl has got? Something like a two-piece swimsuit? Whatever you say, I *was* sick with longing, I did so want one like hers. Then, quite abruptly: have you been over there recently? Have you seen how the place looks now, with all those super-smart villas? I'm often over there, I said. And she said, glancing at me in that masterful way of hers: you simply can't tear yourself away from it, from the sucking-hole – can you? One day I reminded her that there were still things out there that belonged to her. And she (not very interested): what things? Things that belonged to them, I said. Which *them*? she asked. Our parents, I said. She looked away. I have nothing that belonged to them, she said. And I: yes, of course you do. A shawl, for instance, and jewellery – those earrings. Don't you remember, blue sapphire earrings? At least, you told me that the stones were precious, real sapphires, and the earrings had been our mother's. And she: I own nothing that was theirs; and I (again): but what about the shawl? She: the shawl, maybe, yes; and then I: and what about all the rest of your new stuff, where did it come from? And she: he gave it to me; and I: who did? Johannes? And she: no, him, Mr Carsten. I was silenced, just sat and looked out through the window. I remember it as a clear, bright day. When the tram swung round a street corner, the sunbeams pierced the grimy window panes like sharp spears of light. But what about all the photos? I said then. And Minna turned and smiled at me for the first time. Her old Cheshire Cat smile, stretching her lips from cheek to cheek until they looked like pulled rubber bands, had changed into an arrogant, ugly grimace: a smile like a slash across her face. Haven't you noticed how we're never in the same photo, you and me? she asked. They might have wanted to take pictures of us one at a time, I said. Why would they want to do that? she said. Come on, I said, whatever, we're brother and sister. What makes you think that? she replied, to your knowledge, is there anyone who believes that? Are we the slightest bit alike? This was the Minna I knew, who with one word could hurt me deep inside. Suddenly, it was as if time had stood still: again I was the little boy who sat with his face pressed flat against the window, staring at the farm where my sister was, and waiting for her to come home, but only the pale whitey came and dissolved everything around me – forest, farm, telephone poles, road signs; not even the ever-glowing light on the stable wall could penetrate the fog. Why did you go up there, to Mr Carsten? I asked. She shrugged. What did he want from you? She shook her head. The question seemed not to trouble her; rather, it was beside the point, even meaningless. He wanted to shag me, I suppose, she said without much conviction. When he didn't get what he was after, he was just like all of them. Tried to make up for it, said he was sorry. As if that made any difference, she added. Then she got up and got off the tram. Even though it had not reached her destination. That was the last time. I went along and waited at her stop on Jernbanetorget, day after day, but never saw her again. After several weeks of waiting, I went back to the collective on Markveien. A woman there told me that Minna had gone abroad. She was not sure where. Maybe India. Later, I heard that she had gone to Chile. They left in March 1990, after Patricio Aylwin had succeeded Pinochet as president, and Chicuelo presumably thought it was safe to return to his homeland.

*

I had asked Minna if she remembered the 'sucking-hole', as we called it. It was at the northern end of the beach at Horse Strait. The beach was good for swimming, and Johannes and I used to turn up and help, as our annual voluntary service. At the far end, spurs of flat clay-shale rocks stretched out into the sea. The older children went there in the summer to dive for crabs. At the furthest tip of the lowest of the rocks, there was a bowl-shaped cleft or hollow, of roughly the same diameter as a toilet seat. If you climbed into it and tried to stand on the bottom, you discovered that there was water underneath the rock and also that the current down there was really powerful.

A twelve- or thirteen-year-old standing on the murky bottom of the sucking-hole would have water up to his waist and the smooth upper edge of the rock level with his shoulder blades, which was just the right height for using his elbows to heave himself up and out. But the pull of the current was very strong, the flowing water nipped and tugged at one's skin all the way from the ankle bumps to the belly button, and it was so cold it felt as if one's entire body had gone numb. Minna, as I remember her from the summers when we went swimming from the Horse Strait beach, was a long-legged, lanky girl, whose knees and elbows were sharp enough to hurt if you were trying to push yourself to the front of the queue that always formed on the tip of the diving rock. Everything about her was in uncontrolled motion. When she dived in, she did not keep her legs together and her arms stretched out over her head like everyone else: her limbs sprawled and flapped, often making her splash hip or back first into the water. When she had had enough of swimming and diving, and came back in, she breathed heavily, in fast, noisy puffs, and seemed to have a hard time crawling up on the flat rock. Help, she would scream, or pretend-scream, her arms splashing furiously in the water. When she asked me to slide her down into the sucking-hole, her skin felt the way I imagined a seal's or a dolphin's would, all slippery and smooth. When she stood in the hole, only her head and part of her neck stuck out. I lay down with my cheek against the rock edge so that my mouth was quite close to hers. Her lips were cold and rubbery when she pressed them against my arm. In that moment, all of her was on the surface. Her lips, suckered onto my skin; below her dark eyebrows, her sparkling eyes had an unmistakable expression, which I would always think of as Minna's: at the same time fearful and scornful, with a pretence of submissiveness. And when she asked me to pull her angular, bony body out of the hole, her breath against my face was mildly sweet and sour like sun-warmed buttermilk. Alone, she could not have got out. It is her eyes I remember after she had left the tram, my last sight of her. Their expression was the same: fearful and scornful and pretending to be submissive. Help me, her eyes whispered, while the water, which nobody could see, sucked and tugged at her deep down. Help me up. But I never wholly understood how to help or even with what I was to help her. I was lying next to her, with my face pressed close to hers, but could do nothing.

*

After Minna's move away from the collective in Oslo, I went out to the island more often. I told myself that it was because Johannes needed someone to look after him, but each time I left the island, I understood that I had come because I had nowhere else to be. Though it was a fact that Johannes was in truly sad shape at the time. He had stopped paying for water and drainage after a long-drawn-out struggle with the local council and, once water no longer came out of the taps, he gave up on washing and shaving despite my best efforts. Every time I visited, I brought clean clothes for him and saw to it

that he changed. I bought drinking water in ten-litre containers from the Kiwi shop and, if it had been raining since my last
visit, I filled four or five buckets from the rainwater tub at the
back of the garden and carried them to the bathroom. Usually, there was enough for him to have a bath at least once a
week. He was suspicious of the rainwater as well and would sit
hunched on the edge of the bathtub, with his arms clutching
his knees. The tub had been unused for so long that a streak of
rust had formed between the tap and the drain, and the bottom had become covered by a yellowish chalky crust which no
amount of scrubbing could remove. While I was bending over
the tub to try to clean it, Johannes kept chattering about what
Brekke or van Diesen or some other neighbour had said about
this or that. Mrs Brekke has got cancer of the oesophagus, he
said. Do you have any idea of how many people on the island
have come down with cancer during just the last few years?
Well, you haven't, anyway, I said, and told him to climb into
the bath. And, before he had time to protest, I tipped two full
buckets over him. It made him sink shivering into a corner
and, while he sat there, I washed his hair and shaved him. His
once beautiful hair was still growing well, dense and long, and
his high-boned, shiny cheeks gave his face something of the
innocence of the younger man. But dirt had entered into his
pores by now and remained like a shadow over his skin even
after the shave. A dirty cherub: he had never looked more of
a fake than he did then. The call from Ullevål came one afternoon, while I was towelling his hair dry. I went to answer it
on the telephone in the hall. A woman's voice enquired if she

had reached the Lehmans' house. I remember that my hand on the receiver went completely cold. To gain time, I asked her to repeat the number she had dialled and stood perfectly still while she counted out the figures. Johannes's voice from the bathroom wanted to know if it was the police. He never had any problem with his hearing. I shouted to him that he was to carry on drying his hair, and then the woman's voice at the other end of the line gave my sister's name in full: Marie Sophie Wilhelmine. What has happened? I asked with a sinking feeling, and saw Johannes drop the towel on the floor. He must have heard what I said, or perhaps my face told him all he needed. I turned my back to him and said into the phone that I was her brother, trying to speak as quietly as I could, but even so Johannes must have heard every word, because when I came back into the bathroom, he had climbed into the tub and was sitting there, swaying from side to side, tears flowing down his cheeks as if he were a small child.

*

She had been found floating lifeless in the pool at the Tøyen swimming baths; it was at about half past three on an ordinary afternoon in October, the time of day when the noisy school classes that fill the pool in the mornings have left and exercising adults do their monotonous lengths in peace. A woman who had been swimming alongside Minna for a bit saw her floating and thought at first that 'the lady had just decided to rest' in the water. She swam calmly on but when she came round a second time, she took in the fact the body 'didn't move' and called for help. One of the employees, a pool lifeguard, tried to save Minna with mouth-to-mouth resuscitation and then applied a defibrillator. It was too late. When the ambulance reached the hospital, it was established that Minna had died. The police suspected suicide because there were tranquilliser tablets in the bag she had left in the changing-room locker. Later, suicide was ruled out. The post-mortem examination did indeed find a small amount of water in her lungs but no trace of alcohol or prescription drugs in her blood. Conclusion: death from natural causes. Natural causes? Minna was forty-one years old when she died. Would someone at that age simply expire 'from natural causes'? Looking back now, I'm not sure what tormented me most: that she floated in the water for so long before anyone noticed and realised that she had died, or the insight that I should never have stopped watching out for her, that I ought to have been in some inconspicuous spot in a high row of seats, keeping an eye as my sister swam her lengths. Just as, over the years, I had scrupulously observed everything she did, in secrecy or in full view of everyone. If only I had been there, it would not have ended like that. Or was it the other way round? This was precisely how she *wanted* to die, in complete privacy, seen by no one and, least of all, by me. I talked with Margit, one of the women in the collective and someone whom Minna was probably closer to than anyone else, and learnt that Minna had stayed abroad for only a couple of weeks. Margit had hardly said goodbye when a removal firm got in touch to say that they were to come and pack up all Minna's belongings. There was not much: a table, a bed, a chest of drawers and a few old armchairs which Minna had had mended and reupholstered. The collective assumed that she would want her things to be delivered to a new address, but it turned out that the removal firm had been told to deposit everything in a self-storage unit, with the rent paid ahead for several years. Margit did not have any forwarding address for mail. Much later, in connection with the police investigation, I heard that Minna had decided to live in sheltered housing under her old name. It was utterly inexplicable to me why she kept that name even though she had broken with everything else in her past. She had also made a note of Johannes's telephone number in a worn black notebook that was in her handbag. For many years, it pained me to think that I might have driven her to the brink of suicide with my constant proposals about how we should meet and talk (about Johannes and Kaufmann and Mr Carsten, and heaven knows who else). Perhaps she left the tram the last time I saw her simply to escape from me (and all the rest of them) for good. I no longer believe that to be true. I think she had completed a kind of cycle, moving on from the years of being the person people told her to be, and reverting to what she had been in the beginning – nobody or, rather, *nobody's*. If she really had killed herself, it was an act she carried out the moment she decided to take off and move to a place that no one knew of, and where no one knew her. What happened later in the Tøyen pool only confirmed something that had already been completed a long time ago.

*

They would not let me see her for a long time. First, the police wanted to talk to me. Digging in the archives had produced old reports about enforced care orders, drunkenness, raids to follow up possession of drugs, and more of this kind, a long list. They quizzed me incessantly about Minna's circumstances, people she might have known or met, many such questions, which of course I could not answer. While these *conversations* (as the police chose to put it) went on, my mind was blank and alert at the same time, the way you respond when some enormity has befallen you, something you know will have consequences not only for your entire future but also for your past, and then not just for how the past should be understood or evaluated but also for what you *know* about it. Now I cannot say what was worst, the unthinkable fact of Minna's death or the realisation that I had been lied to all my life: about who we were but also about *what* – what our relationship was, exactly. It took much bureaucratic manoeuvring to persuade the authorities that I really was Minna's brother and that it was therefore appropriate to allow me to see her in the hospital mortuary. There was no trace of pain in her face –on the contrary, she looked calm and peaceful – but around her lips a faint, singular smile still lingered, the rubber-band smile I always associated with her. Seeing it filled me with a strange sensation of being seen by her even though the gaze had left her eyes: she saw me, right through our shared past. When I had pulled myself together, I signed for the few things she had brought with her to the pool: a simple cloth bag for towel, shampoo, deodorant and some makeup things, and a shoulder bag with worn clasps. In one of its pockets, I found the wallet with Indian-style fringes that she had owned for as long as I could remember. The pocket also contained the black notebook in which she had written down Johannes's number. This was how the hospital staff had managed to reach us when I was drying Johannes's hair. My number had not been entered anywhere in her address book. In addition, the bag contained a half-finished packet of menthol cigarettes, a Bic lighter, a few coins and notes, a box with tampons and a sheet of Sobril tranquilliser tablets. The Sobril must have been what had made the police suspect that she had taken drugs before going in for a swim. Underneath all this, I found the envelope from Mr Carsten that I had given to her that day in the tram. It was unopened. I could not work it out. Why carry it around in her bag if she had no intention of opening it? Had she simply forgotten it was there? I tried to remember which bag she had with her in the tram; was it this one? But the fact of her death had changed everything. I could not remember any more. It ended with me taking her things home. At first, I was going to leave Mr Carsten's message alone. But the thought that it might cast a light over what had happened made me have a look after all. It was not a letter, as I had assumed, but an old black-and-white photograph that had been folded once longways. It showed a girl of about three or four sitting on a horse, saddled but with the reins hanging down from the bridle so that the child clearly found it hard to stay in the saddle and was leaning forward with both arms clutching the flanks of the horse. The horse: he was *my horse*, the same white horse that I had looked at from my bedroom window, evening after evening, right through my childhood. The girl on the horse was Minna. Even though the fold of the photo ran across her face, there was no doubt in my mind that it was she.

*

I am not sure how long I can hold out here. The dusk is gathering outside and Mr Carsten will soon decide that he has waited long enough. Anyway, the sacking of the Yellow Villa has surely not gone unnoticed. Simonsen or Brekke may well have notified the police already. They will start a search for me soon. And if they move up here as part of the search, what will *he* do? Some time ago, I adjusted the rifle scope so that I can scan as much as possible of my house and the garden on either side of the drive but, apart from the patches lit by the street lamps, a grainy, hazy darkness is swallowing up the outlines of everything else. Hearing is the only sense I can rely on now, but all I can hear is the never-ending, monotonous whine of a succession of aeroplanes, part of the dense evening traffic above the island, which one by one begin their descent. The cabin lights are switched off before landing, so that only the cone of light near the nose wheel and the blinking lights at the wing tips can be seen as the plane comes past; its body is no more than a long, heavy shadow. Then I hear him, surprisingly close, on the long veranda, clomping and wheezing as he goes.

The beam of a torch slices through the room, but aimlessly, more sliding along the walls than searching for something. The sounds tell me that he is moving around outside the house. Is there a way into the house other than the ones I have already tried to block, some entrance I do not know? I go to the kitchen. Not a sound in there, only the noise of the wind as it surges against roof and walls. I go back into the hall and wait by the trapdoor to the cellar steps. Then I see the sharp torchlight glowing white in the long row of windows facing the veranda. He is moving more slowly now. I wonder if he has brought his hunting rifle. Never mind. He will get through my modest barricades; it is only a matter of how much time he has and how much effort he is prepared to make. I move over to the cellar door under the stairs, pull it up and climb down to stand on the top step. I hear a massive thump near the front door. The solid marble top of the hall table had tipped over and slammed into the floor. I slowly lower the trapdoor but stay close underneath, hunched on one of the top steps, and listen as he drags his heavy leg through the dark hall. His hoarse breathing is interrupted by loud swearing. He must have bumped into something. Now I listen out for the dog, its long, panting breaths, the excited scraping of claws on the hall floor and thresholds. But no, it seems he has not brought the dog. Perhaps he felt no need: he knows that I am here. I tense my body in anticipation of him gripping the trapdoor handles and forcing his way in here, where I am crouching, waiting to see the beam of his torch or perhaps the sole of one of his boots. But nothing happens. He does not come. Perhaps his courage fails him at the last moment. Or else he assumes that he has all the time in the world, that he can easily starve me into defeat. Is that how he thinks? Then it suddenly dawns on me. He cannot get down here because of his leg. And, at that instant, it comes to me how it must have been then. That time, the very last, when I begged you, pleaded with you not to go up to the farm any more.

*

But, of course, you went anyway, all dressed up in the clothes he had given you and looking like a depraved virgin bride: the far too low-cut dress in cream silk, which a woman with a certain hauteur, like Mrs Kaufmann, could possibly have carried off but which made you look ridiculous, and glammed up like a past-her-best diva in all the jewellery he wanted to decorate you with, the outfit completed by a pair of white high-heeled shoes so outsized they threatened to come off your feet with every step, forcing you to walk as bandy-legged as a cow. You must have felt that a touch of vulgarity was required to show off all this finery to greatest effect: you thrust one bony hip forward and placed your hand defiantly on it before you wrapped the matching shawl around your shoulders and left. Once on the road, you quickly lost your stiff-necked self-assurance because your high heels kept getting stuck in the mud. I watched you from the window: you had to pinch the cigarette between your lips to have both hands free for holding the already dirty hem of your dress clear of the muck and gravel. Can I reimagine it now? There is Mr Carsten waiting for you in the yard; his legs in high, black boots are planted far apart and he has put on the checked waistcoat he wears only for special occasions. He feels proud, naturally; you are his own shy little flower. Just to get you to dress up for him is quite a feat. It is a mild evening in August, though in the dusk the air is already as swollen as in September and the sky is grey with light clouds after a long rain that still fills the ditches and the deep wheel ruts in the yard. When you reach him, blushing, sweaty and breathing quickly, he says there is something he wants to show you and, without more ado, takes your arm and leads you past the stables to the paddock that he has laid out and fenced with Kaufmann's approval. Boxer is there, over at the far end and almost blanched out of sight in the hazy dusk. Boxer is the harness-racing roan that Mr Carsten and Weiler, his old chum, have invested a great deal in, time as well as money. All Mr Carsten has to do is make a few clicking noises and the horse comes to them, trotting lightly across the damp grass, and strokes the leather-gloved hand with his soft muzzle. As sensitive as the finest Miss, Mr Carsten says. He costs a lot to keep, but it's worth every penny. Can you guess how much he got in prize money last year? He tells you. The sum means little to you, but the horse is really beautiful. You are allowed to come close and hold his great, warm head in your arms. To hide his limp, Mr Carsten stands with the heel of the boot on his good leg hooked into the low fence rail, while his stiff, calliper-supported leg bears the entire weight of his body. It must hurt but it is a pain he is used to. He sips from a flat hip flask he keeps in his inside waistcoat pocket and lets the cigarette hang in the corner of his mouth when he offers you one. He lights your cigarette, coming so close that you can pick up his characteristic smell, the smell I always found disgusting, a harsh mixture of stable and leather and sweat and ingrained tobacco smoke but with another ingredient that is more than just distasteful: it is somehow swollen, thick and milky. You are side by side, leaning on the fence. Boxer stands a little away with his head close to the ground. An unidentifiable bird gives off a drawn-out burbling sound, followed by a heavy beating of wings from inside the leafy crown of a tree. On the opposite side of the yard, light is spilling out of the downstairs windows along the veranda of the Kaufmann villa. The lamps are on upstairs, too. Presumably, Helga is seated at a window, trying to make out who they are, these figures she can just see standing over by the paddock fence. Of course she recognises Mr Carsten, but who is the short female by his side? Helga thinks that the woman's clothes are somehow familiar, at least the shawl. Because of your bulky outfit, it is impossible for you to climb up on the fence as you would have liked to; it would have been the natural kind of thing for you to do and, if you had, it would have made you feel more at ease. But in this dress and those shoes, all you can do is stand up straight and let yourself be scrutinised. He does exactly that: he looks you over or, more precisely, his gaze is turning you this way and that, as if he is trying to see who you are, or who he takes you to be without these clothes, and distinguish this you from the person you seem to be when wearing them. Aren't you scared? you say to him just to escape his eyes for a while, and: scared of what? he says, still looking at you. So you say: scared that they'll see you, because you're drinking? And he takes the flask from his pocket again and untwists the top and drinks and then he smiles some more and, again, that look in his eyes, and: would you like some? He hands you the flask and you do drink a small mouthful and cannot hide the face you make as the rough alcohol slips down your throat, and then he takes the flask back from you and wipes the rim with his hand before putting the top back on and returning it to his inside pocket. What is there for me to be afraid of? he asks, and seems suddenly to have made a decision. He straightens his body (without moving the heel of the boot, it is still hooked over the fence bar, as if it were stuck). *They're* the ones who should worry, I've been at this farm much longer than they have and will survive the lot of them, and don't they know it. Holding his cigarette just a little way from your face, he goes on: tell you one thing, better not worry about how many masters you serve or what *kind* of masters they are, never mind what they choose to do to you or not, as the case may be: all of it is slavery and as long as you admit it, you'll also be able to take it, all you need is patience. And: how do you mean? you ask. He replies: just look at me now, I own this, and he points across the paddock to where Boxer stands in exactly the same position as before, the white-painted bars of the paddock fence looking almost fluorescent against the dark trees, and he takes in the farm manager's house and the Volvo and the horse trailer parked next to it. My kingdom, he says. But you have stopped listening. For some reason or other, he has stirred up thoughts that you are getting lost in. Then he says: you're cold. Let's go indoors. And you ask: indoors, where? And then he points towards the main house, which seems to float like a gigantic ship in the thickening dusk. Are you crazy? you say, laughing. But he does not pay attention, just flicks his cigarette away with his thumb and index finger, unhooks his good leg from the fence and moves heavily off towards the house with-out turning round to make sure that you are following him.

*

And perhaps that is your big mistake: agreeing to follow him into the Kaufmanns' large villa. Of course that was not part of the plan from the beginning. All you had wanted was to be seen when you *shone* in your beautiful new clothes. He had said that it was fine for you to bring your friends up to the farm sometime. But you no longer had any friends, not among the lads, not anywhere else either. It was after you had told him this that he came by to drop off the fancy clothes and dismissed your protests with an impatient wave of the hand. Some old stuff, he said. Do you think the two old harpies have cause to dress up any more? Better someone use these things rather than leaving them to rot at the back of the wardrobe of some old Miss. I was in my room, looking at you while you tried the clothes on in front of the mirror. Johannes saw you too, even though he never let on. He must have known that it was only a matter of time before the dam burst, the reassuring wall he had kept trying to shore up between us and *what had really happened*. Now you are both standing inside the villa. He walks with his muddy boots well apart on the highly polished parquet in the drawing room, and all the rooms in the Kaufmann home are brightly lit as if for a party. But the hosts seem to have chosen to hide. Small wall lamps have been switched on next to the large painting of the St John's Eve bonfire, the naked human bodies rest on the rocks, and *I am here now!* Mr Carsten shouts straight out into the room, but no one answers and you say: why don't they answer? and he shouts again, *we are here now!* and you join in, WE ARE HERE NOW! and burst out laughing, you cannot stop it, and: come along, he says, and takes hold of your arm. Where is Mrs Kaufmann in that moment? Maybe she is standing behind the door to what was once her husband's study, rigid with fear, her senses alert to the slightest change in Mr Carsten's words and expression. What about Helga? But Helga's face has never been distinct, apart from the broad lower jaw that she moves so frenetically, as if she was obsessively chewing on something. Probably she is also observing everything because, after all, your clothes belonged to her. Her father wanted her to wear them at the reception for the guests from abroad, and it is her dress that Mr Carsten touches now, strokes again and again with his hand, and perhaps you are shrinking back under his arm, repulsed or frightened, but then he says again: there's something I want to show you.

*

It is as if, in a completely dark room, a light is suddenly switched on in front of a painting. For a moment, it is not the painted image you see but your own face reflected on the surface of the varnish and paint. Just for a fleeting moment: then the reflection dissolves and your face vanishes as if it was never there. In the same way, as evanescently, I stand on the cellar floor, watching in the light from the open trapdoor as the two of you climb down the steps. You come first, in your absurdly long dress, and stop after just a few steps so that, with your back to the wall, you can help him. Mr Carsten has not been down here since Sigrid Kaufmann decided to block the cellar entrance from the yard at the back. That was after Kaufmann's death and everything down here stayed just as it was, Mr Carsten says, while he manoeuvres his stiff leg into the gap. He can only get down if you help him to place his useless leg in its specially reinforced boot at a right angle to the top step and then wait as the rest of his body follows, and you, who kicked off your own idiotic shoes ages ago, support your back against the wall while the lantern in his hand casts a flaring light over the roughcast cellar wall that picks out the outlines of both your faces and then deletes them again. Finally down there, he pulls off his thick boot and lets you have a feel of what remains of his paralysed leg: shrunk and atrophied inside a cage of jointed metal struts and leather straps with clasps he can loosen only by using all the muscular strength he can muster in his arms. When I was a child, polio was incurable, he explains, you were simply grateful that you didn't have the worst of it, so at least you escaped the iron lung. And then he went on to tell you what it was like to grow up on the Inner Islands back then, when there was no permanent bridge to the mainland and no drivable roads on the island. His family had been living there ever since the *Danes ruled* over Norway. His mother and father were both Kaufmann's tenant farmers, the *elder* Mr Kaufmann, of course. Though he had met the son already. There were only some seven years between us, he explains. I remember him as tall and thin as a rake, neatly dressed in trousers with braces and an always freshly ironed, long-sleeved shirt that he wore buttoned right up to the throat. He would bring books with him to read outside, sitting back against a tree trunk. That is, when he wasn't watching me and the others at work. It was hard for me to be a harvest worker, what with my leg. I had to learn how to scythe with one hand. One day, when I was sitting down on the verge, he came along to speak to me and said he would find a cure for me. There is a cure for everything, he told me. Including the illnesses science has failed to deal with so far. We are human beings, you know, he said, we don't need to endure hunger or thirst, so why should we have to suffer disease? Only our strength of mind and our imagination can set limits for what we can learn to achieve. He would say things like that. And he went on to speak of a vision he had had (yes, that's really the word he used, as if it had been a sighting or a mirage): one day it would become possible to get rid of all the ancient practices in farming and animal husbandry still in use on the Inner Islands, even though neither the crops nor their management were adjusted to the soil and climatic conditions here. He had been to England and had read about new methods of fodder improvement that he was going to put to the test. Not that this kind of thing was enough for him. The mentality of the farmers out here must also change. It was pointless for just one farmer and his family to work their small plot. Instead, all growing and grazing should be managed collectively, with equal distribution of seed stock and tools. It is futile to toil on the land without the knowledge of what is best for it, he would say. At the time, I suppose I thought it sounded mostly like silly fantasies but, just five years later, he had begun to turn his dreams into reality out on West Island. A total of eighteen hectares of good agricultural land and also grazing meadows for cows and goats had been set aside for collective farming, according to rules for the island that he had drafted; it included an apple orchard and cider press that used to belong to the Sanatorium but had reverted into the Kaufmann family's ownership. This was how it all began, and it soon led to the first colony being set up. Kaufmann advertised to get the right people to join it and in the beginning things moved pretty slowly, but once the word got around they arrived in bigger and bigger numbers: young idealists like himself or ordinary workers looking for a better daily wage. Because I realised that my bad leg meant that I would never farm our old land alone, I joined in as well, and in return, as a sign of our mutual trust, he appointed me to the foreman's position in the collective. We lived in shared lodgings in the old Sanatorium or in a barrack that Kaufmann had had built in the hospital grounds. We were divided up into work teams. Some of the women were asked to cook in the communal kitchen and some of the men to join the carpenters, especially to maintain the tools, together with the engineers who looked after the tractors and other equipment that Kaufmann gradually acquired on the colony's behalf. There were other communal activities, like everyone taking half an hour off in the morning for exercises, at Kaufmann's insistence. The colony grew larger all the time. We already had the farm out on West Island, but after a few years Kaufmann bought up two older farm properties on Holm Island. The Mains Farm was here, of course, and Kaufmann moved in with his young wife. It was when Helga was born a couple of years later that things changed. It is an evil disease, partly because of the way it comes to light only slowly, and then the first symptoms are so vague they could mean many things. But those of us who worked close by his side noticed well enough what it did to him. He grew more and more withdrawn and reserved and glum. I know he saw it as a curse that he, who had wanted to embody happiness and health and good living, should have a child so miserably malformed. Not that the word was ever used, though. Helga was frail, that's all anyone admitted to. And I am told that it was not the worst form of this atrophy that afflicted her, which might have made it harder for him not to put his hope in there being some cure after all. Kaufmann consulted all these specialist doctors, and from the age of just three or four, Helga had to put up with a lot of different treatments. She had to soak in baths of rock-salt brine and sit strapped into various contraptions meant to strengthen her muscles. Just before the war started, Kaufmann went in for experiments with ionising radiation which absorbed him completely for quite some time. The Sanatorium was turned into a clinic and everyone who joined the colony had to have a dose of radiation to give him a large group of subjects to compare. My wife and I went along to be irradiated as well. Yes, you look shocked but he actually found me a wife! On condition that we became experimental subjects, of course. Katarina, that was my wife's name, was the daughter of a farm worker who had been in Kaufmann's employ ever since the time of the first colony. This was before I was appointed farm manager and given my own residence at the Mains Farm, so Katarina and I were lodged down here, in the basement, together with the other farm workers, and she was to serve upstairs as a housemaid and also as Miss Helga's own maid. If you ask me, Katarina went quite peculiar from all the radiation. Anyway, she started to steal things. Mrs Guddal? you say at that point. I remember her, Johannes used to drive out to visit her on Sundays but we were never allowed to come along. Mr Carsten looks at you. The two of you sit side by side on the bottom step, and he has stretched his stiff leg out. In the flickering light of the lantern, his face is at the same time intrusive and remote. You can't understand what it was like then, he finally says, then looks away. He *owned* us, do you have any idea of what it is like to be owned? But you don't say anything. What can you say? After all, to be owned means that someone else thinks you're worth owning and, just at this moment, what are you worth? Mr Carsten goes on talking without waiting for an answer. The war began, and with it all the children came to the islands. I don't know how many Kaufmann had recruited. It must have been several hundred in the end. At least half a dozen of them were from Germany, Franz Lehman among them. He was treated like everyone else, at least at first – quartered on West Island and so on – but we soon realised that he was someone special. He was allowed to come and stay at the farm, and not with us but in the big house. Then he and Miss Helga began to spend more and more time together. I have to say, it vexed quite a few of us that she, who had always been so uppity, should all of a sudden start behaving like an ordinary mortal. For a while, it almost looked as if having this boy around was the one thing that might make Helga better, after everything else had failed. I can't say if Kaufmann himself saw the irony of it, maybe he did. But none of us knew for sure if he, Franz, really was a Jewish kid, though people whispered about it and many claimed to know. I do remember once, it was in the middle of the war and Kaufmann had a visit from a German delegation. A whole banquet was laid on to entertain them. I remember it well, I had to spend an entire day just setting up lights along the roads for the guests' motors – to give them a 'grand entrance', as Mrs Kaufmann called it – and then there was the long veranda and the farm to be illuminated as well. Twenty staff were on duty that evening, all with special jobs to do, and then, when the last course of the meal had been served and it was time for coffee and brandy, Franz was asked to come downstairs. Say what you like, that boy had a wonderful singing voice. Didn't you know that? He was asked to declaim poems and to sing to the gentry and, naturally enough, Helga had taught him to sing in Norwegian without rolling the consonants. Afterwards, the entire company almost went out of control, that's how pleased they were. Flushed faces, a storm of applause. Fancy that, for a little Jewboy. Kaufmann saved his life, no question about it, and later, long after the end of the war, he came back here and brought his wife. And his own children too, you interrupt. After a short silence, you ask: might they have been Mrs Guddal's children? You have understood at last, though perhaps you guessed long before then. Mr Carsten looks down at his shrivelled leg. Franz was going to adopt you, he said, without looking up. After the war, when Franz was over in the States, he and Kaufmann kept in close touch. They wrote to each other while Kaufmann was in jail as well. Apparently, Franz and his young American wife had realised they couldn't have children, perhaps, Franz thought, due to the radiation that Kaufmann had subjected him to when he was here as a child. I don't know if it's the truth. After all, many couples are childless and the whys and wherefores are never explained. But Kaufmann suggested a solution and there they were, come all the way from America to adopt you. As far as the authorities were concerned, everything was in order, the paperwork signed and witnessed, your names added to your new parents' passports. You were free to leave. Except, at the last moment, Mrs Kaufmann did not dare to let you go. She hated Franz, had hated him from the moment he arrived. Not because he was a Jew but because he had barged his way into the family. She called him *the little parasite*. And perhaps she hated him because he was everything that Helga was not, healthy in every way. Besides, she was scared about what might come out in public if she allowed the two of you to go abroad, the whole story about the volunteers coming to the island and the experiments that had come to obsess her husband more and more over the years. Mr Carsten falls silent. And then? you ask. And, because she and I always got on, she asked me to do something about it. And you: so it was *you* who fixed it? Mr Carsten fumbles inside his waistcoat and pulls out the flask, stares at it as if it were an utterly alien object, then undoes the top and takes a long, deep drink. And then: you must understand, he says, that after the colony and all those projects that Kaufmann dreamed up, the inbreeding on the island was something else, you couldn't make it up, and if everyone is related to everyone else, it's that much easier to keep things in the dark. If you two got away, no one on the island could silence you. Besides, there was no telling what Lehman really knew and whom he could have told and what the outcome might be. Not just for the people on the farm but for everyone here! A brief silence and then you ask: what happened afterwards? Mr Carsten stares at you. In the dim light around the cellar steps his face seems to hover, freed from his body, large and alien. What, with them? he says, and moistens his lips, dry from the alcohol. With our *parents*, you say. All I know is what happened to you two, Mr Carsten replies. Then he looks at you again. I never stopped keeping an eye on the two of you, regardless of what you were up to, he says in a voice that sounds somehow hollow, and I'm glad I didn't. So, you had us with this Mrs Guddal, you say. *You* are the child I had with her, Mr Carsten says. As for the boy, to this day I've no idea who his parents are. And, at last, both of you sit in silence and your voices have a quality precisely like the glint in the layer of varnish on an oil painting when the light falls on it: having sounded eerily clear for a short while, they dissolve into white noise and broken silences. A handful of tired, trivial words are all that is left. Minna, in the tram: what makes you think that? Are we the slightest bit alike? Now that I think about it, she nearly always avoided the words brother and sister, and it is also true what she said that afternoon about the Javanese box photos, that there is not one that shows the two of us together. All of them are either of Frank and his wife Elizabeth, or of me or of Minna, always one without the other. And of the person who should by rights also be in a photo, Mr Carsten, there is not even a shadow. Now he is sitting upstairs in the villa with his rifle pointing straight at the cellar trap-door. He has waited almost fifty years for just this: the moment when I dared to return to the place from where I came so that, once and for all, he can erase the error that bears my name, and kill me the way you kill a crippled or malformed animal.

*

You did not come home again after that evening. I remember that I went outside at dawn to look for you. Mornings at this time of the year are usually still light and mild, rich with the smells of freshly mown grass and damp soil. But the whitey

233

had rolled in over the island during the later part of the night and was now lying, heavy and clammy, over everything, and in that bitterly chilly air nothing can be heard or seen, not even the sound of the grasshoppers who usually sing in the field verges until late September; there is no light to see, no starry sky, nothing. Now I wonder of course if, even as you agreed to go with him into the basement, you had already realised that his bad leg meant he would never be able to climb back up the stairs without your help. But it might have struck you first when you had been down there for a while and he had become, as he used to say, *well oiled* and what had begun with big talk and flattery ended as such things usually do: with reproaches and accusations. He said that you never bothered to come and see him up at the farm, never admitted to knowing him in front of others and always took the side of those on the island who spoke ill about him behind his back. But in your heart of hearts, you'll have known the truth, right, Minna? You knew who your real father was, even though you didn't want to say anything or want anybody else to know? But you stood your ground. How did you do it? was all you said. And so he tells you, speaks of the years that followed Kaufmann's release from prison and his decision to refurbish the old basement apartments into a 'cottage hospital' for the farm workers who later became his patients and whom he insisted that he could treat and cure, even though many were already so severely ill they were beyond all help. Their beds were down here, Mr Carsten explains, pointing at the hospital cots, which twenty years later are still lined up in

234

the corridors and in the narrow wooden pens. He stored an entire pharmacy down here as well! Mr Carsten selects a key from his bunch, unlocks a metal cupboard, more than a metre in height and fixed to the wall next to the wash basin, and shines his torch on the shelves: brown medicine bottles, packs of bandaging and containers of disinfectant. He hands you a small pharmacist's vial to look at and you ask: what is this? Arsenic, he says, tasteless and odourless, and easy to give to people in doses that can't be traced. *So it was you!* This you say in almost the same triumphant tone of voice as earlier, upstairs in the drawing room, when you shouted (then, together with him): *we are here!* And perhaps he smiles but, by then, he might also feel that he has said too much, and that you are going to slip out of his grasp. Perhaps he even gets angry. Or not: maybe he becomes ingratiating, his voice honeyed as he begins to plead. Minna, he says. He takes a step closer to you, he wants to touch you, hug you. You used to let me in the old days, he says, when you were little! Actually, I'm not sure I can hear him say this, but his expression is easy to imagine: his grotesque face is distorted by his intention to look trusting and tender-hearted, which only makes him appear even more loathsome and ugly. But, all the same, you might let him touch you because you already know what you will do next. Perhaps you even let him undress you, remove these borrowed things, since that is what his shaking hands insist on doing. He knew he could take them off you any time, was that not the reason why he had made you put them on in the first place? And perhaps he takes his own things off, too, and stands there with his pathetic hard-on, snivelling in the shadowy light. I couldn't stand seeing you leave, he says, I just couldn't bear it, and he staggers towards you as if to put his arms around you. Perhaps you let him do it, allow yourself to be hugged close to his woeful, trembling body, limping and unbalanced now on its shrivelled stump of a leg, until all that is left to you is the certainty that this is what he wanted, always: to drag you down into the same stench and darkness from which he comes himself. I push him – and you – out of my mind just as I imagine you must push him away, very forcefully now, because his heavy body is almost suffocating you as he tries to wrestle you down onto the floor. You have picked up what remains of your clothes, grabbed his boots and prosthesis in passing and you are already halfway up the steps when he realises what is happening. Before he has managed to stumble to the bottom step, you are in the hall and have slammed the trapdoor shut. Up here, above ground, dawn is breaking and the fog has caused a faintly rippling, coppery mist to form everywhere, making the outlines of the farmhouses and outbuildings look as if drawn in black ink on almost still water. You walk through the damp grass towards the paddock and Boxer, who stands at the far end, unmoving, as if listening for something in the vague, somehow metallic shadows. He snorts loudly and comes to you slowly while you pour the contents of the pharmacist's vial into his water trough. Then you leave. I do not know how long it takes you to leave the island, or which route you follow: you might take your usual shortcut across the meadows, or prefer to go around the back of Brekke's place to avoid being seen by any of the neighbours. When the first planes are coming in to land, screams and angry voices are heard from up on the farm. But by then, it is daylight and I am awake. So is Johannes, though he may not have had any sleep that night. We stand together under the trees in the garden and watch as a police car comes up the road, turns right at the crossroads and continues towards the farm. Seeing it reminds me of the day in late winter when Kaufmann died. Then the convoy of cars also drove slowly and without lights. I wonder if anyone ever saw you leave, walking along in your dirty dress, torn at its low neck, with those high-heeled shoes in your hand. You followed King's Road all the way to the bridge and crossed to the other side, to what had so far been *the mainland*, a place neither of us had ever believed was truly real.

*

All those nights when Minna had gone out I lay awake in my upstairs room in the Yellow Villa, sometimes asleep, sometimes not. I must have slept now and then because I remember dreaming that I was lying awake in another room, exactly like mine except that there was no axolotl on the ceiling. It was only when I realised it was not there that I understood I must really be asleep and only *dreaming* that I was awake. But when I tried to wake up from the dream, my eyelids would not open, though it could have been that my eyes were already wide open and looking into darkness much greater and deeper than the darkness I usually fell asleep in and woke up from.

This was the moment when I understood that the *other* darkness was the real one. All that I felt or heard, all the ordinary, safe sounds around me – planes in their banking turns over the island, Brekke's dog barking at the end of its long lead, Johannes's footsteps as he crossed the landing outside my room, the mumbled weather report from the radio in the kitchen and the grinding noise of the larder door hinges when it was opened, the smell of butter sizzling in the frying pan as Johannes was preparing the midday meal – all this belonged to a world that was most certainly real and true but which did not exist in the place where I was. Not then, and not now, either. But what was this other world where I was when I slept, dreaming that I was awake? Was it not the same place that the old historians referred to as the world of the *monstrous ones*, godless beings with no name and no family? I wake with stiffened joints and the tendons in my neck are taut and hard, as if in cramp all night; I struggle to haul myself out of the cot, fumble in the dark through the narrow cellar passage until I finally get back to the kitchen alcove and stand there, holding on to the enamelled sink with its ruined, rusty tap that has not had water flowing through it for decades. I listen upwards, into the house, to try to make out if Mr Carsten is still about.

Though whether he is waiting or not seems no longer of any consequence. For the first time in my life, I feel larger than him, I have now grown to be part of this house, the place he forced me to leave. It has taken all this time for me to be grafted back into the family tree, to become one with the past, like the damp rising from the bottom of an ancient sea into the house, and with the woodworms crawling throughout its walls, slowly grinding the wood into grains and flakes and dust. I go up the cellar steps and shove the trapdoor open with my neck and shoulders. The handles hit the wall with a harsh, cold sound. No one can have been here for many hours. I hunker down for a while on the hall floor to catch my breath and then reach for a pair of dusty rubber boots that has been left under the stairs. The boots are a bit too tight but I manage to pull them on. The marble table top that fell over when Mr Carsten barged in is lying on the floor, but I shove it out of the way and go outside to stand on the long veranda. The dark is still solid around me and, within it, rain is drizzling down and dumbly soaking into soil and leaves and clay. The rain might well be the same as the rain of yesterday and of four weeks ago. Further away in the damp mist, the farm manager's house, his car and parked trailer stand as they always have. Has Mr Carsten fled the field or has he just gone into hiding? Halfway across the yard in the dark, I stumble on something unexpected. I cup my hand around the beam of the torch to hide the light and carefully bend back the wet grass. In front of the toe of my boot, the blank white of an eye stares up at me. The dead dog lies flat on the ground with its tongue like a stiff piece of blanket between its teeth. It strikes me that I have forgotten my rifle in the cellar. The silence makes my eardrums bulge as if the procession was still under-way but makes its presence felt only as this unbearable internal pressure on the ears. Somewhere inside the thumping of the drums, inside the rustling of the rain, I hear Minna say what she said then, about Kaufmann: you must promise me to kill

239

him, promise to kill him for my sake. In the pouring rain, she sounds feverish, and almost as if she is laughing. I walk to the manager's house. The door is unlocked, the handle moist and sticky with rain as I pull the door towards me. I let the torch sweep over the flowery board on the lobby wall. The red ear protectors that hung there earlier are now gone. Oddly enough, I seem to know already where they are. I give the door to the room a hard shove with one shoulder and then stop and stand helplessly with my hands held out. Mr Carsten is seated on the bench at the kitchen table with the red ear muffs on his head and the gun he has shot himself with still jammed into the crook of his left arm. The upper part of his body is twisted back at a strange angle, as if he had been about to fall forward over the table but the force of the shot threw his body backwards again. Behind him, the kitchen wall is covered with a dark, reddish sludge, a partly set mix of blood and brain tissue that has run down to the floor in long congealing strings. His head, or what remains of it below the absurd ear muffs, is leaning over a little so that, from the doorway, the paralysed side is still directed towards me with its ghoulish half-smile and staring, lifeless eye. The air is thick with the cloying stench, a combination of blood, stale alcohol and vomit, and when the flies that have already been swarming around the corpse begin to buzz around my eyes and lips as well, I can no longer keep my retching down and run out of the house, squeeze myself in between the stack of logs and the rainwater butt and throw up. It has rained so much tonight and the previous nights that the butt is full to the brim. I fill my palms with water and press them against my face, then rinse out my mouth and splash water over the back of my neck. A breeze makes the water surface ripple a little; all that I can see of my reflected face is a shadow that fades and disappears when I straighten up. When I go out into the yard again, a few crows take off from the dog's cadaver in the grass and fly cawing into the dark between the outbuildings. Other than that, the only sound is the monotonous rustle of the rain. Back in Mr Carsten's place, I go through all the loose odds and ends on the kitchen table and then the bedside one. The receipts with Mr Carsten's signature are not where I put them yesterday. He must have known that I had been here and wanted to see him, presumably also what I wanted to see him about. Perhaps it was the only reason why he broke into the house yesterday. All he needed to know was if I had sought refuge in the cellar, so that I would not hear the shots when he killed the dog and then himself. But others must have heard them quite clearly. During the long silence on the island between the landing of the last evening flight and the take-off of the first one in the morning, the sound of shots from a hunting rifle would carry everywhere, and should have woken all the neighbours, especially since the noise would have been followed by the barking of Brekke's dog, which is always tethered outside at this time of the year. But there is not a soul in sight. I walk out into the yard, stand where Mr Carsten stood yesterday and train my binoculars at the Yellow Villa. Despite the dark, the letters of FUCKING NAZI on the garage wall are easy to make out against the coarse cement, as if the intention was for the words to be seen from the farm. Through the slowly

241

falling rain, the indistinct sound of a car engine is growing stronger. At first so distant it is hard to pick up at all, the rasping noise of the gears is becoming audible. I hear the driver changing down and then, quickly, up again. It comes from down the hill. The Speedfreak, of course: Skakland's son, who zooms from house to house, stuffing newspapers into people's letterboxes. I cannot tell how many nights I have lain awake, waiting for Minna to come home and, towards the early hours of the morning, hearing the silence pierced by precisely these sounds, as usual feeling that, yet again, my long wait through the night has been in vain. But now the insistent throb of the engine noise reaches me from another direction; it is a kind of acoustic distortion, like the visual one of looking down at the Yellow Villa instead of, as in the past, looking up at the farm from down there. In the same way, the entire familiar landscape has changed into another that is itself and not itself at the same time. Now I can also see the beams of light from headlamps as the car comes along the road. They flicker nervously over the curtain of trees at the other side of the field, then sway and seem to retreat for a moment while the car, accelerating furiously, comes up the long slope from King's Road. But Skakland takes the steep turn far too sharply. The headlamps shine into my eyes and, just before I get dazzled, I have a quick, strange glimpse of the car as it upends in slow motion, topples over and tumbles into the field. The engine is suddenly quiet but the headlamps are still on, their light seemingly stuck in the nearest tree tops. It is a while before I fully grasp what has happened. I turn quickly and run back. My first thought is to pull the gun from Mr Carsten's hands (since he is likely to have fired only twice, there should be at least three cartridges left in the magazine), but it does not take me long to realise how silly that would be at this stage. Instead I go back down into the cellar and pick up Johannes's old rifle from where I left it yesterday, leaning against the foot of the steps. Still not a sound from anywhere, as if the entire island has been lowered into a deep bowl of silence. I cross the slightly sloping and scoured grassland below the edge of the forest, the meadow where the white horse, mine and Minna's horse, used to stand dreaming next to its white-enamelled tub, then into the field where Skakland's car lies on its side, as if stopped while falling, its windscreen half ripped out of the chassis and so broken up by a fine network of cracks that it has become opaque. I walk around the car, shining my torch into it through the other windows, and then see the Speedfreak tipped forward with his chest pressed against the steering wheel. Scattered sheets of the daily papers lie draped all around him, over the passenger seat and the bonnet. I reach in through the gap in front, push the door handle down and manage to tug the door open. Skakland stays immobile, his body still squashed against the steering wheel. He must be conscious because his eyes follow me, as if closely observing my every move. Is there a spare petrol can in the car? I ask. He scrutinises me with the same seriousness as before but says nothing. I root around behind the front seats and get hold of a plastic container that I had already caught a glimpse of among the bundles of newspapers in the rear, then reach into the car again and release the bonnet catch. Underneath, the engine is burning hot. I rip out the fuel feed, walk round the car, twist the lid off the tank, shove the hose inside and suck. The cavities of my mouth and nose fill with the nauseatingly greasy taste of petrol before I put the end of the hose into the container I have in readiness; once it is half full, I screw the top on and then try to get Skakland out. Somehow I haul his heavy body up on my back. Instinctively, Skakland clings to my shoulders and, sagging at the knees, I drag both of us along to the remains of my childhood home. Both the front and the back doors of the house have been left wide open. Broken furniture, shattered glass and bits of clothing are strewn everywhere in the grass and on the drive. I remember how Johannes always warned us when we were children against leaving toys outside overnight. You never know what kind of folk are out and up to no good, he used to say. Still, for all his years on the island, he was never subjected to anything like this. By now Skakland is definitely unconscious and doesn't resist as I haul him upstairs. It takes a long time to strap him into the lifting gear that Johannes installed here. Just as I have him in place and ready to be winched up into the attic, he seems to come to. His glazed eyes are darting about inside the bloody mask of his face and he flaps about and strikes out with his arms so wildly I fear the whole block-and-tackle machinery will break free of its attachments. But when I have forced him into the Steib sidecar, he calms down for a bit, settles with the back of his neck resting on the top of the seat and sits gazing up into the ceiling. It apparently did not occur to the vandals to do anything about the books that Johannes stacked along the walls; they left the

diaries as well. I quickly push as many as I can into the rucksack, where I already have the notebooks and photographs I
brought down from the Kaufmann villa. The rest of the books
I dump on the floor, as many as I can get at before the dust
swirling up from the wooden floorboards of the attic becomes
so thick I can no longer breathe. Then I walk backwards with
petrol pouring from the open can but taking care not to spill
too much at a time. Only when I have reached the steps do I let
the petrol flow freely, some of it soaking into rags, and start
fumbling in my jacket pocket for matches. The paper delivery
man sits in the Steib sidecar, staring at me in amazement until
what is about to happen suddenly hits him. But the flames are
already forming a massive wall between us. On the other side
of the billowing smoke, I see him make a forlorn attempt to get
up. I throw the rucksack with the books through the attic
hatch, jump down myself and then start running with the
rucksack in my arms. I get out through the broken cellar door
and onto the drive. Behind me, I hear the roar of the fire as it
eats the dry timbers of the house. By the time I am in the garden, the flames have already ripped through the roof and are
bursting through the upstairs windows.

*

Dawn. The sirens of fire engines have fallen silent and the red
glow of the fire has died down. Only the rain remains, within
the strangely bright space it seems to create. I take the rowing boat out on the lake, as Johannes and I did when we took

Minna to her last resting place on a still day in November. The forest was soaked and as heavy as lead; all we could hear, apart from the rhythmic hammering of drops on bark and leaves, was the dull clatter of the oars as I put them in the boat, then the light splashing against the bow as I waded out in the water, pushing the boat while carrying the carefully wrapped brown cardboard box under my arm. I climbed in, hooked the oars into the rowlocks and began to row out to the middle of the lake with long, grinding strokes. Johannes is sitting aft, hunched under his yellow plastic raincoat, which is covered with white droplets like strings of pearls. He pretends to look out for birds. Oh, it's still there! he calls out, it's the bittern. In the thickening mist and rain it is practically impossible to make out anything among the reeds and, anyway, he is almost blind by now. I pull in the oars, take the urn from my lap. The ashes trickle between my fingers and transform into white butterflies like the swarm that fluttered around Minna when she was running along the water's edge. Before dispersing, the flakes of ash gather into a fragile cloud over the grey, pitted surface of the lake. There is no name for it either. Johannes sits there, slumped under the raincoat with his face turned away. He, too, is no longer among the mortals, and the boat is drifting further and further out. I let my arms dangle over the gunwales and lightly touch the water, which is almost warm against my skin, despite the rain. Now the first plane of the morning is approaching, the usual faint whine growing first more solid, then into an ear-bulging roar. I hear rather than see the birds rising, their wings snapping against the water.

The machine tears itself free from the tree tops and glides low above me until the steady beat of the blinking wing-tip lights slowly vanishes over the forest. The rain becomes heavier, the lake's surface more deeply pitted. Beneath the surface, long, heaving swells lift the boat. The far shore disappears in the mist and I drift helplessly over the darkening water as if over an open sea.

Also by Steve Sem-Sandberg

THE EMPEROR OF LIES

In February 1940, the Nazis established what would become the second largest Jewish ghetto in Poland in the city of Łódź. At its heart was the ghetto's leader Mordechai Chaim Rumkowski, a sixty-three-year-old Jewish businessman. Mysterious, ambiguous and monarchical, 'King Chaim' forced adults and children alike to work punishing hours in workshops to provide supplies for the German military, as thousands of others were transported and never seen again. Was Rumkowski an accessory to the Nazi regime driven by a lust for power, or was he a pragmatic strategist, actively saving Jewish lives through collaboration? Steve Sem-Sandberg draws on genuine chronicles of life in the Łódź ghetto to create a compelling meditition on power, corruption and compromise.

'Irresistible . . . absorbing from first page to last . . . Dickens would have been very pleased with this novel.' *Guardian*

'Fiction of true moral force, brilliantly sustained and achieved . . . stunning.' Hilary Mantel

'[The] cinematic richness of detail . . . invites immersion in the way few contemporary novels of serious ambition do.' *New York Times*

www.faber.co.uk

ff

Also by Steve Sem-Sandberg

THE CHOSEN ONES

Winner of the Prix Médicis étranger

The Am Spiegelgrund clinic, in glittering Vienna, masqueraded as a reform school for wayward boys and girls and a home for chronically ill children. The reality however, was very different. Through the eyes of a child inmate, and a nurse, Steve Sem-Sandberg explores the very meaning of survival. This extraordinary novel offers invaluable and compelling insight on an intolerable chapter of Austria's past.

'Extraordinary . . . has a rare and raw power.' *Sunday Times*

'You don't so much read Sem-Sandberg as stand in the fiery wind of his prose . . . This novel is as bright as a cloudless June sky under which, behind walls and doors, we go about our inexplicable human business.' Sebastian Barry, *Guardian*

'Meticulously researched and laden with history but such is Sem-Sandberg's skill that it does not feel this way . . . Historical fiction at its most raw and disturbing' *The Times*

ff

www.faber.co.uk